THE

MONEY

A novel

DAVID SHAWN KLEIN

Black Rose Writing | Texas

ISBN: 978-1-68433-637-1
PUBLISHED BY BLACK ROSE WRITING
www.blackrosewriting.com

Printed in the United States of America
Suggested Retail Price (SRP) $19.95

The Money is printed in Georgia

*As a planet-friendly publisher, Black Rose Writing does its best to eliminate unnecessary waste to reduce paper usage and energy costs, while never compromising the reading experience. As a result, the final word count vs. page count may not meet common expectations.

For Eva

THE MONEY

ZHUKOV WHO IS NOT ZHUKOV

I was standing at a mirror in the men's room at the Jay Street courthouse, rehearsing my argument to the D.A. on behalf of Amber Waves. Amber was facing an assault-and-battery for pushing Mariano, her super, down a flight of stairs after he'd drilled a peephole in her bathroom ceiling. She couldn't afford to spend months in lockdown or she'd blow her gig lap dancing at Crème de la Cream, which would leave her with no money for Prednisone and asthma pumps for her kid Alex. That meant Alex would be forced to live with Amber's sister-in-law, whose birth name, Amber swore, was "Raggedy-ass ho." I was so wrapped up in keeping the Waves family intact that I hadn't heard the seething Russian the first time he spoke. He'd appeared at my neck with an obvious disregard for the concept of personal space.

"I *said*," he insisted. "Are you lawyer?"

I turned and looked him over. He isn't big, I thought. But he might be quick. Under his jacket: Shiv? Pistol? Chainsaw?

"I pay cash," he explained.

"What do they say you did?" I asked.

His complexion was the color of his nicotined fingers. He had dry ice for eyes, with jagged bloody slashes. One of those eyes fumed like it was measuring me for a butcher's drop cloth, the other glared down at the bulky gold cross that hung from his neck, as if frozen in a sort of purgatory.

"Whole job is go to Brighton Beach," he continued. "Pick up papers. Deliver to D.A. For fee, five thousand."

Incoming traffic started getting heavy, so I suggested we find a few quiet feet of corridor. He pushed past me with a slight hitch, as if his torso and legs had been screwed together not quite flush. He was like a walking mace. One of those sinewy bantams hardened by some obscure rage.

The corridor along the courtrooms, usually crowded with the panicky and desperate, and their clients, was strangely quiet.

"What kind of papers are we talking about?" I asked.

His mutinous teeth gave rise to a shroud of herring, onion, and Winstons. "They think I am Anatoly Zhukov, and I am Anatoly Zhukov. But I am not the Anatoly Zhukov they are looking for. Also, I am not the Anatoly Zhukov they are not looking for. And that is the problem."

Practice law long enough and you don't even blink at stories like that.

"But what exactly have you been charged with?" I asked.

"First of all, is ridiculous. I am not in this country long enough to know how camera goes into parking meter."

"Cameras in parking meters—why would someone do that?"

"For the *credit* cards—what kind of lawyer *are* you? Click, click, you take picture, you have identity. When you have identity you sell identity. Brighton Beach."

He produced a large brick of cash from his leather jacket.

"Second of all, I didn't do it. I'm not lowlife hustler. With my brain, if I was criminal, I would be big picture. No, I write address. You pay for papers. Give them to D.A. and get me out of this."

"I can't mule forgeries, I'm a lawyer. Why not let me work a deal? Do it the straight way?"

Zhukov Who Was Not Zhukov spat through his teeth: "I never said forgeries! And I can't make deal. If they figure out who I am, between INS and Bratva, is big trouble."

"So you're a Russian national, right? On an expired visa. Or no visa?"

He was right in my face, like an enraged Doberman held in check by nothing more than a last vestige of fraying rope. "Do I *look* Russian to you?"

I allowed as perhaps he didn't, it must have been the lighting.

"*Ukrainian,*" he said. "There's *difference.*"

"Okay, but you're obviously out on bail, why don't you fetch your own papers?"

"Didn't I just tell you feds and Bratva, you want me to show my face in Brighton Beach?" He thumbed the cash like a deck of cards. "Five thousand for papers," he said. "And five thousand for fee."

I had a vision where his deck of presidents came up straight flush for Shatterproof, my fighter. Shatterproof was a single father. He'd tasked me with getting him a medical clearance so he wouldn't get barred from his upcoming fight. He needed the purse to feed his kids, Rafe and Kendra. The commission was insisting on a CAT scan of his brain. But Shatterproof had suddenly decided he was claustrophobic. Also that a scan was a violation of one or another of his constitutional rights. The real problem was that he suspected that a CAT would show a bowl of jello cratered with knuckle marks. Shatterproof had a glass jaw and nothing but disdain for fighters who covered up. Better to die with honor than duck and weave, or take a count—except for the complication that he was single-fathering his kids. But his heart was as big a bullseye as his head, so he was destined to a lifetime ten rounds against himself: the proud warrior with two sweet-faced kids who wanted him to keep tucking them into bed at night.

So Zhukov's presidential straight flush seemed like a pretty decent solution: I could give my fee to Shatterproof and he could skip the fight.

Then Olivia would almost certainly talk to me again.

Because if I saved Shatterproof's brain and helped him feed his kids, she'd see I was a good lawyer, after all. A lawyer who did Important Work. A month earlier her father, an eminent Rhode Island judge, had tapped a contact to get me a job doing "real" law with a thousand other partners in a glitz factory at the Hudson Yards. It was called The White Firm, and each of those thousand partners lived up to the name. Just walking in the front door you got snow blindness. Olivia had nearly begged me to jump at the opportunity, because at my age, she said, "The window was closing." I'd told her if The White Firm were my only window, I'd prefer to jump. She'd barely spoken to me since.

"What are you waiting for?" Zhukov asked. "Take the money."

On the other hand, if Olivia knew I'd given the D.A. fake ID, even in a good cause, her deep freeze might make me a pioneer in husband cryogenics.

My father would never have hesitated to take Zhukov's money. He'd been a lawyer, too. Though his had been less the practice of law than a carnival midway, with its false fronts, rigged games, and peep show grotesques. He'd loomed so large across his gold rush boomtown, slapping backs and slipping cash-stuffed envelopes into palms and pockets, "fixing" accident sites in the dead of night and "getting our story straight," swearing undying loyalty with fingers crossed behind his back, and even, here and there, trying a case in actual court, that he'd been known with much affection, but also terror and loathing, as the Mayor of Brooklyn.

I kept my clients strictly small time: boxers with losing records, DUIs and doored cyclists, bankrupt bodega owners, lap dancers with asthmatic kids. Olivia hated my crew of misfits, because, she insisted, I wasn't living up to my potential. It was why she'd asked her dad to get me the partnership offer in the first place.

I said, "Sorry, but I'm not taking on new clients at this time."

His laughter was the mocking death's hack of the cigarette addict. "No, you're too busy for man like Zhukov. But not too busy to pick up new client in toilet."

He moved in close to cut off all avenues of escape. Pressed the cash into my hand. All I could see was Shatterproof and Rafe and Kendra, smiling around their dinner table. Olivia hugging me because I'd kept a family together.

I thought, Who says she needs to know the ID was forged? I can have it both ways, help Shatterproof *and* win back Olivia.

"Five thousand to move some papers," Zhukov said, leaning in kissing close. "Easiest case you ever had."

THE LIE

I opened the door to our apartment and was immobilized by Cipka the Polish nanny's feverish perfume of orange groves, infrequently bathed flesh, and talcum. If Cipka was still home, it meant Olivia was working late.

Gabriel interrupted a Transformers-induced rampage to leap into my arms. I tossed him into the air well above my head, for Cipka's sake stifling the urge to crumple to my knees. She seemed to look on more with amusement than interest. Better that way, I assured myself. It would be exactly like me to fight for my wife while pursuing our nanny, and it had not been working out all that well, the being exactly like me.

We lived in a loft in Tribeca of the Beautiful and Rich. That was all Olivia. She was Vice President of Branding at P²R³, one promotion away from a corner stadium atop its four floors, each roughly the size of Switzerland, in the Jorgen Heimlich-designed cathedral of commerce called the Ice Palace for its giant glass slabs that jutted out like guillotines, where P²R³ had its offices. If we'd had to get along only on fees from The Krakow Law Group (the "Group" was entirely aspirational, unless you count one Krakow, divided against himself), we would probably have been crammed together in a railroad apartment in Hell's Kitchen.

Before I could ask Cipka why Gabriel was still wreaking havoc, Olivia rocketed in.

"Just home now?" she said, kissing me somewhere beneath my eye socket.

"Just home now," I replied.

"He's still awake?" she complained to Cipka.

I said, "I'm holding out for a bedtime story."

"I *meant* Gabriel," Olivia snapped.

Cipka was already vaulting over our threshold. "He wanted to wait up for you," she chimed, nearly sprinting down the corridor. She was studying for her business masters at NYU and worked late only in emergencies.

Olivia nodded disapprovingly. "*Discipline*, Cipka. It's called bed time for a reason."

Then: "Henry, shut the door."

Then: "Gabriel, do you know what time it is?"

A cocktail napkin had drifted to the floor where Cipka had hurried away. It was embossed with blood red lettering that spelled out *Anarchy*. On the back she'd written some sort of schedule, with precise, businesslike handwriting. *Anarchy* had once been called Tally's, an old-school topless bar down the dark tunnel of Varick Street. It had been reclaimed by young professionals, women included, and christened *Anarchy* through whatever mystifying force of cultural reversion recovers hipness from the played-out. I'd often passed it when I avoided going home by taking the long way.

Maybe it's not Cipka's handwriting, I told myself. Maybe the napkin belonged to her friend and back-up nanny, Liis. Clearly, some level-headed fact-finding was in order. As always, Olivia placed her satchel against the coat closet and dropped her keys in the ceramic Tyrannosaurus Gabriel had made her for Mother's Day. I pocketed the napkin before she had a chance to ask what it was and why I needed to hide it.

Meanwhile, Gabriel was rampaging through the apartment while the Power Rangers cowered. "Did you *not* hear me tell Cippy it was bed time?" Olivia asked.

It was always entertaining to see Reason, as played by Olivia, work itself into a froth of lip-biting frustration in the face of Chaos, as played by Gabriel. Reason never could reason herself into grasping how a six-year-old boy could behave, well, like a six-year-old boy.

"I've got him," I told her. "With luck he'll still get into Princeton, even going to sleep, say...thirty minutes late?"

"*Twenty.* Then I'm taking no prisoners."

Gabriel and I built a tower of blocks, hiding his green army men in strategic positions. We blitzed our tower with cloth Spidey balls and cheered as a couple of dozen soldiers got crushed to death. Finally, subdued by blood and gore, he slumbered over my shoulder as I carried him to the rocking chair, where I rocked him to sleep.

Then Olivia did her tucking and kissing, and then we were alone.

Pretty much the entire loft was furnished by Joss & Main. Crazy expensive, but, I was forced to admit, they made insanely comfortable stuff. I knew it was Joss & Main because she'd repeated the name with the hushed urgency of prayer when we were tussling over whether we could afford it, until I came home one night to learn she'd decided we could.

The one piece we hadn't mortgaged our future for was Gabriel's rocking chair. Scratched, battered, stained with coffee and cigarette burn and God-knows-what. It had the tiniest squeak that no amount of oil could silence: Whenever you thought you'd found the sucker, the sound moved elsewhere. Olivia's grandmother had been rocked to sleep in that chair, and so had any number of Cartwrights after her, Olivia included. She liked to say she held that chair in trust for future Cartwrights. So when Gabriel was past breastfeeding she'd left it out in the living room, not minding how it clashed with her beloved Joss & Main.

Neither did I. With all our goose down, calf belly, and polished kapok, the place I felt most comfortable was that old oak rocker.

Now that Gabriel was sleeping, Olivia undressed in our bedroom the way she did every night, leaving the door open while I rocked and watched from the living room, like a moviegoer stealing an imagined intimacy. She let out her hair, bending her long white neck *just so* to study her buttons as they came undone.

"The web is the great alchemizer of rumor into fact," she said, slipping an oversized Harvard sweatshirt over black Capezios. "Gossip hardens on impact and just *try* to substitute truth for bullshit. But I'm not taking the hit to my career. I'm *not.* Just because it was my idea. *If* it turns out to be true."

"Circle the wagons," I advised, not letting on how fuzzy I was about what she was getting at.

She shook her hair free, looking like the ballet dancer she once hoped she'd be, and like the young wife of not so long ago, flush with expectation for our life to come. I felt a pang of tenderness for all those dreams.

She came down the hall, not so much toward me as in my general direction.

"But it can't be true," she said. "TajWear using child labor in India. It's just some Twitter mind fuck. Toxic internet gossip. I wanted the firm to partner with Taj's foundation—you're going to laugh—but, to do *good*."

She looked to see if I was laughing at her innocence. I could have told her about my day: how I'd reunited Amber Waves and asthmatic Alex, with Amber only having to do a short stint in anger management. Or how Amber hadn't been able to pay my fee, but had offered a fifty-dollar bill, two free passes to Crème de la Cream, and a hand job (I took a rain check on the hand job). I could have told her about Zhukov's money, and Rafe and Kendra, and my only option for helping them. But Olivia rarely asked about my day during her dispatches from the front. She hadn't for some time, since I'd failed to deliver on the potential she'd whimsically invested me with.

She said, "You think I'm being naïve, don't you? That a PR firm can make a difference?"

Olivia was sincere and open and uncynical. Where I grew up in the Mayor's Brooklyn, goodness was defined as progressive shades of less bad.

She'd come so close I could feel the static of her mind at work: piecing out what damage she may have done to her career, calculating options and risks, feeling her way through uncertainty and bravado toward a battle plan.

"If the firm supported Taj's charity...*Taj*, Henry. The *rapper*," she continued, standing over me as if she were a prosecutor making her closing argument. "And there was this secondary benefit for the firm in the afterglow of his celebrity...still it really *was* about his charity, about doing our share. Taj has so many businesses going, besides touring and recording. How could he have known? I mean, child labor in *India*. How could he have *known*?"

She poured herself a glass of white wine, took a sip, and sat in troubled silence.

"Is anything bothering you?" she finally asked, with what sounded like genuine concern, at once violating the longstanding dynamic of our marriage. She had skin so perfect that makeup was superfluous, and her deep black eyes could shred you with intelligence, but also with this strange, magnetic stillness that made you keep staring back, even while you were getting a balls-out shredding. In contrast, I was the kind of guy whose tie flew out in all directions, a sign of the mayhem within.

I asked what she meant by "bothering."

"You seem distracted."

I sighed rhetorically. "Someone posted an anonymous rumor on the internet that your rapper Taj has been exploiting children in India. You talked Lee into funding Taj's charity in the first place, and now you're afraid of the blowback to your career."

She brought the glass to her face for another sip, as if to mask conceding with a furtive smile that I really *had* been paying attention.

I said, "See, Liv. I do listen."

"He's not *my* rapper," she said, waving off my proof-of-attention as a meaningless conversational non sequitur. "And I'm not afraid, per se. You're doing what you always do, changing the subject. I'm just saying you seem off, and do you want to talk about it?"

More than I can say, I thought, reaching into my pocket and fondling Zhukov's cash.

If I told her how I planned to use it, she'd accuse me of being like my father. But all I wanted was to help Rafe and Kendra, and impress my wife, enough to end the long Tribeca Winter of our marriage. Was that the same as the Mayor's Beemers and Patel Phillipe watches?

"Henry," she repeated. "Do you want to talk?"

She would tell me to give it back. Give the money back at once. Clean-slate the whole Zhukov deal.

She'd be right. It was way too slippery a slope from helping Shatterproof and winning her back, to cashing in my legacy as the Mayor 2.0.

So, first thing in the morning, I'd rush over to Court Street and tell Zhukov thanks but no thanks. It would be like the whole thing had never happened. Which meant that the lie I was about to tell wasn't a lie, after all.

"You're reading me wrong," I said. "I'm four-by-four."

"Be that as it may," she answered, with a break in her voice. "Be that as it may."

Then Gabriel woke from a night terror. She gave him a warm bath, singing "Zoom Golly Golly," her voice humming along the bathroom tiles. He went still and silent as a doe. I rolled Zhukov's cash into a black nylon sock for safekeeping. Then, eyes shut, I rocked our old chair, singing "Zoom Golly Golly" along with Olivia, soft and low.

THE NAPKIN

Church Street Boxing was at the top of a lung-busting flight of stairs. Inside it looked like the owner had bribed the city's building inspector with boxing lessons for life in exchange for tearing up a sheaf of condemned notices. Across the warehouse-sized floor, Wall Streeters dressed in TajWear Beat Downs sparred with ferocious sincerity among journeymen pros in threadbare Champions trying to keep sharp for one more payday.

Shatterproof was in the ring working with Chulo, his trainer. Shatterproof's kids, Rafe and Kendra, sat on folding chairs just outside the ring, their faces buried in homework resting on their laps.

"Hey, lawyer!" Shatterproof called through his mouthpiece, dancing backward and waving a glove hello. "Got my clearance?"

Chulo, a short, sturdy Dominican who was almost a double for Cheech Marin, but with nothing like Cheech's sense of humor, cuffed Shatterproof's ear. "What are you, Oprah fucking Winfrey?"

Shatterproof threw a right cross into Chulo's body armor that lifted his trainer into the air.

"That's it," Chulo said. "Keep your head in the ring."

I'd first met Shatterproof four years earlier, after Paulie Mishkin, an old law school buddy, had buttonholed me in the lawyers' room at Manhattan Supreme with the sort of "once in a lifetime" business opportunity that was so great it made his forehead weep with sweat.

"Dude," he'd said, assembly-lining pistachios between his teeth and machine-gunning the shells onto the floor. "I'm going to let you steal a piece of the next middleweight champion of the world, Abdul Rahman."

"I don't know anything about boxing, Mishk, and where would I get investment-level money?"

"Borrow it from your wife, she's rich."

"Don't go there—"

"Okay, okay. Jeez, calm *down*." With an unbuttoned shirt sleeve he wiped the beaded sweat that boiled from his hairline. "But look, you gotta take Abdul off my hands. There's this consortium I represent."

"A *consortium*," I said. "Of what?"

"These Senegalese dudes. Looking to start a little neighborhood bistro," he said defensively. "I was doing some work for them, permits and whatnot, the build-out. So I'm, like, holding a bunch of their investment money in escrow. But at the same time, things got tight around the office. Couple setbacks a case or two. You know how it is, one day you're flying high, it's like those magic cobblers I read to my kids: Every morning you wake up and instead of shoes there's stacks of Benjies all around your bed. Then, like *that*, you come crashing down, hemorrhaging cash and plummeting toward a Chapter Seven. So I figured, my Senegal buddies weren't going to need their escrow money for a good few months. They'd never know it was missing until it wasn't anymore."

"But they did."

"I was able to come up with almost all of it, pretty much. But if I can't find the rest, like, *now*, they're going to stove my head in. That's what they said, man," he added, coughing up a pistachio shell. "Stove it in."

I gave him half what he needed. Never did find out where he got the other half. Not long after, Paulie lost his license over something concerning a client's wife, ten thousand dollars, and a gun. Last I heard he was working as a freelance insurance investigator somewhere in California after winning early parole for his legal clinics in the Watertown Prison library. That's how I came to own a piece of Shatterproof. After his first year of fights I gave up hope of seeing a return on my investment.

But now, with his shirt off, dancing and jabbing, it seemed he could dismantle a fighter twice his size. He was all marbled muscle that somehow moved with speed and grace, and his head reminded me of a Greek sculpture at that museum Olivia made me go to one time for some charity. He was gifted, that much was certain, and it still shone through despite the battering that life, and Shatterproof himself, had unleashed on his gift. The main thing about him was that his eyes were sad--but like they'd always been sad, long before he'd started being called Shatterproof behind his back. Possibly even before his wife left him with the kids to make a better life for herself in a state down South that she hadn't bothered to name. I really liked him, liked him a lot. For his potential, and for how his years in the ring had revealed that it could never be more than that, just potential. And for how he kept feinting and jabbing at futility, always looking for that knockout punch. And for those kids.

"You disappeared on me, lawyer," he said, hanging over the rope after Chulo had released him for the day. "The fight's in a week."

My liking him was how he kept me in the game, trying to get him cleared to fight, hoping to convince him not to.

"I'm working on it," I assured him.

"You're working on shit." He glanced over at Rafe and Kendra. "Sorry, kids." Then to me, "I need this fight."

"Shatterpr—"

"Hey!" he snapped, gesturing toward his kids with his gloved hands.

No one was allowed to call him Shatterproof in front of his children.

"Abdul. I can't think of many ways to feed and clothe your children if you're in a coma. Plus it takes all the fun out of bedtime stories."

"I'm a warrior, ain't born to sit on my ass some night watchman. Sorry kids, about the ass."

Suddenly his muscles did this weird St. Vitus thing, like he was plugged in to some QVC instant weight loss contraption. It only lasted a couple of seconds. "Cold in here," he said quickly. Then he barked, "Chulo, where's my robe, man? I'm going to get sick standing here all sweaty before the fight."

Chulo had Shatterproof's gear laid out on a bench a few yards from the ring, packing it carefully into a bag. He glanced up with a look that said his man had taken a hard right and lost his way in the backward count.

"Get me cleared to fight, lawyer," Shatterproof said without waiting to hear from Chulo about the wayward robe. "There's no way my kids go hungry."

"What if I paid you *not* to fight?"

There was a gunshot of laughter from Chulo.

Shatterproof hung his wrapped hands over the ropes. "Deal. So write a check for..." He did a fast calculation in his head. "Four hundred K."

Chulo chuckled, "Unless he got the cash on him."

Shatterproof looked at me like he couldn't believe he'd been burdened with a third child. "Four hundred K is what it'll take for me to retire and get my kids through college. Unless they don't get scholarships, then I'll need a bunch more. But my two will get scholarships. So just the four hundred. Or, let's keep it simple—get me a clean scan."

Chulo froze in the middle of zipping up Shatterproof's bag.

Shatterproof nodded at me with sorrow and derision. "I got the only lawyer in the city his client has to do his thinking for him. A clean scan, it's the only way."

Chulo tore the zipper across the rest of the bag. "Piece of shit bag! Fucking zipper broke!"

Shatterproof kept staring at me. "They sell piss for a tox screen," he said. "They sell healthy brains."

Rafe and Kendra were bent over their schoolbooks. Gabriel would soon be the age for homework. Given the havoc he'd perpetrated on *The Very Hungry Caterpillar*, I imagined we'd have our work cut out for us, Olivia and I.

"My kids eat," Shatterproof told me. "Or they starve. That's on you, lawyer."

"There is this guy," I mused. "A doctor in the Bronx. Sonny Liang."

Chulo deflated like a punched-out speed bag.

I didn't get many accident cases, so I'd never done business with Sonny Liang. I'd heard his name whispered fondly around the courthouse for his willingness to write medical reports that could miraculously turn a hundred-thousand-dollar case into a million-dollar one.

I'd actually met him once, before my freshman year at Georgetown. The Mayor had offered me a summer internship in his law office—and accepted it for me, too. I'd wanted to lifeguard because the pay was good, and because the heroic authority of a lifeguard high up in his chair, combined with the ocean air and the heat, tended to drive women into a sexual frenzy. The Mayor tried to bribe me with a sixty-dollar steak at the Palm, but when he saw I still didn't want to work for him, quickly resorted to his favorite rhetorical device, the Stabbing Fork.

"I don't give a damn what you do after I'm dead," he fumed. "Schmucks with their *legacies*. Their scholarships and hospital wings. And to be honest, I don't lose a minute's sleep worrying you'll throw your gifts away, some high school teacher. So you can take your old man's firm or you can leave it, you get out of college. But you can't reject what you don't know. Especially when we're only talking a summer. Just one summer."

For a taste of what perks came with the legacy he couldn't give a damn if I took or rejected, the Mayor let me ride along the night he treated Dr. Liang and a judge named Scottie Walsh to dinner at Sparks, followed by ringsides at the Garden. We traveled in a limousine driven by a guy wearing an actual limo cap. All I remembered of Dr. Liang was the imperious cloud of cigar smoke that engulfed his head.

Shatterproof wanted to believe Sonny Liang would cooperate in giving him a clean bill of health, but had seen enough to know that in life, as in boxing, you have to keep your elbows in and your chin down—hope has a vicious right.

"He can scrub a CAT?" he asked with narrowed eyes. "Has to be clean as a virgin's—" He swiveled to his kids then glared at me like I was the one with the profanity problem.

I said, "They call his office Lourdes on Grand Concourse for the miracles he performs on losing personal injury cases. If he can heal the healthy by proving they're disabled, surely he can work similar wonders the opposite."

"I'm no opposite. Put a Kodiak bear in the ring, by round two he's staggering, eyes puffed out like apples, can't find his corner. It's just the commission, this CAT. They're like the government, interfering in a brother's livelihood."

Chulo untied one of Shatterproof's gloves. "Lawyer," he spat. "How my boy's gonna pay for a healthy brain?"

"You deaf, Chu?" Shatterproof hurled the glove to the canvas. "Henry's fronting the scan. I got the only lawyer in New York gives a shit. Sorry, kids." He leaped over the ropes and looked me dead in the eye. "I owe you, lawyer." Then he knelt before Kendra to tie her shoelace. "How're you walking around, your laces like that?"

"What worries me," I said, gesturing toward his kids, "is what will happen to them if anything goes wrong in the ring."

"Didn't you hear?" he laughed. "I'm shatterproof."

Then, because I wasn't laughing along, he added, "Just get me my fight. I'll be fine. Least 'till they're twenty-one and on their own."

ANARCHY

The Krakow Law Group occupied a narrow storefront on Desbrosses Street, which in winter siphoned the frigid air from the Hudson into a tunnel of concentrated misery. It had once been a slaughterhouse, a bit of history I'd learned only after I'd moved in and decided to believe it was simple coincidence and not a portent of my career to come.

My neighbors included a tax accountant and a professional photographer. The accountant once informed me, with a look of reverent longing, that the photographer had a sideline in pornography. Then there was Geneva Moon Sprite, who taught small group yoga and gave holistic massage. She'd once offered me a fifteen-minute sample as an inducement to buy her Chakra Release package, and though I was curious just how holistic her massages got, I declined. There were also the inhabitants of a handful of apartment buildings that had been renovated in a Desbrossesian straining toward the hipness of Gansevoort or Hudson, but no neighbor had ever stopped in with a legal problem and the cash to fix it.

I had a street-level office, roughly the dimensions of a steamer trunk. My only window was the one near the door, facing Desbrosses, that the landlord never cleaned because he would have needed a power drill, though an occasional ray of sunlight would gasp through now and then.

No receptionist or other superfluous staff supported the Krakow Law Group, because a cell phone and a few free apps can get you through the day just fine, without payroll taxes, Christmas bonuses, or emotional meltdowns suitable for reality television.

My cell went off, but the screen showed only a number, no name. My clients often phoned from burners and prepaids, but a chill of intuition warned that I should check the number against the one Zhukov had scrawled on a torn-off matchbook cover. He'd seemed desperate enough to expect I'd already been to Brighton Beach, and unbalanced enough that it was a bad idea to tell him I hadn't. The number was a match. Decline.

I flattened Cipka's napkin on my desk. It was definitely some sort of schedule. Olivia wasn't taking my calls because I wouldn't admit something was bothering me, so I took the long way home through fast-falling night. Ericsson up to Sixth Avenue, Sixth to Watts, then to *Anarchy* for an answer to the mystery of Cipka's cryptic napkin. Ten minutes in, Zhukov called again. If it were possible for a wind chime ringtone to sound menacing, mine did, so I powered down altogether.

Finally, I came to *Anarchy* and its familiar green muses. One sitting on her knees, cupping her breasts; one tossing her hair; the third with palms provocatively on hips, inviting or cautioning, or, I supposed, both. "Walk on by," I'd always warned myself those nights when I'd stopped to squint into the smoke glass window. "Once you cross that threshold there are further thresholds, and it gets easier to keep crossing."

Somehow, I found myself inside.

Grasping a Redwell stuffed with files I had the very best intention of getting around to reading, I crashed into shoulders and stepped on feet and compulsively apologized as I headed for the constellation of upmarket bottles arrayed behind the polished mahogany bar. I'd never been a drinker, so I ordered what the guy next to me was having, which turned out to be an Irish Pipe Bomb.

I'd always imagined *Anarchy* would be a time machine to a bygone era, a grimy crossroads of Wall Street and Jersey Shore, paved with cigar ash and jizz. Yet everyone was exceptionally well behaved and very nicely dressed. Let's say that I was the only one clothed by Men's Wearhouse. Beyond the bar, dancers writhed in scarlet wire birdcages set on three-foot platforms. Red light bulbs winked around the platforms. There was table service for dinner, and room to mingle with a drink in hand.

Then I saw Cipka in a birdcage.

I blinked and it was still Cipka, dancing away. A woman behind me shouted for a Train Wreck, so I told the bartender make it two. Cipka braided her filament of G-string around a finger. I was pissed as hell: Someone had inhaled my drink when I wasn't looking, so I was forced to order another.

I'd been right to hide the napkin, after all: Olivia would have killed her. But as a lawyer, I'd taken an oath to defend every citizen's right to fundamental due process. She might have a perfectly valid, or even heart-rending, explanation. I owed her the benefit of the doubt. Talk it out in a private booth, over a couple of Train Wrecks.

She saw me push through the crowd and her look went from panicked calculation to defeat, then back to calculation, as she glanced down at her nakedness and up at me.

"What are you doing here?" she said, reaching through her cage and taking the glass from my hand. The skin between her breasts glistened like cellophane. "I thought you were one of the good guys. A bowling-night-with-the-boys type."

I must not have been looking her in the eyes, because she glanced again at her half-naked body and shrugged. "It's just dancing, Mr. K. You have other ways I can make my B school tuition, besides the life-altering money you pay me, I'm all ears."

"Well," I said, working out how to explain it all to Olivia. "You are pursuing a career, there is that."

She seemed to read my mind.

"Gabriel needs me, he loves his Ci-ka. And I'm crazy about him. Just don't tell her. 'What she doesn't know...'"

A bouncer planted himself a few feet away and studied me impassively.

I said, "You want me to lie."

"Not unless you're ready for me to explain to Olivia how you knew I've been dancing here all along."

"But I didn't."

"So *you* say."

The bouncer's impassive stare turned surgical.

Cipka said, "Now please back away from the cage, sir. Our bouncers fracture things first and ask questions later. I'll finish my shift and find you."

The bouncer took an almost imperceptible step forward, so I hustled to the bar where I asked the waiter to recommend a drink with a kick, and he suggested something called a Sazerac. I gulped my Sazerac and tried hard not to stare at Cipka. Instead, I blinked at the liquor bottle Milky Way behind the bar and worked at a plan for keeping everyone happy. There had to be a way to keep the four of us intact that didn't involve lying again to Olivia.

Then Cipka tapped me on the shoulder. She was dressed in jeans, and the contrast of her blond hair against a red sweater, along with her peach complexion that was still flushed from hours of dancing, made it seem like she was almost on fire. "Let's get out of here," she said, grabbing my hand. Then, as if reading my confusion, "You're going to let a young woman travel alone through this big bad city this time of night?"

We cabbed it up to 58th and Third.

"Well goodnight, then," I said as we pushed into her lobby.

"I thought you were old school. See a girl to her door."

At her door she said, "Someone could have broken through the window, or climbed through my microwave or whatever. Lurking inside with evil intent."

She lived in a studio apartment with a fine view of a bricked flank of Bloomingdale's.

Her walls were bare, her surfaces clean. The furniture, Ikea. My Sazeracs and Train Wrecks converged into all-out peristaltic mutiny: Her place was built on stilts and the stilts were swaying wildly. I ran full throttle for the bathroom, leaving off the light to protect myself from the sight of irreparable reality staring back from the mirror. Cipka's surprise at seeing me at *Anarchy* echoed in my head. *I thought you were one of the good guys.* Feeling around in the dark, I found her toothpaste, hurrying a gobby mass around my mouth, then to the faucet where I shocked myself alert with cold water.

I stumbled out to find her lolling on her bed, flipping through a copy of *O* and sucking an orange mint against her upper palate with a sibilant whistle. Her window shade threw off alternating bars of light and shadow. Mint wrappers littered her nightstand like silver snow. Also, she was naked again, this time not half.

"You're a very attractive woman," I stammered, swamped by the mulchy perfume of her feet, the ruttish smell between her legs, and bittersweet orange.

"Yeah, I know," she said, studying another page.

"I'm a little fuzzy on something. What exactly is happening here?"

She turned to me with the same bored look she gave Oprah. "An insurance policy. If you turn me in about *Anarchy*, Olivia will Instagram it to her entire crowd. I'll never nanny again. You know how she likes to talk."

I stuttered, "I'm not following the insurance thing."

She laughed. "Sure you are. You've got something on me. I'll have something on you. After you put something *in* me."

"I want you to know, I've never done this before."

"Then what's Gabriel, adopted?"

"I mean with someone other than Olivia."

"Relax, Mr. K. She's not here. Want to look under the bed?"

Just then it hit me that I'd lost my Redwell.

"Shit!" I said, "I forgot something."

She laughed again, "You really are one of the good guys. I like good guys. I like them the way a dude likes to pop a virgin."

"A Redwell," I explained, sort of backing toward her door. "One of those brown accordion files that lawyers carry?" She hadn't seen it. "It's got privileged information. If someone gets hold of it, that could be an ethical violation. I probably left it at *Anarchy*. Do you know what time they lock up? Why are you laughing? I have a *duty*."

"I'm sure you do," she said, wrenching open my belt and tugging at my zipper. "Want to avoid a violation."

I slipped off my pants and emptied my pockets as if my Redwell would suddenly turn up among the loose coins and Wrigley's.

"What's that?" she asked, as my cash-stuffed nylon sock thudded to her floor.

"Just some legal papers."

"In a *sock*."

She sat at the edge of her bed. "You look like it's a contract on your life or something. Give it here. I want to see what you don't want me to see."

Cipka had a very persuasive way about her, possibly because she was naked and in bed. I told her about Zhukov and his Brighton Beach forger, and what was hidden in that black nylon. I assured her how first thing in the morning I'd be giving back his money. The one thing I didn't confess was how I'd lied to Olivia.

"Take it out," she commanded. "I want to see."

Apparently responding to my look of flustered confusion and tortured hope, she added, "The *money*."

I stacked the bills across her sheets.

"Wow," she said. "What's my end?"

"Your 'end'?"

Draping herself in hundreds, she said, "For being the voice of reason. Making you keep it."

"It's not mine to keep," I explained, sounding as if I were lecturing Gabriel.

"The guy's going to jail, right Mr. K? Without his ID? So in jail, what can he possibly do to you?" She sat up hard against the bedboard, covering herself with a blanket that she bunched in a fist at her throat. "Wait a minute!"

All I could think about was the trifecta at the end of that perfect belly, but the erotic energy was sucked clean out of the room by the one force in the universe more powerful than sex.

"We sell it back to him!" she said. "It's balls-ass brilliant! We go to Brooklyn, pick up the forged ID."

"*Possibly* forged."

"Whatever. You tell your Ukrainian, I've got your papers, where's my fee? He says, I *gave* you your fee. You say, Be that as it may."

I had no idea what she was talking about.

"You take him for twice the money. See? What's he going to do? He's stuck in jail."

"I always wondered what they teach in business school."

"That's why I'm an A student."

"Yeah, but you forgot something. I'm supposed to hand the ID over to the district attorney."

She shrugged. "Same difference."

"I don't think you're following: I'm a lawyer and there are rules."

"*Rules!*" she laughed. "All there is, Mr. K, is wanting and getting."

"You sound like my father."

"Then he was a genius."

"Actually, the genius almost went to prison. Instead he got cancer and died."

She shrugged. "Reap the whirlwind."

Throwing the blanket aside, she covered herself with money again.

All those times she'd breezed by, arm-loaded with steaming laundry, or grocery bags brimming with food, or Gabriel's brightly-colored sand toys, smelling of suntan lotion and sea, with barely a nod or smile my way.

Now I had only to cross a foot of shadowed floor.

"I can't do this," I said. "I mean I've never with anyone except...not at all sure that I can do this."

"The Tunnel of Love," she cooed, opening her knees, and with her fingers, opening more than that. "One ride, ten K."

THE FORGER

Cipka and I rode an antiquated Q an hour and a quarter to the ocean end of Brooklyn. Every lurch and jerk, the helpful announcements from the conductor that sounded like an attack of wild parrots, every single molecule of light rebuked me for the Pipe Bombs. I pretended to sleep to avoid a heart-to-heart with Cipka about why I'd backed away from her tunnel of love, and how it wasn't her, it was me. Generous Cipka pretended not to know I was pretending. But a jolt of uncertainty ripped across my belly: Did she still plan to use as insurance my getting as far as the ticket booth to her tunnel of love, even though I'd declined to ride?

Olivia had been less big-hearted when later that night I'd banged home, fumbling through the dark and into bed, the alcohol and the reproaching memory of naked Cipka prompting me to ignore the voice in my head that warned that this was a night best spent on the sofa.

"You're never late," Olivia murmured, half-asleep.

"Big case tomorrow. Had to write this epic motion."

"At the local bar? You reek."

"You'd be surprised."

"At what?"

"Tell her," my good angel whispered. "You always would have." But my fallen angel said in honeyed tones, "You can set this all straight. You can set it straight and get everyone back to normal. And besides, as the saying goes, *What she doesn't know won't make her fire the nanny.*"

"I'm not sure," I'd answered. "I'm not sure what you'd be surprised at."

She showed me her back.

The Q finally gasped to the last stop. Below, the el thrust a corridor of darkness across 86th Street. We stepped out into the feeble October sun, searching for the address Zhukov had scrawled on a matchbook cover. His money banged against my thigh, bruising a clot headed straight for the heart, because I knew his friend with the papers couldn't be right, but I also knew I was going to keep looking until I found him.

Cipka wore a light brown jacket with a short fur stole and tight yoga pants. That summer, Olivia and I had taken Gabriel to Saratoga to see the horses. We walked through the must of early morning grass, and stables, and horses damp with perspiration. Cipka smelled like that all the time, like April bloomed between her legs. I berated myself for letting her come to Brooklyn. Or was I the one tagging along?

"It strikes me that our imagination has probably run away with us," I said as we walked up Brighton 14th·, squinting at the building numbers. "And the papers are perfectly legal."

She exhaled impatience. "*Legal!*" She took out her phone and in under a minute had Google-mapped us to a sprawl of Miami Modernist yellow brick and smoky terrace glass. We headed for the elevator through a vast Baroque lobby with Chinese carpeting and crystal chandeliers. "Look, your Russian *needs* his ID, right?" she said. "Legal or whatever. Where there is need, there's a market."

We entered a mirrored elevator and I studied my shoe to avoid the refracted Krakows with their looks of contempt, pity, and terror. Cipka squeezed my hand.

A woman answered the bell. Late thirties, with a sexy, go-fuck-yourself ennui, wearing a Trump Plaza bathrobe that hung open over half-moon breasts and peach-colored panties.

I had no idea what was supposed to happen next.

Cipka said, "We're here about Zhukov."

Without a word, the woman disappeared into the bedroom.

"If cops rush in with guns and badges," I told Cipka, "you're explaining it to Olivia."

"I'm not afraid of *her*."

"*You* only live there part time."

She popped a couple of mints, exhaling fresh cut orange. Then sidled over to the coffee table and pretended to study a large glass frog, while actually spying on our forger through the half-opened bedroom door. I stayed put inside the front door, asking myself, What *evidence* do you have this woman is actually a forger? For all you know, Zhukov is completely legitimate.

Directly across the room a large window seemed to frame all of Brooklyn. I'd grown up not far from here, in a tan brick apartment building grandly called Ocean View Manor. It was just me, the Mayor, and Nina, his First Lady (well, first among many), in a ten-room penthouse. The Mayor often "worked late," which meant he might not show up for days. Days when Nina kept the apartment as clean and quiet as a mortuary. But then he'd breeze in again without warning to parade through every room spooning ice cream from gallon containers, emptying his pockets of so much cash it seemed like the magician's scarf trick, strewing cocktail napkins with scrawled deal numbers, and phone numbers, shouting war stories from the legal trenches at the decibel level of a boom box.

The Mayor spent so many weekends working on his newest "blockbuster case" that we never got to shag baseballs or build model airplanes, or learn how to survive on acorns and leaf dew if we should happen to get stranded in the wild. But he did give me something far more useful: career training for the day his firm became Krakow & Son.

For instance, there was the Sunday he drove us to a Waldbaum's in Bay Ridge. He loved war movies, so we had to pretend the supermarket was Normandy. He crouched, skulking down the aisles like he was dodging sniper bullets. If I even hinted that I thought he'd gone nuts, they would have had to scrub my body from the linoleum. Instead, I sort of half-skulked behind him, until he located Target X: an aisle with no customers and lots of large glass bottles. Walking his fingers up and down rows of Italian tomato sauce pretending to search for his favorite brand, he stopped at a family-sized Del Monte, swiveled right and left, and edged it off the counter until it splattered across the floor. My job was to document this "egregious lack of reasonable maintenance" with the camera he'd shoved into my school bag.

But my brain had shut down, and the camera had become a Rubik's Cube. "*Take the picture,*" he hissed. The muscles in his neck swelled like suspension cables on the Brooklyn Bridge, the lightning bolt vein in his temple detonated. I looked away to see red sauce hemorrhaging from the shattered glass. "You take that picture and take it now!"

But I couldn't find the shutter release—the camera felt as jagged as the bottle of Del Monte.

"Fucking kid!"

Then somehow he had the camera and was snapping out shots.

The next thing I knew he was zipping my bag and pointing at the exit. He had this look in his eye that he got sometimes, like he was my age again and playing the prank of the century. Suddenly he shouted, "*Run!*" galloping away with big, goofy, loping steps.

I knew there'd be alarms and sirens, and cops storming in, dozens of them, to drag me off in cuffs. I ran, but it could not have been like any Hollywood war movie, because I was thirty pounds overweight, asthmatic, and so athletically gifted that I was in danger of tripping over my own sneaker.

He screamed with laughter, "Better lay off those Twinkies."

"I struggled to keep up, laughing even more hysterically than he was, and wondering why, since it was all so funny, I couldn't stop crying.

"Hey! Hey, you!" Zhukov's friend was forcing an envelope on me, the old-school kind from the days of interoffice memos, stained with coffee and finger grease, held together by rubber bands. Her fingernails were raptor claws painted crimson. I rocketed back from Brooklyn-then to Brooklyn-now. She said, "What's the matter with you? *Take it.* It's what you came for."

With a gasp of exasperation, Cipka took the envelope. "Thanks," she told Zhukov's friend, her voice shaky and breathless. "See you when I see you."

She seemed, all at once, different somehow, and not in a good way.

Confused, the woman said, "What about me?"

"What about you?" Cipka parroted, looking jacked-up and terrified.

Suddenly she was speaking in tongues, but the woman understood, and it made the blood drain from her face.

"Don't speak Russian to me, Polish twat," she told Cipka. "Pay me or give me back my envelope."

"Come take it," Cipka answered. "Russian ass whore."

I reached into my pocket to get the cash.

Cipka told me, "Put that sock back in your pants."

The woman retreated a step, opening her fists to fan foot-long nail-talons. She seemed to be deciding whether to leap at me first for hesitating with the sock, or at Cipka, for telling me to.

Cipka told me, "Walk backward to the door. Keep your eyes on her hands."

To the woman, she said, "You and I are renegotiating, puta."

"Puta isn't Russian," I explained, gripping the sock by its black nylon tail and holding it out toward Zhukov's friend. "It's Spanish. Plus, I'm not sure renegotiation is our ideal play. It is Brighton Beach: think what relatives she must have."

I tried to dig the cash out of the sock, which turned out to require a pretty fair amount of work. Zhukov's friend stepped back on her left foot, something I'd seen Shatterproof do before dealing a lights-out left hook. Her breathing accelerated.

"It's not a gun, it's not a gun," I said quickly. "It's your money."

"We can do this," Cipka said imploringly.

Finally, I had the cash in my fist. "You can count it," I told Zhukov's friend. "It's all there."

She pointed her chin at Cipka. "Ass whore? It's Poland that's ass whore of Russia."

Cipka, who read "Goodnight Moon" so lullingly that I would often fall asleep before Gabriel did, lifted the glass frog from the coffee table and slammed it against the woman's head.

Zhukov's friend fell, upending the coffee table, head bouncing like a soccer ball from table to sofa arm, hitting the floor with a sickening thud. There was blood spray all over; blood clotted the forger's hair.

"Shit," Cipka observed. Then, "Is she dead?"

She wasn't. She groaned something in Russian that I expected wasn't "Nice to have met you," dragging an arm and hip to prop herself up to her knees.

A voice that sounded a lot like mine said, "We've got to get out of here. Leave the money and let's go."

Cipka had stopped hyperventilating. It was hard to tell if she was breathing at all. Her eyes were glassy, but there was a hot stain of color on her cheeks. She tiptoed around the widening Rorschach of blood oozing from the woman's head and gathered the money. The woman fought like hell to get to her feet. Meanwhile, my sock had flown across the sofa like a used condom. Cipka grabbed that, too.

"The fuck," she told me. "Let's go."

Somehow we were in the elevator.

"Nothing. Happened," she said. "We belong here. Stop breathing like that, someone's going to notice. Everything's normal. Just two people in an elevator."

A trail of the forger's blood ran from her lip to her cheek. I glanced at myself in the elevator's mirrored wall: I was okay. She flinched when I raised my hand to her face. I nodded to the mirror, and when she looked, she let me clean the blood with a thumb. Then she forced my thumb into her mouth. Her eyes condensed to jungle green, like a leopard in estrus, the kind who just after climaxing kills her male. When she finished blowing my thumb it was clean.

We ran full out, finding our way back to the train station by keeping the elevated tracks in our sights, but winding up near the beach instead. She pulled me under the boardwalk, biting my lips and snaking her tongue into my mouth with an urgent, pleading whelp. I placed my hand on her breast over the stole.

She repeated, "Do you think she's dead? Do you think she's dead?" as if homicide were an aphrodisiac. Then she tried to shove my hand up under her shirt.

"We should get out of Brooklyn," I said. "There'll be police."

She rubbed the front of my pants and made that urgent sound, over and over.

"You knew you were going to steal the money all along." I said. "You planned it."

She pushed against me, grinding and snarling.

"That thing with your Polish outrage," I continued. "You set her up, Zhukov's forger. Taunted her so she'd taunt you back and get you pissed enough to have the courage to hit her with the frog so you could steal the papers and keep the money."

She undid my belt and went for my zipper. "You think too much, you know that?"

I pushed her blouse up to her neck and her breasts popped out, pale and pink and lovely. She looked both ways to make sure no one was watching. Her sudden modesty sent every corpuscle of blood rushing to my head.

A police siren wailed in the distance. All I could see was a cruiser barreling at me with the forger at one window and Olivia at the other.

"I'm so sorry," I gasped. "But I'm an attorney; can't afford to get arrested. Can you see that?"

She pushed me backward with a look that suggested I was lucky there were no glass frogs around. Then her mouth moved, but whatever she said was drowned in the thunder of an oncoming Q. She took my wrist and we ran again, and at the station climbed the stairs two at a time, disappointing the conductor by slipping into the car a microsecond before getting caught in the door and dragged down the platform. We sat and I tried to plead two counts of guilty-with-an-explanation, adding my boardwalk hesitation to last night's retreat from her Tunnel of Love, but she was jacked on violence and sexual frustration. All she kept saying was, "Call Zhukov now, *call him now.*" It took a lot of convincing before she agreed to wait until we weren't in a subway car filled with strangers. Then she launched into a warp speed blow-by-blow of everything that had happened from the moment we'd hit Brighton Beach. Finally, she dropped off to sleep in the heavy ocean sun beating through the windows.

Zhukov had scrawled his cell number on a torn-off matchbook cover from a place called Exotica. I took the forger's envelope from my pocket, trying to convince myself that it was all in my imagination and the papers were legitimate, after all. It was the sort of envelope, filled with cash, or dummied permits, or witness statements, that the Mayor had handled countless times without a shred of ambivalence. But then, he'd enjoyed the gifts of self-confidence and simplicity of thought that had, like recessive genes, skipped a generation, consigning his offspring to a mind as densely tangled as the half-dozen rubber bands that held the envelope shut because the glue had dried.

The Q made its dreary way forward, but I felt I was traveling further and further from home. At Prospect Park a white guy with Rasta hair and tats got on, treating us to a tune from his radio from which all the music had been removed. It jack-hammered Cipka awake.

"Why are you staring at Zhukov's phone number?" she asked. The nap had calmed her, she seemed herself again. "Are you repenting what can't be changed?"

I said, "I'm not giving this to the D.A. Won't cross that line. But we can sell Zhukov his papers, we can do that. You'll get your money. And Zhukov can hang out in the Court Street men's room again until he finds some other lawyer to negotiate his release."

"Sounds like a plan. So why do you look like hell?"

"Because I'm wondering, once he's free, what's to stop him from tracking us down?"

"Why would he do that? Oh! You mean revenge for his Russian bitch? God! Relax, Henry. Obviously he wants those stupid papers so he can disappear again. He's not going to do a *lawyer*. Why are you looking at me like that?"

"You're out of focus. I see two of you: one is stroking Gabriel's hair, the other's using a frog for a bludgeon."

"We're making it work," she said. "Just trust your Cik-a."

"May I plead guilty with an explanation? About last night?"

"It's only sex, Mr. K. No worries."

She was so uncomplicated that she made me feel sad for myself.

I said, "You know what they say about the third try…"

She took my hand. "I like you anyway. You make me laugh."

"You have lots of great qualities, but I can't remember ever seeing you laugh."

"I laugh on the inside," she said, with a pang of hurt.

Back in Manhattan, we climbed out at Chambers Street and Cipka shoved me under a scaffold between the green subway gate and a Duane Reade.

"Call him," she said. "Call your Russian."

"Ukrainian," I reminded her. "And he probably already heard what you did to his friend."

"You don't know that they're friends, you don't *know* that."

"The prudent thing would be to take some time to think through our side of the story."

"*Prudent?*" she said. "Fucking *prudent?*"

But she glanced at her watch, sighed and backed down. "I have to pick up Gabriel from school. Decide what story you're going to tell Zhukov. You can call him without me, but I have to be there when it goes down."

"When it 'goes down' you'll be there," I lied.

Squinting those almond eyes as if they were an X-ray into the soul of Henry Krakow, she said, "You better hope I am." Then she raced off to fetch Gabriel from the Sunflower School.

We'd nearly killed a woman, nearly had sex under the boardwalk, conspired to steal money that belonged to my client—and it was only two in the afternoon. But there was more to do. Time was running out on Shatterproof and the commission. I wasn't looking forward to another long slog, this time to Dr. Sonny Liang way up in the Bronx. But at least I'd have time to work out how I'd lie to Olivia about Cipka, the frog, and the forger.

DR. SONNY LIANG

Dr. Sonny Liang's office was standing room only. Neck braces, crutches, slings, canes—there was even a guy with a back support worn *over* his clothing. The reception desk was empty; no one answered the dull thud of the little silver bell. I knew someone would have to appear eventually to collect the next patient, so I staked out a Krakow-sized width of wall against a door frame without a door, that I figured led to the examining rooms.

On a rickety coffee table the *Grand Concourse Gazette* featured a photograph of Olivia's client Taj. He wore a body-hugging electric silver suit and a scowl, hand-in-hand with an equally aggrieved DAna (whose anthems of heartbreak, with their broken-voiced sobs and anguished growls, rising to full-throated protestations of defiant survival, had become the background music of American life). The headline screamed, "200 HUNDRED CHILDREN = ONE SILK SUIT." I didn't have time to read the article, because a thickset woman charged past, almost knocking me over on her way to the reception desk. Her crew cut hair was white and her skin was chalky black, and she wore a pilled cardigan over a nurse's uniform whose buttons threatened to explode like shrapnel.

"Escobio," she called, with the emphasis in the wrong place, Esco*beeo*, which didn't faze the Spanish guy in the blue overalls and an arm cast from wrist to elbow. "Sit down, Mr. Escobio," she snapped. "I didn't say come with. You're next, five minutes."

She gathered a bunch of forms against a clipboard and snapped them into place.

"I'm a lawyer," I told her, as if I were apologizing for being a lawyer. "Henry Krakow. Can the doctor squeeze me in for a few minutes to talk about a case?"

"Which case is that?" she asked, creasing her brow and turning to a computer that appeared to have been the very first on the market.

"Oh, we're not working together yet. I want to see if he's available for something new."

She brightened at the prospect of a trial lawyer bearing the gift of a new patient, and with a hand on each armrest pushed off from her chair. "The doctor is in a procedure," she said, coming out from behind the glass. "You can wait in his private office; it won't be but a few minutes."

She led me down a corridor of examining rooms where patients looked up with instantly deflating hope as we shuffled past, until she pushed open a door to reveal what looked like a warehouse for drug company freebies, golf clubs, dusty liquor bottles, boxes of Nica Rustica cigars, decades worth of family photographs, and prominently displayed photos of the doctor himself, smiling alongside faintly recognizable men who wore the unmistakable smarm of the politician, real estate developer, or Wall Street trader. Two of them were more than faintly recognizable. They'd followed the familiar road from indictment to plea deal, to minimum security prison and early release, to lucrative speaking engagements where they "paid my debt to society" by recounting their rise and fall and harrowing climb back to plush jobs as lobbyists and white-shoe lawyers.

Dr. Sonny Liang—he actually *was* born Sonny, according to his diploma and license—had managed to keep his record, if not his reputation, pristine.

The doctor breezed in, at least as much as six-foot-four can breeze after a lifetime of cigars, filet mignon on the dime of grateful plaintiff's attorneys, and leisurely Sundays tooling around in golf carts. His lab coat had survived years of laundering, with the frayed cuffs and ghosted stains to prove it. Apart from affection for the congeniality of his medical opinion, the world of personal injury viewed Dr. Liang with fascination bordering on the occult for his having been born half black and half Chinese.

"*Mister* Henry Krakow," he chimed, reaching out a massive hand. "I recognize you from around the courts, but somehow we've never met."

"I don't do a lot of PI," I said. "What I can get."

He nodded as if I'd made a sage observation—probably he'd decided that my not doing much PI meant I couldn't be of use to him, so why was I wasting his time?

"Your father was a magnificent character," he said. "Larger than life."

"He was that," I said, hoping to move off the subject of the Mayor. Whenever an admirer reminded me how larger than life the Mayor was, I heard, "So what, Henry, does that make you?"

Liang continued, "Truly sorry about what happened to him."

I tried to steer the doctor away from what was, for me, the most ancient of histories. "I've come about a case."

He leaned back in his chair to work a rubber band in his fingers.

"I have a client who needs a CAT scan," I continued. "His head. And of course an expert to read it."

"Car accident?" he asked. "Falling object?"

"I know you like the fights."

"Not cage, I hope. That's the rage now, but all those flailing limbs, where's the art in it, where's the beauty?"

"No, I've got a boxer. Old school."

He wasn't listening, lost in his reverie of the tragedy of progress. "*Mixed* martial arts! Many things cannot make one thing. That's called chaos." In one breath he removed a cigar from a desk drawer, snipped the end, lit it, took a drag, and said, "But where are you going with a fight case? Who's your pocket? Sue the commission and they'll make sure your client never works again, not even as a corner man. But you'd know *that*, the Mayor's kid. What's his name, anyway, your fighter?"

"Abdul Rahman? He's a light heavy."

"Never heard of him."

"Abdul's a road warrior," I said as if I were apologizing for him. "He's also got these two little kids he's raising himself. Log enough hours in the ring, you get dinged up, and he's got this fight on Saturday."

"I'm not following," he said. "Who are we suing?"

"I need a clean scan." I said. "So he can get cleared."

Liang threw his head back and laughed. "You think there are no more surprises, then the Mayor's son shows up in your office." He leaned forward over his desk, scribbling furiously on a prescription pad. "Whatever you've got going, it's way over the head of us mere mortals."

"No, I really need to get him cleared. For his kids."

"Magnificent," he said, nodding with appreciation and holding out the prescription sheet for me to take.

"Abdul hasn't got insurance, I'm not sure he can afford—"

"I'll talk to the lab," he said, handing me a brochure for a place called ARC Radiology. "I'm friends with the owner," he added with a fugitive smile. "I'm sure he'll quote you a price you can handle."

He bounced from his chair to hustle me out with a hand on my back. "A favor for the Mayor's son."

Shatterproof would never know what it cost me to help him feed those kids.

At the reception desk Dr. Liang patted my shoulder and shook my hand. "When you phone the lab, ask for Perry." He took a new chart from the nurse, called for his next patient, and disappeared through the doorless door frame to the examining rooms.

I studied the slick brochure. According to the brilliantly-colored alphabet rainbow, the ARC in ARC Radiology stood for Accommodating, Reliable, and Congenial. It was way out in the Bronx and Shatterproof lived on upper Broadway, but he would have walked to California barefoot for a crack at Saturday's purse.

One last fight, I assured myself. A final payday for a running start on a new life.

I pocketed the brochure and prescription along with Zhukov's envelope and made my way out of Liang's waiting room. All I had to do now was deal with that guy Perry, figure out how to explain the forger and frog to Zhukov, sit with Shatterproof and a legal pad to figure out his new career. Then I'd finally win Olivia back, once and for all.

Coming home, coming home.

THE JUMPS

"Straightway, they didn't teach in law school how to answer phone?"

Zhukov sounded so cheerful that I thought maybe he hadn't heard about Cipka and the green frog.

"Sorry Anatoly, big trial. Couldn't get away."

He seemed to laugh in his silence. Then he said, "You ever see that movie where Bobby De Niro's lawyer puts knife in back and sends him to prison?"

The sun was beginning to set over Gabriel's favorite park, not far from our apartment. Leaning against a tree at the east entrance, I listened to Zhukov on my phone. Gabriel and a bunch of other kids ran in random patterns, crashing into each other and laughing hysterically. A smattering of nannies sat on benches, huddled against the cold. Cipka sat alone with her legs crossed and her phone on a thigh, underlining a book. She wore tan suede boots and skin-tight jeans, and a chestnut jacket with a flared collar that crowned her light blonde hair and pale complexion. Immersed in her underlining, she bit the corner of her lower lip, ripe and cherry red.

"But I'm here now," I told Zhukov. "Ready to conclude our business."

"De Niro, all he wants is get revenge. So when he has first chance—when he has *his* first chance, *his* first chance," he emphasized, as if memorizing a rule. "Always place possessive or article before noun. Article is 'it', 'the', 'a'. I'm getting rid of accent. Is not easy. It *is not* easy. I work every day with YouTube guy. When I talk like American, then I'll take American name. Thinking of Steve. Steve West. Like

Kanye. Disappear into America forever. Of course, now I'll probably have to find new forger to make identity. Anyway, for payback, when De Niro has his first chance, he fucks lawyer's family but good. See, I remembered *his*, but is *his* article, or what?"

Now I was on my feet instinctively moving toward Gabriel.

"You hired me to avoid attention," I told Zhukov. "You're not going to do anything to invite it."

Gabriel saw me and cried *Daddy! Daddy! Daddy!*, crashing at breakneck speed into my arms. Cipka glanced up and, seeing the look on my face, put her book on the bench and marched toward me, tearing off her headphone.

"Let me tell you something, Straightway," Zhukov laughed. "Never sign up client in toilet"

"Play with me," Gabriel insisted, tugging my hand.

Cipka had reached me with a look that said she'd do far worse than Zhukov ever could if I tried to back down from our plan.

"But you're right," he sang. "People going all over Brighton Beach smashing frogs into other people's heads. Who needs that kind of attention?"

"Listen, I can explain."

"Usually lawyers rob you with leather briefcase and bullshit words."

"Rob you? No, that's not what happened—not exactly."

"And speaking of blood, Helena has plan to drain yours onto a drop cloth and sink your half-alive body in Atlantic."

"Helena, is she the woman in Brighton Beach?"

"Me, all I care is you finish what I paid you for."

Cipka heard me mention Brighton Beach and midnight flashed across her pale blue eyes.

Zhukov said, "Do you feel me, Straightway?"

"I feel you—but I can't take your papers to the D.A. if they're what I think they are."

I gestured to Cipka not to take seriously what she was about to hear.

"I propose to give them back to you," I continued. "And all the money. Every dollar."

Dead silence on Zhukov's end. Finally he said, "Okay. Tonight."

"Can it wait for tomorrow?" I asked, Cipka nodding yes and mouthing, "I have to dance."

"Can it wait for tomorrow?" he mimicked, dropping any pretense of good humor. "I told you I have *no time*."

He made me repeat the address for our meeting and ended the call.

"When's the drop?" Cipka asked. "It better not be tonight."

I let Gabriel pull me away. We played tag, Gabriel-style, meaning that I always had to be It. Darkness fell, threatening to end our summer in October. I chased Gabriel, shouting and laughing, the wind on my face cold and fresh, tie flapping over my shoulder, shirt flying out of my pants. The mothers and nannies watched me indulgently, if queerly. Finally, as the playground began to empty, I missiled back to real life.

"Time for dinner," I told Gabriel. And to Cipka, "It's just as well you have to dance and can't come with me."

Gabriel said, "I want to dance, too!"

I said, "I'm planning to tell Olivia everything. No more secrets."

"Oh, yeah?" she said, raising her eyes with a dubious smile.

"Well, about Zhukov and his papers, anyway."

Gabriel repeated, "Daddy, I want to dance like Cippy."

We'd arrived at my apartment building.

"I heard you repeat the address," she said. "Now you're hoping I don't blow off my shift so I can beat you there and do the deal my way. Better to take me with, Mr. K. Better the chaos you know than the one you don't."

"But what's to stop you from pulling another Brighton Beach, this time on Zhukov?"

She shrugged. "Reap the whirlwind." Then she thought a moment and said, "Too bad we have to take the subway all the way to the ass end of Brooklyn twice in one day. We don't even know what your Russian's going to do to us, or *try* to do, you know, about the frog thing."

"What frog?" Gabriel asked, climbing onto my shoes and demanding that I walk him.

"We could take Olivia's Jeep," she added.

Walking Gabriel in circles on top of my shoes—he seemed to have gained twenty pounds overnight, I said, "Or you can stay home. For both our sakes."

She said, "I have to bring Gabriel upstairs, but you can't come up yet, 'cause you're never home this time. Olivia keeps the keys in Gabriel's tyrannosaurus. I can take them and beat you to Coney Island and cut my own deal."

I opened my jacket to show her the rubber-banded envelope. "Without these?"

Her eyes flashed midnight again. Then she shrugged. "One problem at a time."

Finally I relented. "Meet me at Om Cooking. You know the place, Hudson and Vestry. It's small and out of the way. If Olivia catches you with your hand in the tyrannosaurus, I must disavow all knowledge of you and our mission."

"I don't get caught."

• • •

Om Cooking was a hole-in-the-wall on a quiet side street. It only served "earth sensitive" food. There were two small tables and a counter with three stools along the counter. The lighting was low and the walls held sparkling black & white photos of 50s-era jazz musicians, though I never could get the connection between alfalfa meat loaf and Chet Baker. They were still brewing their evening blend, so I sipped the dregs of an Embrace the Day roast, took Zhukov's envelope from my pocket, and put it on the table.

One of the Mayor's favorite maxims was, "What you don't know can't get you indicted or testify against you in exchange for immunity." In this case, he was right—I should just give Zhukov back his papers and be free of him. But what if they weren't forgeries? What if I'd read the whole thing wrong?

I emptied the envelope onto the table. Zhukov Who Was Not Zhukov had been born, according to his birth certificate, Steve West, a child of the wheat belt with a trucker's license issued out of Texas.

While I was hustling it all back into the envelope I got a call. It was Kendra.

"Daddy's on the floor and he wants you to come over."

"What do you mean Daddy's on the floor? Can I speak to him?"

"He's sleeping."

"On the floor?"

I thought, Shatterproof's dead and this is her way of coping, saying he's asleep.

"He got the jumps and fell down," she explained.

"I'll be right there." After I hung up I realized I had no idea where he lived. I dialed his cell and Kendra answered and gave me the address, precisely articulating each number and spelling out B r o a d w a y.

Cipka pulled up in front of Om Cooking, honking Olivia's horn.

"You were supposed to just bring me the keys," I told her. "How'd you get it out of the lot?"

"The garage guy remembered me from summer when I took Gabriel to the beach."

I told her to slide over so I could drive, but she wouldn't budge.

"If you bang it up," I said, "there's no sneaking it back."

"Are you kidding?" She gunned the motor to scream through a Stop sign onto Hudson Street "I drive like a nun."

I locked my seat belt into place. "Take the Highway," I said. "We need to make a stop."

"Weapons?"

"I have to see a friend. Broadway and 105th."

We made it in what felt like under five minutes, weaving through a chorus of angry honks, a smattering of bitches, a cunt or two, and a half-dozen middle fingers. Cipka double-parked across from Shatterproof's with a promise that if I took longer than ten minutes she'd drive the Jeep through the door and up the stairs.

He lived on the third floor. I knocked and called Abdul? Kendra? I tested the knob and pushed into a long, narrow corridor. Directly across from me was a kitchenette, but no one was there. A bathroom adjoined the kitchenette, separated by a thin plasterboard wall, which must have made for some interesting meals. I followed the hushed voices of Rafe and Kendra toward the end of the dark corridor where a pale light glowed. About two-thirds of the way, a door opened onto a windowless bedroom that was more like a closet, with a bunk bed and flimsy wooden desk. Finally I came to a large open room with two windows overlooking 105th, where a six-foot-two marvel of chiseled muscle and bristling hostility was tucked under a blanket on his sofa looking like he'd flash-forwarded from thirty-five years old to eighty.

"Lawyer," he whispered, sounding surprised. "You came."

Rafe stood guard above his father's regal head, shifting his weight from foot to foot, his face a mask of manly composure that couldn't quite hide his utter helplessness.

Shatterproof tried to push himself up against the armrest. "But I don't need you after all, must have swallowed funny. Yeah! Dinner went down the wrong way. Kids went to call the police and I knew they'd take me to the hospital. If the commission found out, my fight's good as dead, even my only choking on a chunk of sirloin. I figured Straightway'd know what to do, but it was a false alarm. I'm okay."

"Where's Chulo?"

"Chu's a trainer. You see me training?" With a long troubled breath he made a final push to sit straight up. "I need him focused, no distractions. You feel me?"

"But Abdul—"

"I'm asking if you feel me."

"But—"

He turned away from me. "Kendra, what do I always say about but?"

She looked up from her book, placed her hands together on the open pages and recited, "Butts are for sitting and for getting whupped."

I said, "You couldn't spank them if your life depended on it."

Kendra suppressed a giggle and lowered her head. Shatterproof gave me the evil eye.

Olivia's Jeep blared insistently from the street.

"I'm calling that lawyer's hex down on you," he told me. "Where you have to do whatever I tell you."

"I think you're referring to privilege, and it doesn't mean I have to do whatever you say. And in any case, I'm not strictly speaking your lawyer. I'm just a businessman protecting his investment."

The Jeep started in again. This time Cipka just sat on it until a dog started barking and someone yelled, "Cierra la puta boca!"

"Listen," Shatterproof said, leaning forward and softening his tone. I strained to hear him.

"I got the jumps, that's all. It happens you go to war as much as me. I can't tell Chulo because he'd climb into the ring himself before he'd let me fight. But you're a lawyer, you see my meaning?"

Cipka laid off the horn.

"I do," I said with a shudder of resignation. "See your meaning."

Kendra closed her book onto a bookmark bedazzled with sapphires and rubies. "May I show you out?" she asked, leading me down the corridor to the front door.

"Hey lawyer!" her father called. I stopped, but before I could turn back, he added. "You really did come."

The tumblers fell into place behind me. I touched the left breast pocket of my jacket, as if Zhukov's forgeries could somehow have disappeared since the last time I'd touched them, fifteen minutes earlier, and the time fifteen minutes before that. My five-thousand-dollar fee would almost certainly cover Shatterproof's clean CAT scan, or at least I hoped it would. But now I had this idea about a fresh start. I pictured a modest but comfortable house, with separate bedrooms for Rafe and Kendra, so far north from the brutal city you could feed deer on your front lawn, and Canada would be "just across the way." That would take serious seed money, much more than my fee alone. The kind you get from meter-hackers with forged immigration papers, who, as Cipka had pointed out, had to pay whatever you told them, no matter how much, because they had everything to lose.

Hustling down the stairs, I hesitated before opening the door. 105th had grown ominously quiet. I held my breath before stepping out to the Jeep and whatever new mayhem Gabriel's nanny had in store.

THE NEW ARRANGEMENT

We turned onto Mermaid Avenue in Coney Island, a few blocks from where we were supposed to meet Zhukov. I checked my cell again to see if Olivia had called to find out why I was late coming home. As we passed 23rd Street I reminded Cipka for the fourth time to make a left when we hit 26th.

She laughed, "Kinda nervous? I know what you're planning, Mr. K. Don't forget I'm a Henry Kravis Scholar. Free ride all the way."

I asked her what she thought she knew I was planning.

"Walking back the deal with your Russian."

"I wouldn't keep calling him Russian. Certainly not to his face."

"See? You're scared shitless. That's your problem. My guess is you think you're going to give him his fake ID *and* return your fee to make it up to him for what you did to his forger."

"What I did," I said, looking sideways at her.

"But I've got your back, and that's your good fortune."

I told her, "Now you've missed 26th and you're about to do the same at 27th."

She parked in an unlit lot behind a bank and broke open a fresh pack of mints. "And by the way, in my apartment that night, and under the boardwalk? When you couldn't pull the trigger with your hot nanny? Don't tell yourself that was about Olivia. That was fear, too."

She popped a couple of mints into her mouth and the car exploded with oranges.

"I hope you're not planning to get *that* close to him," I said.

She started walking toward the ocean.

"They help me think."

I followed her toward the beach. "I'm not afraid of you," I said, "Or what we were going to—and by the way, you're taking the wrong street."

A highway pile-up of Polish consonants crashed back at me. "*Think*, Henry. Boy, for a lawyer, you're not that bright. We have to come in stealthy." She marched up a concrete ramp onto the boardwalk and headed back toward 26th Street. "You want to just stroll up and say hi we're here? What if there's an ambush?"

The ocean at night looked black, and so did the sand. The arcades and food and souvenir shops were locked tight behind gates. I clutched my collar against the cold as if that would protect me from the deepening chill, or whatever waited further along in the dark. I finally caught up with her.

She found another off-ramp and we followed it down toward a banked light to the outskirts of a large derelict lot with a construction trailer about twenty yards to our left. A cross made of wood planks had been grafted to the top of the trailer cab. Figures moved behind the windows. About twenty yards opposite the trailer where the night began to swallow the lot, there was a three-story brick building with a scaffold. Tools and planks were scattered everywhere. The trailer door opened and Zhukov walked out, craning his head left and right to make sure he wasn't walking into an ambush. He marched over to the brick building. We followed, feeling our way along unsteady ground of wild grass, sand, and garbage.

I whispered, "Head back for the Jeep. *Go.* I can't have you get hurt."

"My Jewish cowboy," she said.

There was a flare of sulphurous light; Zhukov had lit a cigarette.

He wore his black leather jacket, the giant Orthodox cross dangling between his half-zipped zipper. He took a drag from the cigarette and leaned back into shadow. The lit windows in the buildings across the vacant lot on Mermaid Avenue seemed as reachable as stars. I picked up a stray wood plank that hadn't made it onto the stack.

Zhukov laughed. "Is that how you prepare for meeting with all your clients, Straightway?"

"Only those who want to meet me in an abandoned lot in the middle of the night."

"It's not abandoned." He nodded toward the trailer with its warm light. Squinting in the dark, I saw he had a large button pinned to his jacket that read, NO SANDY $$ NO CASINO.

Zhukov eyeballed Cipka. She put a hand on her hip as if to say "Have at it."

He peeled his lips into a smile to reveal teeth like a vandalized graveyard. "So you have my papers?"

Cipka leaned close to me and whispered, "Trade big. Did you see his limp? What can he possibly do to us?"

Zhukov nodded toward the trailer. "In trailer are social justice warriors. Rich oligarchs are trying to steal their Hurricane Sandy money to build casino." He spat. "We have to stop casino and get money to Sandy victims. That's my problem. When you do work of God you can't always be looking over shoulder for immigration." He flung the half-smoked cigarette: an arc of red ash sizzled a little too close to Cipka. "*Do you know what you did to me?*" he said.

She lurched for him but I grabbed her wrist.

"Wait a minute," Zhukov said, looking Cipka up and down. "I knew I recognized you. Aren't you the twat that gave me a happy ending at the Lucky Body Spa over in Sheepshead Bay?" I stepped between them with the plank raised. He didn't flinch. "My purpose for hiring you was to be invisible," he said. "Now because of your duck, Helena thinks we're partners in ripping her off and she's taking contract."

"Actually, it was a frog," I said.

His eyes became colder than the ocean air. "Let Helena send torpedo. Next morning she goes for mail and finds his hand. But if I kill torpedo I'm less invisible, then I'm no use to bosses. And if no use, then you really disappear. So we're back to give me my papers."

Cipka said, "They're in a safe in his office. The combination to the lock is a two with four zeros."

Zhukov threw his head back and laughed. "Twenty-thousand dollars!"

I reached for my jacket pocket, but Cipka gave me a look that said don't be an idiot, we have him and can walk away with twenty-thousand dollars, plus the forger's five and your fee. A thirty-thousand dollar payday. I had a vision of Rafe and Kendra feeding an apple to a deer on their front lawn.

Zhukov lit another cigarette though he was still working on the last. After a couple of long, brooding drags, he shrugged and asked, "What choice do I have?"

I said, "Do you think you can get me the twenty-thousand by tomorrow?"

"*Sure*," he said. "I *was* going to take my time, chill out with feds and Helena's torpedos. But for you and your Polish bitch..." He headed back to the trailer. "Stay by phone. Don't make me chase you like today or I'll find you and torture you until you give me papers. And your ass whore I'll sort of marry."

He stalked back across the lot to the trailer, dragged his bad leg up the stairs and through the door.

Cipka shrugged. "Like I said, easy payday. And by the way," she added, strolling back to the boardwalk, "we're going to need a gun."

JUDGE RAT

Cipka flopped into the passenger seat. "That was *crazy*. I feel like I just came. You drive."

She asked me to drop her at *Anarchy*, so we headed back to the city up the Belt Parkway on a mid-October night. That vortex winter the TV prognosticators warned about made a sudden early appearance. I rolled up my window, but Cipka kept hers open, letting the cold air howl in.

She waltzed through *Anarchy*'s black curtain as if she hadn't reaped the whirlwind of our last couple of days, but inhaled it. I flashed on an afternoon, her first December as Gabriel's nanny. No clients called: The city's lap dancers, drunk drivers, tax scofflaws, and unlicensed dentists were all distracted by fast-approaching Christmas, so I locked up early to head home. As I hiked through snow still undefiled by dogs, I spotted Gabriel and Cipka at Finn Square, a small triangular park on West Broadway that you could see a quarter mile away because of its goofy orange sculpture. They hurled snowballs at passing cars until the traffic light turned red, then ran to hide behind the heap of orange metal. After a few moments, Cipka peeked around to see if the light had changed to green, and when it had, they scooped fresh weapons from their snowball stockpile. She bulls-eyed a taxi flush on the windshield. The cabbie stopped in the middle of traffic and shouted something I was grateful I couldn't hear through the deafening horns and curses. Cipka and Gabriel high-fived. At Olivia's insistence, he'd worn a parka that made him look like an avalanche rescue tent.

Cipka lifted him coat and all to tickle his neck with kisses until he couldn't stop laughing.

Now I wondered as I put *Anarchy* in my rear view: with the violence, extortion, and sort-of sex Cipka and I had shared, how it would feel the next time we were all together: me, Olivia, Gabriel and his Ci-ka. How would that work?

Then it hit me that I could have followed her into the bar to ask about my lost Redwell. I tried calling her cell but there was no answer. At home, instead of driving into the parking lot I idled outside. It was nine-thirty. Olivia, faithful congregant in the Church the Day Runner app, would already have raced Gabriel through bath, book, and tuck, not only on principle, but to rob me of my Gabriel time as punishment for being late.

Instead of going home, I uncrumpled Dr. Liang's brochure and dialed the eight-hundred number.

"ARC," the voice on the other end said as if it couldn't care less.

"I'm looking for Perry St. George. My name is Henry Krakow. Dr. Sonny Liang told me to call."

"Jesus Christ not on the *phone*. I'm reading film, come now."

"Now?" I asked, double-checking my watch.

But he'd already hung up. All I wanted was to nod off to the squeak of Olivia's rocking chair. Instead, I drove east to the FDR, calling Cipka again. She still didn't pick up. If I couldn't reach her by the time I finished my business in the Bronx, I'd stop in at *Anarchy* on the way home and find my lost Redwell myself.

ARC Radiology was a one-story putty-colored brick building that sprawled across a good chunk of East Tremont Avenue. St. George hadn't bothered to keep the large double front doors unlocked, so I pushed open a side door on 169th Street and followed down a dark hall to an empty waiting room, calling, "Perry St. George?" Behind the reception desk was a small office with no hint of life. An arrow pointed down a flight of stairs to the CAT scans.

I followed a dark tunnel with walls and carpeting the color of advanced rigor mortis. The scan rooms were several feet apart. The only light came from behind smoked glass at the end of the corridor, so I pushed open the door and stepped inside to where someone was hunched over a console.

"Perry St. George?" I said.

He shot straight up, twisting his body to block me from seeing whatever he'd been up to.

"That's the thing about lawyers," he growled, tossing his houndstooth jacket over the console. "You never see them coming."

A tail of bills peeked out from beneath the jacket, but he was glaring at me and didn't notice. He was short, his head shaped like a ship's anchor, his eyes black holes of indignation that never met yours directly.

"Dr. Liang told me to call," I said, searching his face for why he seemed familiar while trying not to be obvious about it. "I didn't mean to come up at you like that."

"Yet you did," he said.

So far he was neither congenial nor accommodating. I was hoping I could count on reliable. Then I remembered: *Perry St. George*! I flashed on that face as I'd last seen it, in a perp walk, not exactly hidden beneath the raincoat he'd thrown over his head to frustrate the mobbing photographers. That was about five years earlier. He'd been an OATH Health Tribunal Judge. His job was to preside over appeals by restaurant owners unhappy with their inspection grades. But he got caught selling A's, and indicted, and the *New York Post* grafted his head to a rat's body, dubbing him "Judge Rat," a double entendre, for the scores of vermin he'd unleashed on his unsuspecting fellow citizens, and for his betrayal of the public trust. Soon the entire city talked incessantly of its Judge Rat. There was a final viral outrage when the D.A. and criminal court judge made him a suspiciously generous plea deal, and at once the media moved on. New York forgot, and the restaurant business picked up again, public confidence restored by the mere forgetting.

I said, "I have a client."

"Are you wired?"

"Am I what?"

"*Wired.* Are you wired—do you suffer moron-related hearing loss or are you just an idiot?"

He angled his body like a fighter, measuring me, but still avoiding eye contact.

I said, "Search me if it makes you feel better."

He snorted, "*Krakow junior!* Liang has this delusion that M.D. means he can diagnose character. He's never been caught at anything so he thinks he's immune. But I'm serving a life sentence in his basement running the scans—I see inside people." He suddenly shifted gear. "Brink of trial, or looking to force a fast settlement?" he asked, like a Starbucks barista asking if you want room for milk.

"Neither, I have a fighter."

"He has to come in, actually go through the scanner, register at the front desk. That does two things. By involving the girls and the radiologist you multiply your moving targets if there's an investigation. That's one. The other is the radiologist will authenticate your film on trial, if God forbid you actually go to trial, which one look at you tells me you never have."

"What's it going to run?" I asked, for Shatterproof's sake ignoring the insult. "My fighter's got two kids. Money's really tight."

"It's not how much, in your case, but *what*. Or gratis, one might say. Depending how you look at it."

"I'm not following. Maybe if you tried English?"

He circled to his left, like Shatterproof angling to unleash a flashing jab. "An exchange of favors," he explained. The circling stopped and his anchor head settled into a seabed of grudge and shame, retribution schemes, lost chances and dead dreams. "The thing is, I need a lawyer. But you'll do."

He sat, gesturing toward an empty chair. "A hearing's coming up. Family court. There's this kid. Okay, it's mine. My kid. Zakiah. Women use their children as weapons and nobody gives a shit, it's morally reprehensible. If I had the time I'd spearhead legislation. So anyway I make this small mistake—well a big one in that I married the woman in the first place. She's chief RN at Jacobi Hospital so money's no problem, and she let me slide on support payments because I had some trouble a while back and managing this place is the best job I can get, but that's history I don't need to get into. It pays a whopping forty thousand a year, and try living on that in this godless city."

I glanced again at his houndstooth jacket hiding what seemed a small mountain of cash.

"All the pressures, the things life does to you," he said. "Sometimes you need to blow off steam. So I scrape together enough money for forty-eight hours in Vegas. It's maybe three in the morning and I'm driving the strip with this nice young lady, and the next thing I know my zipper's open and she's taking a stroll down south, if you know what I mean. So for kicks I snap a selfie. She's licking me like a Mister Softee and I'm driving with my phone between my elbows trying to snap off shots to send to her phone, but fuck me if I don't send one to my ex Mattie instead. So then Mattie says if you can afford Vegas you must be hiding money. I protest I was there on a package deal, and she gets this look I know all too well, like a shark heading for a tuna. Then her lawyer finds out my rental car was a Porsche Spyder. Now she's coming after me for child support, arrears and future."

"Sorry," I said. "The one thing I won't do is get guys out of child support."

"I *want* to take care of my kid," he snapped. "But Mattie's got more than enough money, and all this is she's jealous about a blowjob."

I said, "Why can't you do the hearing pro se?" He still seemed to assume I didn't know he was a defrocked lawyer, so I explained. "Pro se means represent yourself."

"Does it, ass wipe? I told you, I had a problem a while back. Bad enough a judge sees my name on his docket, but if I show my face I'm sunk. Someone else has to plead my case."

"Why me? I'm not a regular at family court. Why not hire a heavy hitter? Someone with a name?"

"Your name will do. The judge is Trumble," he said, with a look that suggested we were playing Texas hold 'em and he wasn't sure if I was sitting on a full house or a pair of twos.

I had no idea what he was getting at.

"Stop with the innocent shit," he snapped. "Judge Augie Trumble. The one they call Jenny Craig, because he can't stop stuffing his face. You hold an IOU on him."

"I've never heard of Augie Trumble, and I don't hold IOUs."

"Well, your father did. Liang warned me about your bullshit hapless lawyer act. You've probably got Trumble's marker in your IOU safe, with all the others. But whether you do or don't is immaterial. Like the rest of us, he'll believe you do. Considering it was End of Days for his career before your father worked his magic, all you'll have to do is show your face in his courtroom and squat out a steaming mound of bullshit."

"I never worked with the Mayor," I said. "I don't do IOUs, I don't blackmail judges, and I never get scofflaw fathers out of child support."

"You do if you want that CAT."

• • •

Olivia's Jeep clock faded out at 10:30 when I shut off the motor. Home, finally. The parking lot attendant stared at a small TV with his feet up in a garishly-lit booth, ignoring me as I dangled the keys to signal I was done for the night. I leaned in to put the keys and a twenty on his desk, which he acknowledged grudgingly, never taking his eyes from the TV, a telenovela.

"That's *Destilando Amor,* right?" I said. "I represent one of the actors. Well, an extra, but still."

He pocketed the cash, his gaze locked on *Destilando* without a hint of pleasure or interest.

"The car never left the lot today," I said, referencing the twenty. "If anyone asks, like my wife. Bueno? El auto no para ir garage a hoy."

"Unh," he replied, leaning forward to turn up the volume.

At home, all was quiet. Gabriel slept beneath his Spidey blanket. I stroked the lightning bolt vein at his temple whispering "Daddy's home." He turned on his back, stretched like a cat, and mumbled something in unintelligible sleep talk.

Then I remembered I'd forgotten to drop in at *Anarchy* to find my Redwell. I phoned Cipka, but again got only voicemail. Her epic silent treatment was beginning to annoy me, especially if it meant she was planning to rip off Zhukov all by herself.

Olivia was sitting up in bed with an iPad on her knees and a set of Beats wrapped around her head. She wore gray sweats and a rumpled

T-shirt—no one did rumpled like Olivia. Her hair was pulled back punishingly and held in place with a barrette. In the couple of months since she'd learned that her sniper-like eyesight was in decline, she'd taken to wearing large black-frame glasses that apparently didn't help her see objects up close, because she didn't bother to look up as I came in the room.

I said, "Pulling an all-nighter?" She didn't answer, so I tried a bit of fawning charm. "Taj is lucky to have you. He goes to sleep a child laborer, but when he wakes, you'll have made him America's Favorite Rapper again."

She was as thrilled to see me as the parking lot attendant had been.

I said, "I was preparing for trial. So deep in Westlaw I forgot to call."

She looked up, incapable of hiding, even behind those forbidding glasses, that I had hurt her in some way. "Say again?" she said without moving the Beats from her ears.

"I'm sorry I'm late. That big case. Trial prep."

"Which client?" she asked. "Your exhibitionist dentist?"

She resumed beating at the keys on her iPad.

I put on my own sweats and tee—with me rumpled was nothing but rumpled.

I said, "I saw an article today in some local paper about Taj's India problem."

"You think I care about a *newspaper*?" She finally slid the Beats to her neck. "Social media—heard of it? Have you heard of social media, Henry? In hours, mere hours, it can destroy you. It doesn't matter how much money you have, your connections, or fame, or pull. When the Twitter mob comes for you…" Her voice broke. "We had to kill his feed. No Instagram, no Snapchat. He doesn't *exist*. And you think I care about a *newspaper*?"

I sat at her feet and patted the mattress. "My favorite social media is called Serta." She didn't smile. I worked my hand up her calf for a massage. "I'm just wondering whether my user name and password are still valid." She dragged her feet back beneath her knees.

"Child labor in India," I scoffed. "A rumor, probably started by a rival rapper. An internet drive-by assassination."

She said, "TajWear doesn't do its own manufacturing, it contracts out to another, completely independent company. *They* run the factory, do the hiring and all that. And you're right, no one's even confirmed that there is child labor going on over there. But we're not talking about facts, or truth. One thing the internet is unsurpassed at is moral outrage. Like someone flicking a cigarette out a car window and the next thing you know half of California's burning."

A killer idea came to me, one I was certain might save her career, and maybe even get our marriage back on track. "You know what you should do?" I said. "This is perfect. Taj writes a song of protest about child labor. I mean not just India but the worldwide phenomenon. One of those big anthemy numbers, 'Don't They Know We're Children?' or 'For the Children' or whatever. Gets a bunch of his famous musician friends to sing backup. Then he donates the record sales for scholarships for the kids who work in his factory. Wait! Half to the kids, half to the group that exposed him in the first place. Take the fight to the middle of the ring."

She seemed to think it over, so I reached to stroke a bare arch beneath a pink pilled leg warmer. Then she raised her eyes in that way she had of condensing my idiocy to a single gesture. "A *song*," she snapped, kicking my hand away, setting her earphones in place, and getting back to beating up her iPad. "Stick to law."

"You're not the only one going through a tough time," I said.

She stared right at me and into my soul, icy and penetrating. "I'm sure I'm not."

"What do you mean?" I asked carefully, because I suddenly realized that Gabriel may have understood more about that green froggie than he'd let on.

"You haven't been yourself," she said.

"My lifelong condition," I replied.

"Don't be funny."

She gazed down at her keyboard.

Finally she said, "Are you having an affair?"

I shot from the bed. "That's crazy."

"Why is it crazy, Henry? People do it every day. Why is it crazy?"

"All I do is go to work and come home again. Who would I do it with?"

A blush like a bruise darkened her face. "*Please*. Ask your mother. Ask your mother how hard it is for a lawyer out in the world to find women to screw."

I spun away and headed for the door. "Tell my clients their cases aren't big."

"What? *What?*"

"You said I couldn't be working late. But I doubt my clients would agree their problems are insignificant."

"I never...no human being is insignificant. It's their cases, the legal complexities, and I don't know, *wider* significance. If you did antitrust, or international or election law, you'd be deep in it, an influencer, and not a guy making gritty street deals. You have so much promise, but...and you think you're funny, but it's a tragic funny. It's not your job to atone for your father—but we're off the subject, and I can't do this anymore, throw my life away waiting for you to find yourself. I can't."

"All I did," I said, slamming the door behind me, "was work late."

I stopped to check Gabriel again, hoping our voices had roused him from sleep so I could comfort him as we rocked. "Gabriel," I whispered. "Are you having a nightmare?" He never stirred. Alone on the rocking chair, thinking about my life, I said, "This is not what I'd meant." Then I shuffled the last few days into what I hoped would be a map back to when Olivia and I never noticed how far we'd strayed from our dream of who we were and who we would become. Strayed in burning our days in the business of living, the blur of getting by.

KERMIT

In a flurry of light she was gone, in a flurry of light she returned. Three mornings a week Olivia rushed out precisely at four-thirty to swim exactly sixty-six laps. This was one of those mornings. Somewhere between flurries I'd fallen asleep on the rocking chair with Perry St. George's file open on my lap. By seven she was home again banging around the kitchen, so I didn't have to worry about oversleeping and missing his hearing.

Gabriel walked in all scraggle-haired and blurry with a green creature in his fist, to climb onto his chair at the kitchen table. Olivia brought over Cheerios for Gabriel and a bowl of gluten-sugar-and flavor-free granola for herself. She spooned granola dry and read the *Times* on her tablet. I carried over a mug of coffee.

"Who's this?" I asked, nodding to his green friend.

He looked at me as if we hadn't come from the same gene pool. "Kermit, of course."

Olivia said, "It's a gift from one of your clients. I picked it up from the doorman coming up from swimming."

"Strange time to deliver a gift," I mused.

Gabriel spooned some Cheerios at Kermit's face and Olivia said Kermit isn't hungry, cut it out.

"You know your clients," she said without looking up.

"Did it come with a card?"

Olivia shrugged.

"What do frogs eat for breakfast?" Gabriel asked.

"Flies," Olivia answered. "Isn't that gross?"

The blood pounded in my head. "Kermit is a *frog*!" I said.

Gabriel said, "Of course he's a frog Henry, he's green."

Without looking up from her *Times*, Olivia asked if I would mind taking her turn walking Gabriel to school, she had to get to work for an early Come-to-Jesus over the TajWear debacle.

Think straight, think straight...don't let them see anything's wrong.

"Well can you?" Olivia asked, from somewhere far away.

"Can I what?" I asked.

"Are you paying attention?" she snapped. "Are you paying attention *at all*?"

JENNY CRAIG

Zhukov wouldn't answer his phone and his voicemail was disabled. I left yet another message for Cipka to find out if maybe she'd sent Kermit, her idea of a joke. Coming out of the subway at Jamaica Station and heading for the courthouse, I thought, there's got to be a way to fix this before I see Judge Trumble. To fix it all: Zakiah St. George, Rafe and Kendra, Shatterproof's brain. Kermit. But by the time I passed through courthouse security, the best I could come up with was panic and grief.

A lawyer flew past arm-loaded with files.

I called to her. "Do you know where I can find Judge Trumble's part?"

"Who?" she asked. Then, "Oh! You mean Jenny Craig. Just follow the trail of Doritos."

I finally found his hearing room. He was running well behind schedule, so I sat and watched while he mumbled interminable questions to each side's lawyer. The regulars waiting impatiently for him to call their cases exhaled elaborate sighs that he seemed not to hear, sharing looks of disbelief and resignation. His pockets were stuffed with treats, his arms fat-stunted with fleshly waddles—he leaned to each side to slip out chips while rolling out comments at the rate of a word a minute.

But when his clerk called St. George's case and I introduced myself, Trumble turned eggplant and his clerk had to rush him a glass of water. St. George's file had financials I was certain had been compiled by the most scrupulous of accountants, but Trumble barely listened. His forehead beaded with waxy sweat and he never reached for a single Dorito. He just kept waving away my argument with rumbled impatience as if I were a panhandler on the subway coughing up the newest strain of hepatitis. Successful but confused, I fought my way out of the building in a blur of heartsickness, but Trumble's clerk found me to ask if the judge could have a minute in chambers.

Trumble leaned down against his blotter as if it were protecting him from a harrowing downfall.

"Are we good?" he asked. "Is it finally over?"

I said, "Your Honor, I have no idea what you're getting at."

His clerk banged in with a message, but Trumble turned on him with flaming jowls and he banged out again. He sat back and pulled out a bag of Doritos. Seemed almost to cry. "Just tell me whether we're good and you'll burn your file. I can't take the strain, my heart. I have a *family*, for God's sake."

I couldn't keep insisting I had no file, because he might go on to tell me what was in it. Whatever it was, it was worth his screwing Zakiah, so he deserved to spend his days in a purgatory of uncertainty. But in fairness, who was I to judge, since, simply by being born the Mayor's son, I'd now become Trumble's partner in whatever soul-selling bargain they'd worked out? One of us, at least, had suffered enough at the Mayor's hand. Before slamming the door behind me I turned and told him, "Paid in full."

•   •   •

"You better pony up," I told St. George from my seat on the J train to Manhattan, after I said congratulations asshole you beat your daughter out of child support. "When can we come in for Abdul's scan?"

I'd come up with a way for Shatterproof to avoid keeping that date. To never fight again. To get on with his life. But meanwhile, the only way to protect my family was to schedule the scan, then give Zhukov everything: ID, money. All of it.

But Zhukov's phone was still dead. That meant staking out his construction trailer in Coney Island until he showed up again.

There were two ways that could go. One, well. Two, being dumped in the Atlantic with cinder blocks for flippers. About a year prior, a client had given me a set of Samurai swords as security until he could pay my fee. I never heard from him again. So, I'd head to the office to get a sword, then to Coney Island to find Zhukov.

We rumbled passed Sutphin, then Woodhaven, St. George's file on the seat beside me, out of sight. I desperately needed sleep, but I was afraid Zhukov might call, or Cipka. At Cypress Hills an old Chinese couple got on. The train was overheated; I fought to keep my eyes open. The woman seemed to smile at me.

I wanted to cry, *Are you the Xiaos?* But she offered no cookie and he walked without canes.

The next stop was Crescent Avenue and Sunset Park. Was there time to search for them, to search again for the Xiaos, to make them understand? I was a kid, just a kid. So how could I know what would happen when they welcomed us in, the Mayor and his junior partner? How could I know?

But no time for Sunset Park, got to finish Zhukov, get Rafe and Kendra their lawn and deer. The rumbling of the train was like my rocking chair, irresistible. Mrs. Xiao and her cookie, light and sweet, a Hershey's kiss in the middle ... the Mayor and his junior partner ... *Sign paper and whole life change. Big house! Cadillac car!*

Zakhia ... Zakhia ...

You better eat that cookie, and like it, too.

THE MEAT LOCKER

The J finally arrived at Canal and I climbed out into daylight. At Desbrosses Street I tried Cipka and Zhukov again, with no luck. The shadows deepened and the temperature fell and I hustled faster, the streets filling with menacing Kermits, taunting Kermits, snarling Kermits. When I finally hit my office I didn't notice that the door was open and the lights were on.

Then I did notice.

The entire brownstone had been turned on its head and shaken violently. Chairs, computer, phone, lamp, file cabinets—even my desk, a polished oak colossus that Olivia had surprised me with for a moving-in present—hadn't merely been upended, but thrown. Glass crunched as I walked across scattered file covers and confettied papers. My first thought was that Zhukov had come looking for the envelope with his ID, except nothing suggested an orderly search. This was all-out destruction. It was personal.

Again the sound of crunching glass—but this time I hadn't moved. With a shriek of terror I spun around. Chulo was standing in the door.

"I didn't hear you come in," I said.

"Yeah, that's kind of obvious."

"That's why I called out."

"Lawyer, that was no call-out. That was my wife when she sees a mouse."

He crunched over to my desk, which was on its back, legs up like a wounded beast. "I like your style of organizing, hefe," he said. "When you want something, you don't have to search around, it's all out in front of you."

"Someone trashed the place," I explained.

"Damn, your observation skills are finely honed."

My computer was on the floor against a corner. He lifted it with his foot, bending to study where the cord had been severed. Then he looked back to my front door.

"Is Abdul okay?" I asked.

"It's funny, 'cause the lock was done clean. Your friends were definitely not on a first date with B and E. But then they come in and it's like a house party: two parts meth, two parts booty, shake 'em up in a too-small apartment and BOOM. Anything missing, like valuables or whatnot?"

"I'm not Skadden Arps, Chulo. No Matisse originals hanging on the walls. Or Faberge eggs."

He scowled. "Faberge eggs! What's that? From a French chicken? They were looking for secrets, maybe. Maybe you got a divorce case, one of your rich lawyer friends or some stockbroker, the wife thinks her man's stashing the goods away in one of those Swiss bank accounts?"

"No blue chip divorces, no."

"Well then someone has it in for you, that much is clear."

He walked over to my phone and inspected the severed wire, poking at its underside. Glancing up to catch me studying him, he shrugged. "I was a cop back in DR, so long ago I never think about it. But do something long enough it's like a tattoo so deep in the skin you can't get rid of it. You got my boy his scan?"

"I did. Just have to arrange the when. So you're a cop—I wouldn't have thought."

"Was. And if you have to arrange the when, you didn't get the scan. Hey, lawyer, you *know* you ain't lifting that desk without an army."

"I could," I said, dropping it back the eighth of an inch I'd managed to pry it from the floor, "if you helped. Maybe there's a message or clue underneath. People don't break into an office, trash it until it's unrecognizable, and not leave some sort of sign why."

"First of all, it would take at least three of us to lift that thing, and one of them would not be me, 'cause of my diabetes. Also, I'm no office cleaner."

I righted a chair and sat with my eyes pressed against the heels of my hands.

He slipped off his black beanie and held it in his hands. "My boy's a thing of beauty, but that damned chin! I used to ask God: Why give a guy stallion legs and a warrior heart, but a chin like a schoolgirl's cherry?" He shifted his weight from his right foot to his left. "Look, if Abdul fights, I pocket some money. Believe me, the rent's always snapping at my ass like a bulldog at a Chihuahua. If I done what they said I did when I had the badge back in DR I'd be rich I wouldn't need the money. But he grows on you. And those damn sweet-face kids. And I got other ways to pay the bills, I survive."

"What are you saying, Chulo?"

"I just *tol'* you, you can't let him fight."

"You think I can stop him."

"Use some of your slick lawyer talk. Tell him they're out of clean CATs, the commission caught wise. You're the one makes a living offa bullshit." He balled his hat in his fists. "Me, I just got these, and a wisdom of ring sense in my head. But there's this one move I thought of: He can be my assistant, learn to train, to work the corner. Less money in it, but he gets a reputation, a trainer in Chulo's tutelage. Soon enough Wall Street's riding up in limos for hundred-an-hour lessons."

"Yeah, Wall Streeters in Lululemon. He'll jump at that."

He slipped his beanie back onto his head. "I'm with him day after day, and I can tell you, he takes this fight he ain't Abdul Rahman ever again."

He marched to my front door, spun around to face me. "I was never here, you got that?" Then he turned up the collar of his hunter's jacket and walked away, not waiting for my answer.

The door shut behind him. I surveyed the muddle that was now my office. My computer looked as if it had been dropped from a window. The phone numbers for most of my clients, plus the numbers for the lawyers and paralegals, bail bondsmen and judges' clerks, doctors and insurance adjusters, and everyone else I did business with day to day, that I still wrote on index cards because I was too lazy to save them in my cell, covered my office like paper shrapnel. My landline appeared to have been severed between someone's teeth.

I took out my cell phone to call Cliff, my computer guy who was also, in a pinch, my phone guy. Besides moonlighting as a freelance computer geek, he assistant-managed a Verizon store in Chelsea. His mother, Emma Mott, was Olivia's secretary. She'd raised Cliff without a husband, so Olivia was hellbent on giving a hand whenever she could. That was how Cliff managed to keep his position as head of IT for Krakow & Associates, despite his habit of declaring a problem absolutely finally fixed, a dozen times or more, before actually sort of fixing it.

But just as I was about to speed dial Computer Guy, someone texted a video without a message from an unidentified number. Cliff would have shaken his head in sorrow to see me download an anonymous attachment, but it was a good bet the video had something to do with my trashed office.

The download finished and Cipka was on my phone, stripped to a camisole and panties, hands tied to a meat hook, hanging in a row of animal carcasses. Her flesh was bone white against the bloody swine in the icy air of the freezer.

A newspaper was skewered to a cow with a butcher's knife, presumably to show proof of life, but it was photographed from too far away to make out the date.

I brought the phone to my lips, "Don't you think you've seen one too many movies?"

She just kept hanging, breathing out tufts of cold air.

I put the phone on speaker. "Now that I know the real Cik-a," I chuckled, "I'm not surprised. Fake ransoming yourself for my Zhukov money."

She was doing a great job of pretending not to hear me.

"Who's holding the camera? Liis? Or is it one of those selfie tripod things?"

Then Zhukov called, talking against the background of Cipka on her hook. He said, "I couldn't find my ID in your office, so I took your ass whore instead."

I wasn't buying any of it.

"It's not a good idea to fuck with clients, Straightway," he continued.

I brought the phone close to my face: Cipka did look pretty terrified.

"It plays havoc with trust," Zhukov added.

"Listen," I said, wishing I could strangle him through the phone. "I know people who will ship you back to Russia in Ziploc Baggies."

I really didn't know anyone who could ship him back to Russia in Ziploc Baggies, but I said it with what I hoped was sufficient conviction to make him believe I could.

He screamed. "*Ukraine!* You freaking idiot!" Then he totally lost it in a flare of Ukrainian curses. Then he shouted, "Cut off her ear!"

A male voice with a Russian accent said, "Which ear, 'toly?"

After a terrifying pause, Zhukov said, "What an intelligent question, Vasyl. Since each ear is so uniquely different from other. I DON'T CARE WHICH FUCKING EAR YOU CUT OFF YOU BRAINDEAD APE! WHICHEVER LOOKS BETTER ON CHAIN AROUND YOUR NECK."

Cipka just kept hanging there breathing out cold air, but in the background I heard a squeal of muffled terror.

I said, "I've been trying to give your money back, and your ID, but your phone's been dead. Do you really need a kidnapping charge along with everything else?"

Suddenly he was calm again. "You'll get your ass whore back. But first I have job for you."

"I want to talk to her."

"And I want to lick that girl Kardashian's ass like ice cream cone."

"You threaten my child, that's menacing, child endangerment. Plus kidnapping. I'm a lawyer, don't mess with me."

"Yeah, you said lawyer over urinal. I told you at beach Helena has men looking for me, because of toilet lawyer and his stripper."

"Helena would be your forger? The one with the frog growing out of her head?"

From the other end of the call came a sound like flailing electric cable.

He said, "She thinks I sent you and stripper to fuck her over. But she can't kill me because of the work I do for casino against Heredarans. But if she only takes my eye, maybe casino bosses won't be so mad, is what she's betting. And which of these eyes do you think she'll leave me with?"

"I hope it's one that can see the guys coming up behind you in the prison shower when I put you away for life."

"Okay Vasyl," he called. "Cut off the bitch's ear. No, make it a tit."

Cipka tried to scream inside her gag.

I said, "No! Wait! What about the job? You want me to do a job."

"Rip the tape off her mouth," Zhukov told Vasyl. "I want him to hear her suffer."

While the video Cipka continued hanging in slow motion, from somewhere off screen she said, "Wait a minute! I *knew* I recognized you, Zhukov! Weren't you lead float in Ukraine's Gay Pride parade?"

I shouted, "Zhukov, don't! You wanted to disappear into America."

But Cipka just kept coming. "Ukraine sucks Russia's cock. Ukraine gets down on its knees and looks in Russia's eyes while it's sucking its cock."

"*Are you insane?*" I shouted at my phone.

"And licks balls," Zhukov added, laughing. "Tape her up again, Vasyl. She has dirty mouth for nanny."

Cipka's curses were muffled by Vasyl's fresh tape over her mouth.

Zhukov said, "She'd make good soldier, Straightway. But even the hardest bitch, when she sees her titty crawling across the floor..."

"*You want to disappear and I can help you!*"

"I know you can, Straightway. I know you can."

"I could talk to Helena. Explain what really happened."

"True, and while you're explaining she'll tie Hefty bag over your head and fill pockets with bricks and throw you in Atlantic Ocean."

"What can I do to get Cipka back in one piece? Tell me what to do."

"I can be real player here in this country," he mused. "Not just criminal but legitimate, like Donald Trump." Suddenly, as if I'd scoffed at his ambition, he raved, "You don't think I can?"

"I never said that! I'm a firm believer that if you can dream it you can be it."

"You think I'm nothing but wharf rat? All I can do is be muscle whole life? In Ukraine I come from long line of master builders. My father from his father from his father. But I'm going to be bigger. I'M GOING TO BE BIGGER THAN PAPA. I'm going to be huge player, go home with my American dollars and buy his company right out from under him. Then we'll see who's wharf rat. Success is in Yushenko blood," he added, sounding almost mournful.

I didn't point out that he'd just revealed his real name.

"But now is complication," he mused. "That I have to always looking behind me. First homeland security, then D.A., and now Helena."

"Please don't take this as a failure to empathize, but my nanny is hanging in your meat locker."

"You put her there, not me. Not me, Straightway. *Straightway!* What bullshit. I did my research. Like Trump says: 'Always learn everything about guy you're doing business with.' So now I know who you really are. Is best news since I snuck in from Canada and they make me take garbage lowlife job as shestyorka, and I see how soft and lazy Americanized bosses are, like low-hanging fruit, and I move up like that to krysha, protecting our interest in casino."

"I don't get what you're asking me to do."

"INTERRUPT ME AGAIN AND VASYL WILL GUT YOUR STRIPPER BITCH AND FUCK HER INTESTINES."

He took a slow, calming breath. I sat on my upended desk vowing to myself that the next time someone asked me if I were a lawyer, I'd lower my head and walk away.

He continued, "So where was I? Shestyorka...krysha...Yes! So then what happens, cops find out I'm rigging parking meters and I need professional ID, fast. Other problem is, with parking meters, I didn't get permission from bosses. Why? Because they would never give it and risk attention on casino. So I rip off meters and keep money for myself. But with arrest, bosses must find out, and when bosses find out, I'll disappear, but not in way I intended. So then I need lawyer, someone outside casino scheme, to get ID and get me off hook, one, two, three. And with you I hit Mega, because you betray me with

Helena, so I have to find out who you are, so how to hurt you. And who you are is perfect"

"Who do you think I am?"

"I don't *think*. Zhukov never thinks."

"Yeah, I'm guessing you're famous for that. But who am I supposed to be?"

"You're not 'supposed' to be anyone. You *are* son of Mayor of Brooklyn."

"I never worked for my father, not a day. I'm my own man."

"We are never our own men," he scoffed. "Blood is blood. You know why Atlantic City is failing? It was built on swamp. From shit foundation only comes shit, any builder knows that. Coney Island has *history*, has name. That's where we build greatest casino in world. Los Mansos Herederan think I'm helping them rebuild their church because I *care*. But I really work for bosses. But bosses don't know who they'll work for someday soon."

"If you're looking for help with the Russian mob, I don't know anyone."

"Who said Russian mob only?"

"I'm not my father, I have no connections. I hold no IOUs. Whatever it is you think I can do for you, I can't."

"The Luna Park Casino and Hotel," he said grandly. "It pisses on Caesar's Palace."

"The Russian mob is building a casino in Coney Island? I don't think so."

"I told you not Russians only. When something needs to get done that "good citizens" have no stomach for, like screw over Herederans, bosses take care of, for a piece of action. The real players, the ones who give bosses piece of action, they trade stock in casino with every judge, politician, and bureaucrat who can get it built fast. But how to know who's willing to do favor? One guy, who knows everybody, and all things about everybody. Who is that? Take guess. Your papa!"

"I told you I don't know anything about his business. Give me my nanny and I'll give you your ID and every dollar of your money, and you and your casino friends can take over Coney Island and grind the Herederans to dust. We never met."

"I know your father like brother. How? He's criminal. Hey, that makes me your uncle! Welcome to family. I'll tell you how a criminal like your father operates: take and take and take. Shake his hand, like *that* you're a one-armed man. All those big-time players, the judges and politicians that he corrupts with stock to get casino built, are million-dollar casino chips he can use later. How? He must have kept a file on everyone he traded with. He *must* have. Why? So in future he can blackmail for favors for himself. When I have his file I'll own everyone in Brooklyn. No more krysha ever again that everyone pisses on. Instead, king. Then I show papa. I show him good. *You* are wharf rat now, papa! Not me, not me. *You!*"

"The complication, Anatoly, is I don't have it."

"In ten days is condemnation hearing. Los Mansos Herederan and their troublemaker leader Gonzalo Guerrero want to use their FEMA money to rebuild church that Hurricane Sandy blew down. On *our* property, *casino* property. The Church of Saint Jude the Apostle. You know who is Saint Jude?" he laughed. "Patron saint of lost causes. We tell judge the hurricane destroyed the land. 'It's not safe'. State of New York must condemn, so Luna Park Casino and Hotel can fix it up good for all people of Coney Island. Jobs, tax money. Businesses come, more jobs. That's problem for Gonzalo Guerrero and his Herederans. Now we're the do-gooders, so no more funds for them. Problem for casino is judge announces he's thinking to vote for the Herederans and their lost cause church and not condemn. We're afraid to bribe judge because word is he's last honest man in Brooklyn. But for me, that's good news, because if judge votes for casino, if I have your papa's file, I'll own every big player who traded stock for favors to get casino built. But if judge decides to vote against the casino, I can stop him. How? The Last Honest Man in Brooklyn by definition must have skeleton in closet. Papa taught me that. With file I'm sure to find skeleton on judge, then Zhukov is hero who gets casino built. So honest or not, judge is going to make Zhukov player of players. The hearing is in ten days. That gives you nine days to find your father's file. But first thing is go to D.A. and get me off meters rap."

Suddenly the way out for Shatterproof grew clearer.

I said, "You want my file? Only in an exchange, in real time. I hand you your names, you hand me Cipka. Plus the twenty-thousand you owe us."

"I'm warning you, Straightway."

"The twenty-thousand you promised last night when Cipka renegotiated. The nanny and the money. Or I've got a friend in the FBI who'd love to hear all about you."

After more of that electric wire sound, he said, "In ten days if I'm not new boss of Luna Park Casino and Hotel, Vasyl's going to butcher your nanny like cow. Work fast, mini-Mayor, because it's cold as hell in this meat locker."

I was standing now, screaming into the phone that I *told* him I knew nothing about my father's business, and I didn't have a clue about any file, and God help him if he hurt Cipka or TOUCHED A HAIR ON MY CHILD'S HEAD he would wish Helena got to him first. And it wasn't until I was so worked up that my threats were nothing but gibberish that I realized he'd hung up on me the moment I'd started screaming.

THE DISTRICT ATTORNEY

The tax accountant stood in my threshold, staring at the war zone that Zhukov had made of The Krakow Law Group.

"They were tossing furniture," I said. "And you didn't hear anything?"

"It's New York," he shrugged.

I was searching for my keys so I could lock up and head for Brooklyn to buttonhole Zhukov's assistant district attorney before the courts closed for the day.

"This kind of damage can justify a wide variety of losses," the tax accountant said. "Insurance-wise. A Rolex. Stack of bearer bonds. High value collector coins you were holding for a client. The sky, and your imagination, is the limit. They'll fight you, of course. But you sue and settle."

"Need to be in Brooklyn to pick a jury," I said, hustling down the steps. "Already late."

The tax accountant called after me. "Have you photographed the damage? Want me to call Lichteroff?"

The 4 train staggered into the Jay Street-Borough Hall station; now all I had to do was find one ADA in a neighborhood crawling with them. The guards at 120 Schermerhorn switched to hand scanners because the metal detectors had gone down, so the orderly procession turned into a mass of shifting opportunists looking to jump the line. This meant I'd be shuffling forward by inches, so I decided to use the time to call Judge Rat and make an appointment for Shatterproof's CAT scan, but then I remembered that Gabriel needed to be picked up from school and Cipka was otherwise engaged. I phoned Olivia to ask her to call Liis, the back-up nanny.

Emma Mott icily informed me that Olivia was busy in a zero-hour huddle; any and all interruptions were banned. *Any*, she emphasized. *And all*. The upside was she'd be happy to give her a message when the meeting ended.

"Tell her…"

Tell her what? That I'd managed to get Cipka kidnapped by a crazed manic-depressive and his forger cousin, the Butcher of Ukraine?

"Just calling to say hi," I finally said. "Miss her."

The line started moving, but we were stopped again by a noisy scuffle between a male guard with a hand-scanner and a woman in a Zebra miniskirt. I called Leticia Jameson, principal of the Sunflower School, to explain how our nanny had a death in the family, and did they have any sort of aftercare program?

"Your son is not enrolled in any of our aftercare programs, Mr. Krakow," she sniffed.

The consensus among the Sunflower PTA was that dealing with Principal Jameson made you feel four years old again, having thrown a Crayola at a schoolmate.

"One is required to complete enrollment in aftercare prior to the start of each semester," she added.

The guards finally waved me through security and into the court house lobby. I assured Ms. Jameson that Gabriel would be picked up on time, then hustled around asking anyone official-looking if they'd seen Dierdre O'Connell, Zhukov's ADA. No one had, and as the day was ending, the courtrooms and corridors began to empty. Not a soul could confirm that O'Connell actually existed. If I couldn't find her before closing time, Zhukov would have to wait another day, and so would Cipka.

Maybe she'd just finished a trial and gone over to the D.A.'s building at 350 Jay. As I walked, I phoned Judge Rat and arranged for the last scan of the night, at ten. Then someone grabbed my arm and I shrieked—my phone pinwheeled into the air. I caught it before it crashed to the sidewalk.

"You're looking for Dierdre O'Connell, right?" a court reporter asked, suppressing a laugh. He gestured toward a curbside hotdog cart where the hotdog guy kept removing soda cans from an ice barrel and handing them to a young woman in a black pantsuit and jacket, who rejected them one after the other. She seemed to have a huge chip on her shoulder about the hot dog guy, and perhaps about soda in general.

"If you have any last words for your loved ones," the court reporter warned, "you might want to call them first."

I walked over as she was fishing a dollar bill from her purse. "Dierdre O'Connell?" I asked.

She studied me as if I were a glob of something stuck on her hand from a subway pole. "You're a lawyer," she observed in a lilting brogue, but not in a way that suggested being a lawyer was a good thing. "I don't do business at hotdog carts." She handed the dollar to the vendor and snipped at him. "When a customer asks for Diet Coke, they don't want Pepsi. Pepsi is not Coke. Neither is grape soda Coke. Nor is Shasta."

She turned back to me. "Plus, I'm off the clock."

The hotdog guy gave me a vigorous nod of thanks for chasing her away. I caught up with her at the top of the Jay Street/Borough Hall station stairs.

"We have a case together," I said. "Can you give me a couple of minutes?"

She was as lovely as her gaze was withering: numinous pale Irish skin, hip-length strawberry hair, and a figure that, though trussed in black, was curved and rounded in all the traditional places. She snapped, "I have a doctor's appointment, if that's okay with you."

I put her in her late thirties, which meant her career had stalled and she was fast becoming a lifetime assistant DA. Maybe that accounted for her abundant charm.

"We have this case," I explained. "Anatoly Zhukov."

Not a spark of recognition.

"The guy who put cameras into parking meters?"

"And?"

I still hadn't removed his ID from my pocket; it suddenly seemed wrapped not in rubber bands but barbed wire. After a long breath, I said, "You've arrested the wrong Zhukov."

She threw back her head and laughed. A train rumbled beneath us—she glanced at her watch. "I imagine we must have a conference scheduled?"

My phone hummed, it was Olivia. I told O'Connell, "I *have* to take this. It's a judge."

But before I could tell Olivia I needed to call her back, she snapped: "Henry, *what* is going on?"

O'Connell put the Diet Coke in her bag, spun around, and walked off toward the subway.

"Can't talk Olivia call you later," I said.

"There is no later," she said. "I just got a very serious call from Ms. Jameson, and she says that you—"

I held the phone away from my face and shouted, "I'm coming to your chambers right now, Judge...Shasta."

O'Connell turned back with a grin.

I told Olivia, "Judge waiting, really have to run," and hung up on my wife. I hustled over to O'Connell. "I just risked divorce so we can talk about my client."

She said, "You have a problem keeping your lies straight, are you sure you're a lawyer?"

"Anatoly Zhukov, my client—you've got the wrong guy. I can prove it. This whole mistaken identity thing has put his life in danger. Literally and imminently."

She rolled her eyes but paused at the top of the stairs. "You've got fifteen seconds."

Let's be clear about this, I told myself, clutching Helena's envelope but not removing it from my pocket. *You're not giving the district attorney ID, you're giving her forgeries.*

"Ten seconds," she warned.

And haven't you screwed up sufficiently for one lifetime? Haven't you?

I grazed my jacket with my fingers and buried my hand in a pants pocket. "The evidence is in my office under lock and key. Desbrosses

Street in Manhattan. An hour round trip depending how the train runs."

She said, "I kind of recognize you from around court. And I don't know if you're one of those late-life *What Color Is My Parachute*-type lawyers, or the kind who takes the bar for ten years and finally gets lucky, but listen closely: If you tell me you have evidence and it turns out you don't know the definition, every time we have a case I will skin your client alive. You won't be able to make a deal for a jaywalker. And I'll make sure we face each other *a lot*. Blink if you get what I'm saying."

"I know the definition," I told her. "You're on calendar tomorrow morning?"

"Where else would I be?" she said, racing down the stairs and disappearing into the subway.

I decided to make a fast call to Shatterproof to let him know about his CAT appointment before the longer and more painful one to Olivia to explain why I'd hung up on her.

Kendra answered with her precisely articulated way of speaking that I found kind of scary in a ten-year-old. "Good afternoon, Attorney Krakow. I'm supposed to let my father know when you call. Would you excuse me?"

She didn't wait for me to excuse her. I heard the distant sound of speed and sand bags being pummeled, and Shatterproof barking through his mouth guard. Then Chulo was talking to me.

"Uh, yeah. What's up lawyer?"

I got the impression he was performing for Shatterproof, trying to make it seem like we hadn't shared time on my overturned desk. I gave him ARC's address and told him I'd meet Shatterproof up there at ten.

"Speak louder," he snapped. "I didn't get that."

I said, "Sorry Chulo, I tried. Can't find a way out."

He called out ARC's information to Kendra to write in her notebook. Then, in a muffled voice, he told me, "Too bad, cause I'm watching his girl writing out the address and I'm looking at an orphan."

In the background, Shatterproof shouted something through his mouthpiece. Chulo called out to him. "Nothing, just going over the scan. Get back to work." Then to me, "I can't tell what side you're on."

"Can you get away?" I asked. "You have to see something, then you'll understand."

"I have a feeling the more you help people understand, the more they don't know what the fuck is happening."

"I'm begging you, Chulo. A couple of minutes is all I need. We both want to help Abdul and the kids. We both love him."

"I don't love no one," he snapped. Then, after a pause, "My boy Sanchez is coming up for training around five. You know the Starbucks on Broadway round the corner? You got ten minutes at four-thirty. If this is some stupid lawyer shit, I'm going to lay you flat right there in the middle of the cappuccinos."

On the way to Chulo I called Olivia. She wouldn't let me finish my apology. "Don't dare hang up on me again," she said. "Apparently you knew that Cipka didn't show up for Gabriel? And *you* couldn't bother to call Liis? If Ms. Jameson hadn't called me, Gabriel would have *no one*."

"I've got it handled," I said. "Is it your phone making that sound or mine? I want to tell you everything. So, you've heard of the law of unintended consequences?"

"What are you *talking* about?"

"It starts—this is almost funny—but it starts in a men's room at— you don't hear that sound?"

My battery went dead.

At Starbucks, when I told Chulo I was out of battery and what I needed to show him was on my phone, he looked like he was about to follow through on his promise to flatten me. Showing him the dead phone only seemed to make it worse. But he let me use his to call Olivia back while we walked to City Hall Park so I could recharge at a public port. The prospect of sitting on a bench while the cold air drained the heat from our coffees didn't lighten his mood, but he was turning out to be a surprisingly good sport, if a volatile one, in his red-and-black-checkered hunter's jacket, battered field gloves, black wool beanie, and signature scowl. But now Olivia was refusing to answer her phone, which was probably for the best, because Zhukov to Helena to Sonny Liang to Perry St. George, especially with Cipka thrown in the mix, suddenly seemed to call for a face-to-face with a bottle of Moet &

Chandon and box of Godiva. I plugged in my phone and Chulo and I stood over the charging port watching Cipka hang in her chamois while he listened to the story of how I'd put her there.

"Yeah," he said. "You messed up good."

"As an ex-cop, do you think I have a shot at getting her back in one piece and unmolested?"

He looked at me as if I'd just asked if Shatterproof had a shot at the title.

"What would you do?" I asked.

"What would I do? I'd go get her."

"I don't mean to be disrespectful, Chulo, but this isn't a live feed. I can't exactly ask where she is."

"Why would you, when you already know where she's at?" Shaking his head in exasperation, he bent to where my phone was charging and with two fingers expanded the picture. "See?" I didn't. "Jesus! She's up north, man. Can't you read?" He pointed out that though Zhukov had photographed the ice-picked newspaper so poorly you couldn't make out the date, its masthead clearly read, *The Catskill Mountain News*.

"Go get her?" I said.

"Rescue her ass."

"What time should we leave?" I asked.

"What makes you think I'm going?"

That's when I told him about Rafe, Kendra, twenty-thousand dollars, and the deer.

OPERATION RESCUE HER ASS

Cliff was happy to blow off his shift at the Verizon store to make order out of the chaos that was now my computer, especially because I'd also asked him to use his internet skills to locate the place where Zhukov was holding Cipka. Considering his mother's proximity to Olivia, this meant having to trust in Cliff's loyalty and discretion, which was virtually guaranteed after I promised an epic beatdown by Shatterproof if he breathed a word and got me into even deeper trouble with my wife.

While Cliff grimaced over my tangled mess of wiring, I headed to Olivia's office. Rehearsing the chronology of my last couple of days, along with variations on "It's not as bad as it sounds," I checked in at the lobby security desk, strolled down the trail of blood orange tiles through the Japanese garden with its laughing waterfall and cedar benches engraved with Zen maxims, up to the seventeenth floor reception area, where Olivia waited with arms crossed and a not altogether welcoming look on her face.

"What do you mean, just showing up at my office out of nowhere?"

"You wouldn't answer your phone," I said.

"And what does that tell you?"

I glanced at the receptionist, sitting behind curved pine, pretending not to be listening. Olivia turned sharply and I followed until we passed a corner stadium where a guy barked into a phone while churning an exercise bike. We reached Emma Mott's cubicle and she glared at me as we headed into Olivia's office, which was no less shabby than bicycle guy's.

I scanned her desk and credenza. "At least my photos are still up," I said.

She shut the door and turned on me. "How is Cipka not available to pick up Gabriel from school, and you know that and I don't?"

"Again, I tried to call, but Emma said you were in a zero-hour huddle and refused to put me through."

"And what's the problem? Where is she, anyway?"

"Emma? Right at her desk, glaring up a storm."

"*Cipka*, Henry. She never cancels last minute. What's going on, and why does she call you and not me? Why *you*? It had to be now, didn't it? Now when I'm fighting for my life. You hear about it, over drinks, at the gym, stupid men and their nannies, or someone at work, or online or whatever. You tell yourself, it could never happen to me. And don't you just take the prize, waiting until that moment when I'm losing *everything*. You must have thought, Olivia's at her most vulnerable, now's a good time to really...to really *hurt* her."

She stood between a window and a tall desk chair. She wore a sleek blue suit and her hair wasn't lashed into a severe ponytail as it usually was, it tumbled like glazed wheat, with three strands straying nervously above her left temple, and two across her forehead. Her eyes kept flashing from pain to what I imagined a sniper looks like the moment she spots her target. But no sniper's bullet could tear through my insides like her grief when it broke through again.

"It's not what it seems," I said.

"Oh, god, talk about clichés."

I searched for a version of the truth that wouldn't look like it was my fault Cipka was hanging in a meat locker in her underwear. But Olivia cut me off as I stuttered out a beginning.

"I have options, too," she said.

"If you'll just let me explain."

"And that's what we need to discuss. I know you're going to say it's this crisis with Taj, and your turning down the partnership my father arranged, but it's not. Even though it *was* a great opportunity, and maybe your last, to turn your career around. It's not that, it's...we're not what I'd imagined."

"Not what you'd imagined: husband by Joss and Main."

"See what I mean? And you have no right to take your usual high road. Champion of the little man, looking down from your great height at men like my father, who was only trying to help. Not every successful man deals in IOUs, Henry. Reputation and respect aren't always a bullshit facade. And you have no right, not you, not now that you're fucking…"

She turned toward her window and her shoulders slumped. Then she turned around to face me again with a look of grim resolve.

I asked if she would at least come out from behind the chair. She refused.

I swore I wasn't fucking Cipka. But Olivia kept biting her lip and nodding sadly. Could she somehow know the stuff we *had* done— though, in truth, Cipka had mainly done it to me?

"I need you to move out," she said.

"I told you, I haven't had sex with Cipka or anyone. Including you."

"See what I mean? We need to be apart for a while."

"I'm not ready to move out."

"It's not about *you*, Henry."

"And where am I supposed to go?"

"I don't care," she said, nearly drawing blood from her lip. "I don't care where you go. A hotel, an apartment."

"I can't afford another place."

"I'll pay for it."

"You know I don't do that."

"I don't care just *go*, okay? Please go."

"I can always find a bench at City Hall Park. When Gabriel comes for daddy time we can throw rocks at the squirrels."

She glanced away: It seemed she hadn't thought about Gabriel.

I said, "Are you going to tell him daddy's not coming home? Will you rush home every night to calm him down before bed and rock him to sleep?"

"I'll manage." She had no lip left to bite; tears flowed.

"Liv," I said. "You know I'm not the type to have an affair."

I could see the gears whir behind her eyes.

"That's not me," I continued. "Everything that's been happening, it's all under control. Trust me."

She laughed through her tears. "Trust you."

"What's a few more days when you once promised me a lifetime?"

She finally did come around the chair to stand awkwardly with nothing between us. "You are good to have around now and then," she said. Your idea about a song—don't you remember? You said Taj should write a big emotional song about helping kids, with all the money going to charity. I mentioned it to Lee and he actually liked it. We pitched it to Taj and guess what? He's already writing."

"See? I'm not entirely useless. And you might want to remind Taj that in a song about loving kids, he probably shouldn't be singing about putting a 'cap' in anyone, or showing bitches what's what."

She laughed, tossing her hair. "I'll definitely tell him no caps or bitches."

"So we're good?"

"Not remotely. But you can stay. For now."

I gave a long sigh of relief and reached to kiss her, but she darkened and stepped away. "If Taj's song doesn't work, or backfires into another cluster fuck? That's on you."

"Fair enough," I said, turning around to head out.

"And Henry?" she called as I reached the door. "I never want to see her again."

"I'm pretty sure there's not much chance of that."

The elevator zipped down while the newsfeed on its small TV showed Taj going ballistic on a paparazzo. In the lobby, I passed a bench engraved *All suffering is wisdom* and spun out the revolving door into fast-falling evening. Operation Rescue Her Ass was set to proceed at midnight, after Shatterproof's CAT scan. No need to re-steal Olivia's Jeep, because Chulo's cousin had a souped-up Corolla. Chulo said we'd make it to the Catskills by one-fifteen, one-thirty in the morning. Since everyone would be sleeping, we'd have the element of surprise. There wouldn't be more than one man guarding her, Chulo said, because the cabróns thought no one knew where they had her. Chulo and I agreed that we could certainly use Shatterproof's muscle, but it was best not to let him know about rescuing Cipka and how that fit into our plan for his new life, or he'd never go for it. Instead, we'd tell him Chulo's numbers had hit on MEGA and he was fronting a piece to Shatterproof for relocation expenses, because one of Chulo's cousins had a gym way up in West Seneca developing fighters and he needed a good trainer, and Chulo had sold him on Shatterproof for the job, which was actually true, Chulo told me.

"If my boy has any time to think about it," he explained, "he's not going to pack up his kids and go live in cow country. It has to be boom boom, here's the cash, here's a map, have a good rest of your life."

That meant driving to ARC for the scan, dropping Shatterproof off at home, then around midnight turning back up north for the Catskills. But the entire plan hung on whether Cliff came through on his promise to find the exact place in the Catskills where Zhukov was holding Cipka. And if Cliff came through on a promise involving my computer, it would be a first. I called him for an update.

"Did you find the girl?"

"Pretty much any minute."

"A life depends on it, Cliff. Do you understand the urgency?"

"Yeah, I guess. Pretty much."

Then I heard him cry, "*Shit! Why is everything deleting?*" Then the sound of his phone crashing to the floor.

Then he was gone.

When I'd asked Chulo what kind of paraphernalia we should take for the rescue, he laughed that the only paraphernalia we needed was his and his cousin Rey's fists. That seemed a little overconfident, so I found a hardware store and picked up a wirecutter and rope ladder. Ogled a nail gun (pound for pound, I'd take a nail gun over Chulo and his cousin's fists), but finally went with a silver-headed ball-peen hammer. Then into my cart went three strap-around-the-head flashlights. Along the aisle on the way to check-out, I passed a hopelessly cool set of palm-sized walkie-talkies. What's a rescue, I thought, without "com"?

Leaving the store with my gear, I remembered that Cipka was dressed only in panties and that flimsy chamois. I couldn't expect her to ride nearly naked all the way from the Catskills with Chulo and his cousin, so I stopped in at this place where I'd once bought Olivia what turned out to be an ill-considered anniversary sweater, because I'd picked out a size too large. It was a hole-in-the-wall boutique called

Lushious, that because of the prices should have been called *Maximum Pain*. Finally, ready to rock our rescue, I headed over to my office to make sure Cliff wasn't playing Candy Crush on his cell phone instead of tracking down my nanny.

He was sitting opposite my computer, which he'd set on a chair, eating what appeared to be four burgers shoved into a single bun dripping with goo from one of those chainsaw movies. Next to him on another chair, a bag of fries had exploded alongside a gargantuan soda. A McDonald's shopping bag stood open on the floor. He smiled when I walked in.

"Good news?" I asked.

"Tae a ook," he mumbled through a mouthful of burger.

I stood behind him in a reek of cheese and grease. My computer showed two houses, one behind the other, surrounded by nothing but woods. A single narrow unlit road cut past the main house. It was the sort of lonely road and menacing wood that if you're driving along in the dark, you lock your windows and begin sobbing the Lord's Prayer, even if you're a diehard atheist. In front of a horseshoe driveway leading to the main house, a sign was hammered into the ground: Sbaglio Brothers Meats.

"That's the place?" I asked. "Can I see her?"

He chuckled. "It's Google sat, Mr. Krakow. Not, like, real time. See, the trees are green."

"Then how do you know that's where they have her?"

The McDonald's smelled like end-stage gangrene, so I walked away and threw myself onto my leather chair.

"Process of elimination," he said. "Your girlfriend's in a meat locker, right?"

"She's not my girlfriend."

"Right," he said with a long slurp from his silo of soda. "Nanny. So, you don't need someone with my skill set to tell you the Catskills because of the newspaper. What I did was find us options. Four of them. Two's a slaughterhouse, and two's like these combination meat stores and butcher shops. Now the stores are located near a lot of other places. You're not going to hide a hot kidnapped nanny where maybe someone can hear her scream. One of the slaughterhouses is pretty remote, like on a farm or something. But their website says they're all into organic and humanitarian slaughtering. I figure if you're worried about killing animals so they don't feel pain, you're not, like, hanging women on meat hooks."

"Can you speed this along? At some point we actually have to go rescue her."

He offered me a sip of soda, which I declined. After draining the cup with a barrage of sounds, he said, "Here's what I'm loving. It's called Sbaglio's and their website says they deliver into the five boroughs."

"How does that prove anything?"

"It's obvious, Mr. K. Sbaglio? Italian? Meats in *trucks?*"

"Wrong Mafia." I couldn't believe I'd thought a kid whose solution to all my IT problems was to reboot and cross his fingers had any hope of finding Cipka.

His eyes went wide. "So it is the mob."

"Not exactly. But if it were, you've got the wrong one."

He shrugged. "This is where she's at, Mr. Krakow. I'm telling you. The bigger building in front must be their store. The smaller one in back's gotta be where the fridge is, and maybe where they do the butchering. She's there, I know it."

By eight-thirty, Chulo and his cousin Rey were in my office, crouched behind Cliff and his Google image of Sbaglio Brothers Meats. Rey was a stark contrast to Chulo. Sinewy where Chulo was squat and thick, hyper where Chulo was mainly stoic. Chulo meticulously packed Shatterproof's bag after every workout; Rey reeked of cigarettes and clothes worn unwashed several days beyond the limit of good citizenship.

"It seems dubious to me," I told the cousins.

"*Dubious*," Rey spat.

Chulo said, "What do you think?"

Rey asked Cliff, "Where you work again, kid?"

"Verizon," Cliff answered.

Rey nodded. "Like the kid says, process of elimination."

"So a basic smash-and-grab," Chulo said.

"If we're really doing this," I said, reaching into my Hardware Plus bag and bringing out the rescue gear, "we can't go in blindly. For instance, how many guards are there? Where do they hold her when she's not on the hook? Is she drugged? Are they armed? Is the building alarmed? Is there a dog?"

Dogs scared me witless.

My desk was still on its side, so I laid the gear across the floor.

Cliff's eyes widened when he saw the hammer, but Chulo and Rey nodded to each other sadly.

"Paraphernalia," Chulo explained.

"Pitiful," Rey answered.

Chulo told me, "Let's go take Abdul for the scan. We can figure out your questions and map out the raid on the way to the Catskills."

Cliff balled the greasy McDonald's papers and shot a garbage can three-pointer. "Time to hit the road, guys."

"Great job finding the girl," I told him. "Send me an invoice. Where do you live, we'll drop you off."

"Come on, Mr. Krakow, you gotta let me come with. Google sat's not for field ops, you need eyes on the ground. And what if there's trouble?"

Rey said, "The kid wants to rescue the damsel in distress."

"I'm twenty-two," Cliff told him.

I said, "But you still live at home. And if anything happened to you, your mother would tell my wife, and then Chulo, Rey, and the ball-peen hammer all together couldn't save me."

"I don't like it," Chulo said. "A kid."

Cliff said, "What if you get lost? Does any one of you old guys know how to work Google Maps on your phone?"

Not one of us old guys did.

"Lock and load," Cliff said.

•   •   •

Seal Team Cipka waited for Shatterproof outside his apartment building. Rafe's and Kendra's faces in the window reminded me that I'd missed a second night rocking Gabriel to sleep. *One more day, I promise, and I'll be home again.* Here's how it's going to go down: Tonight, save Cipka. Tomorrow, Zhukov comes up with the cash for his ID, plus an extra five thousand for hanging Cipka in a meat locker, not to mention the trek to the Catskills to rescue her. I give all the money to Shatterproof, who skips out on his fight, saves his brain, and becomes a trainer at Chulo's other cousin's gym in West Seneca. Finally I get to go home for good, to rock and tuck, and tell my wife the tale of my heroics. I hazard a kiss, and she kisses me back, and more.

Shatterproof had to believe he'd be fighting Saturday, until we could force the West Seneca cash on him and he had no time to think. So Rey and Cliff would hide out at the Sultan's Harem on 59th and Tenth, killing time until Chulo and I could get Shatterproof to ARC and back. We hid the rescue gear in Rey's trunk.

The news about the Sultan's Harem put a huge grin on Cliff's face; he asked if I could give him two hundred in twenties as an advance on his bill for having found Sbaglio's.

"Olivia tells me your mom's a diehard Christian," I said as I peeled off twenties.

"I got this, Mr. K. She could, like, waterboard me and I wouldn't say jack."

"I hope so, because I'd get a lot worse than a waterboarding for letting you go to a strip club."

"I'm cool—but you shorted me a twenty."

Shatterproof climbed into Rey's Corolla, waving up to the stoic faces of his kids in the window. "Where's the Jeep?" he asked me.

"There's just so many times you can steal your wife's car and hope to get away with it," I said.

"I hear that."

We were the last customers at ARC. The receptionist gave Shatterproof some sort of iPad to check in with and list his medical history, which he raced through in under a minute. Then a cute but austere radiologist came to lead us downstairs. Perry St. George never crawled out to say hello. An accelerating ache in my belly warned me that his absence meant we were getting a Judge Rat screwing, but when I asked the austere radiologist where's Mr. St. George, isn't Mr. St. George going to help us, the hysteria in my voice rising with the pain in my gut, she said, "I have this very much under control." Looking up from the clipboard to catch my eye, she added, "Attorney Krakow."

Shatterproof turned out to have his own anxiety issue being inside the scanner, so the radiologist let me and Chulo sit in the room with him. While we waited, Chulo stared at his fighter's feet sticking out from the scanner like a corpse in a morgue drawer.

"I known my boy for ten years," he said.

Then we ran out of conversation. His shoulders went slack in the hunter's jacket he'd refused to take off, his fingers were pressed together as if in prayer.

"A fighter comes to you now and again...that tiger in his eye, his moves like they were born into him. Or even just standing there in the middle of the ring, gloves on his hips like, 'let any man in any gym anywheres try and take me'. You think, God *wants* him to be a fighter, it's his destiny. But a couple of years in it turns out you were wrong. You thought you knew but you didn't. Thing is, you don't never know."

The scan completed, we drove Shatterproof home. Then we picked up the other half of Seal Team Cipka at the Sultan's Harem. Cliff swayed out with a goofy smile on his face.

"They got all my twenties, every one."

Rey took over the driving: His Corolla found a speed that made the chassis quake. We were quiet the entire trip, Rey and Cliff pacified by boobs and butt and indigestible beer, Chulo and I thinking about Shatterproof in his scanner, each lost in the puzzle of promise and destiny. Once we hit the Catskills, Cliff navigated us by phone. Rey made two passes by Sbaglio Brothers for scouting purposes, then parked down the road out of sight and killed the motor.

We sat in the fast-freezing car, Cliff beside me in back, blowing rapid flurries of frigid air, stoic Chulo, hand on a door handle, staring out the front passenger window. Rey popped the trunk and threw open his door. "Let's go beat some *ass*."

Chulo walked to the trunk. "We're not beating on anyone unless they make us. I told you that."

I leaned over Cliff and locked his door. "In the movies there's always a guy who stays in the car. He's not less important, he's just the guy who stays in the car."

He turned away and stared toward the house, tuning me out.

Rey pulled the head lamps from the trunk, distributing them among us. "The kid deserves respect. He proved his manhood big time at that Harem place," he chuckled.

"The problem, Rey," I said, "is we only have three head lamps."

This caught Rey up short, but he'd bonded with Cliff over beers and pole dancers and wasn't backing down. "I don't need some bullshit head lamp," he barked.

So Cliff strapped on, flashing the light for the thrill. He reached for the hammer.

"Uh-uh," I said. "The hammer's mine. Don't you have a fighting app on your cell phone?"

He sighed, but I kept my ball-peen.

Finally, I grabbed the handle of the *Lushious* bag that contained Cipka's getaway outfit. Chulo gave me a look that said he was confirmed in his lifelong suspicion of lawyers. Then he saw the walkie-talkies.

"Walkie-talkies?! We're all going to be in the same place."

"If we get separated," Cliff ardently suggested.

Chulo ignored him. "Here's the plan—*walkie-talkies, Jesus.* The big house looks like nothing but a store, so she probably ain't there. Got to be that house round back. I saw one door on the pass-by, but maybe there's another in the rear. I'll handle the front. Rey goes around back to see if there's another way in. Lawyer, you and the kid climb through that window on the side. If there's a bunch of soldados waiting, they'll all come at me when I walk in the front. See? We draw the soldados away from the window. If Rey finds nothing in back, he rushes up to help me beat a path through the door while you and the kid break the window with a rock and use the rope ladder to climb through. It's a flank attack. That way, one of us is guaranteed to make it through to the girl."

We were standing on a deserted road in the kind of sickly moonlight you only see in slasher films, surrounded by woods where you just knew some indescribable evil lurked in its depths. Four strangers, rocking and batting ourselves in a futile attempt to ward off frostbite, armed with headlamps, a ball-peen hammer, fists, a cell phone, and a pink grapefruit Lushious bag. One of us a lawyer, about to commit criminal trespass and God knows what else once we broke inside.

"Ready?" Chulo asked.

We made our way up the road toward the Sbaglio Brothers sign. Then we veered right to the big house. A row of giant hedges obscured the smaller building behind the big house that we thought contained the slaughterhouse and freezer, so we were forced to approach blind. As we passed the big house, Rey glanced in the window and whispered, "I was right, it's just a store, meat and shit."

The smaller building was about two hundred feet down a paved walk. Rey snuck around to the left and headed for the rear. Chulo approached the front door like a surgeon trying to decide where to make the first cut. Cliff and I found the window at the side of the building, but it was higher than I'd thought. Then I saw there was a third building nearly hidden in the woods.

"Cliff," I whispered, hunting around with my head lamp for a rock. "Are we supposed to break the window now, or wait until we hear fighting?"

"*Damn*," he said.

"I say we wait."

"Sounds good to me, but didn't Chulo say now?" He was shivering like crazy—I wasn't sure it was the cold.

A light came on in the big house window. Cliff and I couldn't agree on when we were supposed to throw the rock, so we went to the front and walked through the open door to find Chulo and ask. Two bulbs on frayed twine cast a dim shadow across a massive table made from a slab of wood that was gouged and bloodstained. Blood spray graffitied the walls. Saws, grinders, and knives hung from crude hooks. There were a couple of huge sharpening stones and a rusty electric sharpener. Scattered all around were buckets and shovels, mops and industrial sponges. The smell wasn't the best.

Chulo snapped the wirecutter as he paced. Rey had his back to us, pumping the handle lock on the freezer. Cliff said, "Guys?" Rey swiveled around for his cleaver, saw that he'd left it on the table, and spat, "I'll fuck you up so righteous—" but seeing that it was only us, spat and spun right back to working the lock on the freezer.

I said, "Is she in there?"

"Keep it down," Chulo whispered.

The freezer had one window, but the glass was smeared and no light behind it.

Rey said, "You want me to open the door or you prefer to stare like a peeper?"

"Cipka?" I called. "Are you okay?"

Chulo said, "Are you out of your mind? Whatever was asleep in there you just woke. Maybe they got a pitbull or two waiting to go for our throats, or balls. *Lawyers.*"

Rey gave up on the pump handle, took a pocket knife from his jacket, fanned a set of tools, and went back to work on the door. Smooth was not the word that popped to mind in relation to his lock-picking style.

Chulo laughed and told him, "I pray for Gina's sake you don't bone like that."

"Dumb ass lock," Rey said, jamming harder.

Cliff said, "Hey Rey?"

Rey turned and Cliff took a key from a wall hook and tossed it to him.

"Bullshit," Rey said, inserting the key and leaning down on the handle lock.

Chulo said, "Wait! Rey's right, we don't know what's in there waiting to jump us. We could be outnumbered. First we make a plan."

"It's a *freezer*, Chu," Rey said. "What kind of plan you suggest, a freezer?"

All I wanted was to rescue Cipka. "Why would they have an army in a locked freezer in the middle of the night?"

Everyone agreed that sounded like wise counsel, but Rey and Cliff decided to arm themselves from the display of knives and cleavers, just in case. Chulo was sticking with fists, old school to the end.

"Okay," Chulo said. "I go in first, dead center. Rey and the kid flank out wide. Lawyer, I'll block for you, then you spin off, cut down the girl, and carry her out."

He handed me the wirecutter, so I switched the hammer to my other hand. Then he started the count.

"On three. One. Two. Go!"

We charged. There was a lot of scuffling and crashing until someone found the light.

"Damn!" Chulo said. "She's gone."

The freezer was the size of a small studio apartment decorated with wall-to-wall barbecue.

"They must have moved her," Cliff observed.

I saw nothing to justify his confidence that she had ever been there at all. We moved in deeper.

"Nobody here but us dead meats," Rey joked.

I wondered out loud, "How could they have known we were coming?"

Chulo said they probably moved her a lot, like a feint-and-weave. I searched the cow flanks for the stab wound where Zhukov impaled the newspaper. "I'm not sure she was ever here," I finally said.

"She was here," Cliff said defensively.

Then an unfamiliar voice barked, "Don't move!"

We turned to see an old man, all bone and gristle, with patchy white hair, wearing flannel PJs decorated with Christmas trees, standing in the freezer door and pointing a rifle that was nearly as big as he was. It appeared to be far from the first time he'd used the thing.

"Non uno di voi cazzo mossa," he added. "I'll blow your fucken heart clear outta your chest."

"Where did he come from?" Rey said.

Backing slowly out of the freezer, the old man said, "From above the store, you idiot."

Then he slammed the door and locked us in.

Rey alternately threw himself at the door and beat it with his fists. "Old man," he shouted. "You so tough, let's see what you got."

Chulo said, "Rey, he's just laughing at you—if he's still out there at all."

Rey banged harder. "I'll shove that rifle up your ass and shoot it out your mouth."

"It's really cold in here," Cliff said. His face was a miserable shade of white. He reached into a pocket and lit a joint. "Anybody want a hit?"

Rey immediately turned from the door. "Fuck yeah."

I stared with wonder as half my Seal Team settled in with the joint.

"Chule?" Rey said, offering him a hit.

"You know I don't mess with that shit."

"Mr. K?" Cliff said, clearing the smoke with a hand.

"I'm a lawyer, I can't be found in proximity to marijuana. And what would your mother say?"

"He can't be found in proximity," Rey said, taking the joint from Cliff before he could find a place to hide it. "They already got you on a shitload of other charges."

I said, "The old guy's locked us in the freezer so he can do what?"

Chulo was the only one of us who looked like he had a habit of spending time in meat lockers. "We don't know he's bringing cops," he said. "They could be the ones who stole the girl."

This possibility froze us into a moment of contemplative silence. Then we heard someone at the door.

Cliff cried, "Shit!"

Chulo said, "Spread around, we'll come at them by surprise."

Rey took his cleaver and squeezed against the wall behind the freezer door, to jump whoever or whatever came through first. Chulo killed the light. The rest of us hid as best we could. Cliff was shaking so badly you could hear it over his praying. After a couple of minutes, the heavy door flew open, trapping Rey behind it. At once, the light came on again and the old man marched in with his rifle, this time followed by a much younger guy who looked like he ate an entire carcass every day, right off the hook.

Chulo faced them down front and center, his arms at his sides. Cliff and I had taken cover behind the cows.

The young guy looked Chulo over. "Come out and stand with this asshole," he called to me and Cliff, "or I'll bring you out in pieces."

Put that way, it sounded like a reasonable request, so I joined Chulo, praying that Rey wouldn't try a move. "Cliff," I said, "if I can see you hiding behind that slab, he can see you." Cliff reluctantly emerged to join us, teeth clattering.

The young guy, armed only with biceps the size of ham hocks, said, "What do you think you're doing in our freezer?"

"Outside they got no truck, nothing," the old man said.

"Nothing?" Ham Hocks's eyes creased like he'd discovered crop circles on his front lawn. "No van?"

The old man nodded, *you got it*.

Ham Hocks turned to us. "What kind of thieves are you? How were you going to haul the meat?"

Rey's foot appeared from behind the door. I prayed, *Please don't.*

Quickly, I said, "We're golfers. Wanted to be first on the front nine, but it seems our GPS is broken."

The old guy spat, "What kind of GPS makes you break into a meat locker you got no truck outside?"

Rey slammed the door into Ham Hocks to throw him off balance, but it was heavier than Rey'd imagined, and it barely nudged the guy. With a war cry, Rey tried again, this time unsettling Ham Hocks and coming out swinging. At the same time, the door clipped the old man, distracting him enough for Chulo to take three unhurried steps forward, settling into a fighter's crouch.

An explosion rocked the freezer: The old man had let off a shot. It sounded like he'd held the rifle against my ear. "WHAT THE FUCK?" Cliff screamed. I called, "Cliff are you hit?" Ham Hocks ducked Rey's cleaver and pounded him in the stomach. Rey let out a gasp, *"Motherfucker."* The old man, struggling to get off another shot, accidentally clocked Chulo in the head with the rifle—Chulo batted it away. The rifle hit the floor with another blast and another bullet went flying.

Cliff was sitting in a corner, head buried in his arms, making no sound. I called to him but he didn't stir. Ham Hocks threw Rey against a wall, measuring him for a knockout punch, but Rey lunged, his cleaver swinging wildly through open air, arcing down on his own forearm. He howled. Ham Hocks stepped back in shock. "You sliced yourself!"

Chulo, stunned by the second explosion, pressed the heels of his hands to his ears. The blast had spun the old man around. He fell hard. *"Merda!"*

Ham Hocks cried, "Dad!"

Cliff still hadn't moved. I tried to get over to him, but the explosions and flying bullets and fists and cleaver had pretty much destroyed any communication between brain and feet. Suddenly Cliff raised his head, gazed at the open door and screamed, "RUN!"

Then he blurred by, shrieking, "RUN, RUN, RUN," with Rey at his heels, pressing his hand against his left forearm to staunch the bleeding. Chulo started out, too. Ham Hocks, looking from where his father was sprawled groaning with a hand at his hip to where Chulo was crossing the threshold of the door, made a half-hearted grab for his arm. Chulo spun around to throw a textbook right cross that hit the freezer wall with a thud that sounded as sickening as the groan that erupted, it seemed, from Chulo's soul itself. I was the last one out. All I could see were Chulo's shoulders and the back of his head before I flew by him.

We raced down the moonlit driveway, each trying to outrun the other before the next bullet hit, not registering that it never came, no siren screamed, no cruiser lights flashed. We ran toward the car, but Rey, fumbling for his keys, dropped them. Chulo scooped them up in his good hand, barely breaking stride, and overtook Rey to sit in the driver's seat and slide the key into the ignition. Cliff and I jumped in back. Rey knocked at Chulo's window. "It's my car, I'm driving."

Chulo opened the window a crack: "Get in now or I'm taking off without you, cuz."

Rey slammed his good forearm against the window and marched around the hood to the passenger side. Meanwhile Chulo, anxious to get moving, gunned the motor and put the car in drive, instantly hitting the brake to keep the car from rolling backward—but it lurched forward instead, rolling over his cousin's foot.

"Damn! My phone!" Cliff shouted as Rey howled, Rey staggering over to the passenger door. "I lost my phone!"

Rey got in and slammed the door and turned to Chulo. "What the fuck you broke my foot!"

Cliff said, "I must have dropped it in the freezer or the woods or—no, I had it when we were running."

Chulo, already speeding away, spun around to give Cliff a look that instantly persuaded him not to share another word of grief over his lost phone.

Meanwhile Rey kept shouting, "You ran me over, Chu," and Chulo kept insisting it was an accident, and we should shut up and try to look normal in case any cops drove by. Rey calmed down and Cliff stared out the window, quietly sobbing. Rey inspected the gaping wound in his forearm. "It's not that bad, I only grazed it." He fumbled in the glove compartment until he found a greasy rag and pressed it against the wound. "But when the shock wears off, damn if my foot's not gonna hurt."

Chulo drove in silence, never saying a word about his broken fist.

It wasn't until we'd turned onto the highway that we heard sirens not far off. Chulo kept a steady sixty miles an hour as we joined the light flow of truckers and night-shifters. Rey, murmuring in pain, asked Cliff if he had another joint, but Cliff had fallen asleep.

"We should find a hospital," I said.

"How do you propose we do that," Chulo said. "Ask a cop directions? No hospital till we're so far away there won't be no APBs out, no one watching for four guys who have no reason to be together late at night unless they're escaping from a crime."

That settled the matter and we drove in silence. I noticed for the first time that we still had the flashlights strapped to our heads. We'd left all the other gear behind. I pictured Ham Hocks and his father and the police, standing inside the freezer over a pink- grapefruit *Lushious* bag, trying to make sense of the woman's yoga pants and cardigan.

But the pleasure I took in imagining the theories they'd come up with was cut short by a revelation of failure. Cipka was still missing, and I'd blown a night when I could have been looking for the Mayor's file that Zhukov was certain existed. Shatterproof would have to fight on Saturday, and keep fighting until there wasn't anything he'd be good for.

"Do you know where the kid lives?" Chulo asked, nodding toward the sleeping Cliff.

I told him somewhere in Brooklyn, other than that I had no idea. I took off my head lamp and Chulo, eyeing me in the rear view, brought a hand to his head and spat *estupido,* throwing his onto the seat between he and Rey. The night deepened and we seemed to be driving through time, though it was only 87 South.

Rey groaned. "Do me a favor, look in the kid's pockets see if he's got another joint."

I refused to search Cliff's pockets. Chulo said, "I'll turn off for Brooklyn and we can wake the kid, find out his address and drop him off. Then you. Then Rey and me will go to a hospital."

He wasn't looking for me to agree.

THE DOUBLE DOUBLE-CROSS

My apartment was blanketed by three-in-the-morning moonlight, making it seem like a page out of a Joss & Main theme catalogue titled "Home." It made me want to buy out the store. Like a sentinel on night duty I looked in on Olivia, then on Gabriel. But what sort of sentinel opens the front door and lets *me* inside?

With each squeak of the rocking chair I checked off another to-do for when the sun came up: Get Shatterproof's CAT results; research the condemnation hearing; avoid Dierdre O'Connell; find a way to rescue Cipka that results in Cipka actually being rescued. The squeaks were reassuring, like a shovel in dirt, each one digging me further out of my hole. Then I thought, *Wait a minute—shovels dig you deeper.* Then I was asleep.

The sun burned through the windows. Somehow my overnight bag had made its way to my lap, packed to bursting. Olivia was already dressed for work, her hair tied back so I could see the strain above her ears and along her forehead. Her complexion looked washed out, and so did her eyes.

"You've been in the pool too long," I said, not entirely awake. "What's this bag for?"

She crossed her arms, looking like she wanted to say something I probably didn't want to hear.

"Where's Gabriel?" I asked. "Shouldn't he be eating breakfast?"

"I told him to stay in his bedroom."

With a strange gulping sob, she threw something at me that first made me want to laugh: harmless bits of paper. Until one drifted to my chest and I saw that it was a silver wrapping from Cipka's orange mints. "You made me believe you!" she cried, rushing to the kitchen and throwing open cupboards, then the fridge, punishing the milk, Muesli, and coffee for the sin she imagined those orange mint papers were accomplices to. With another swallowed cry she stepped back from the espresso grinder and her shoulders fell, like some winged creature collapsing in on itself for protection. She held still in that way she had of waging a moral struggle against full-out crying.

"What's with the confetti?" I asked, fighting my own battle against sounding as guilty as I felt.

"*Don't*. Don't you..." She instantly composed herself. "Why was she in the Jeep?"

The overnight bag seemed to grow heavier: What had she packed, everything I owned?

"They *texted* me," she said. "I got a *text*, stupid."

"A text?" I said evenly. I'd never thought, I hadn't even considered, that Zhukov would text her the video.

"God Henry, can't you even *cheat* right? The parking lot. Remember when all those cars were showing mileage the owners couldn't account for?" I didn't. "Gotham Parking never caught whichever parking guy was taking cars for joy rides, so they instituted this new security measure. When you take your car they send you a text. You know: 'Thanks for trusting Gotham Parking'. If you're not *in* your car you know someone's taken it and you can call them and..."

"But I couldn't have had the Jeep last night, I was with a client."

"I'm not talking about last night. They were offline, Gotham. The system was down and they were offline. The texts were backed up and couldn't go through, and then they did, and I got the one from the night before." Now the tears started, though she fought them back. "You looked right at me and said I could trust you and I did."

"Did you ever think that Cipka—"

"*Don't say that name.*"

"That she's the one who might have taken the Jeep?"

Olivia's tears turned to icicles. "And drove it from the passenger side, where the garage guy found the wrappings?"

"What if I told you we were in the Jeep together for a reason, but we never had intercourse?"

She laughed through her tears. "Intercourse, Henry? You *fucked*, okay? You fucked, you fucked. You fucked the nanny, that's why she hasn't come back, she can't. She can't face me. I want you out. *Go*. Just go, nanny fucking fucker."

I took my overnight bag—given how heavy it was, it seemed clear Olivia wasn't expecting to see me again, perhaps ever—and headed for the office.

·   ·   ·

As soon as I hit my office, I remembered that I owed Dierdre O'Connell an early morning visit, so I had to figure out how to buy time before handing over Zhukov's ID, time that would give me a chance to search for the Mayor's phantom file stuffed with an extortionist's fever dream of names of Brooklyn's players. What I would do when I didn't find it and how I would get Cipka safely out of Zhukov's freezer, I had no idea. If I told O'Connell and she got the cops and feds involved, it might turn into a bigger fiasco than my raid on Sbaglio's. One siren, one errant squawk from some fed's earpiece, one leaden footfall and God only knew what Zhukov would do to Cipka in the moments before the cops banged in. Or what the cops would do, for that matter, all those guns and anxious trigger fingers.

Zhukov and his men had neglected to search my bathroom. I picked a fresh roll of Charmin from the half-dozen stored under the sink and dug into the cardboard roll for the seven-hundred-fifty dollars in twenties and tens I'd saved from my occasional cash-paying client, adding it to the Getting-Shatterproof-Up-North stash I'd been holding back from Zhukov. Found my spare suit and shirt, put Zhukov's envelope in the jacket's breast pocket. Headed to New York Sports for a shower and shave. While I was toweling dry, my cell vibrated with an unidentified number. I cupped the phone close to my mouth and prepared to counter whatever havoc Zhukov had in mind with a threat of my own—after all, I still had his papers, and Dierdre O'Connell might also, in half an hour.

I said, "Is this my favorite Polish native?"

"Huh? Hey, I'm not Polish, Mr. K. My family's from Atlanta." It was only Cliff.

"Your name didn't pop up on my phone," I said.

"I had to get a new cell, remember?" There was an awkward silence. "I guess I just want to say I'm sorry. She *had* to be there. I don't know what happened."

"You gave it your best shot. I'm sure if Cipka had lived through this, she would have been grateful for your effort."

"It's funny, I had it narrowed down to two choices, Sbaglio's and Northland's. So if it wasn't Sbaglio's it's gotta be Northland's. We can go tonight. Yahoo Weather's predicting no precipitation and a full moon."

"Let's put the whole rescue thing to bed for now. You've already sacrificed one phone."

"Okay. But if you change your mind, I'm down for black ops. It's just…"

There was an awkward pause. "Just what, Cliff?"

"Well, when you guys brought me home last night, my moms was waiting up for me in the front room. She said she didn't know whether to kiss the Bible she'd been reading or beat me with it, and, well…I can't be your IT guy anymore."

"You told your *mother*?"

"Oh, not everything, I'm no snitch. You're cool. I said we were working on a case."

"Why mention me at all? Why do that?"

"To make my lie more legitimate. You know, that I was out all night doing something serious and not partying. Anyway, I had to promise I wouldn't work for you anymore. But a rescue, that's like a humanitarian aid thing. And besides, I'm twenty-two, I can do what I want. Just please don't tell your wife or my moms is bound to find out."

My wife—of course! Finally, a break.

"Cliff, I need a favor. Make sure your mother tells Olivia about last night."

"How's that, Mr. K?"

"Make sure your mother tells Olivia that you and I worked all night on a case for two nights running. It's important. *Two nights running.*"

He paused as if trying to puzzle out why, finally gave up and said, "Sure, okay."

·   ·   ·

Dierdre O'Connell was giving Judge Roberta Merkin as good as she was getting. It was a motion calendar so there was no jury, just O'Connell battling a lawyer I didn't recognize, whose air of stunted idealism and deflated innocence made it an odds-on bet she was Legal Aid. Judge Merkin came out with her ruling and added, "I pray this was your only hearing in my part, Ms. O'Connell. I'm not sure I can survive more of you today."

O'Connell slammed her file shut. "It's your lucky day, your Honor," she said, huffing past Legal Aid, who looked no less frazzled for having won the motion, and breezing up the aisle. She saw me waiting inside the door, raised her eyes disdainfully, nodded in sorrow, and said, "Follow me."

It sounded less like an invitation than a threat, though her brogue imparted a kind of poetry. I hurried to keep up with her as she stormed past an exit sign into a stairwell.

Standing in front of the emergency fire hose, she said, "We're dealing with a mini flu epidemic and two maternity leaves, so I need to get your scumbag off my desk, stat. What do you have?"

"What do I have?"

"Yes, Mr. Krakow. All single syllable words. Can't make them any simpler."

"I need a couple more days," I told her.

Her pale Irish skin turned a deadly shade of blue. It was amazing how menacing a brogue could sound. "You're playing me, Krakow. I don't care for that."

"What if I could give you something much bigger than some guy robbing quarters from parking meters?"

"Not quarters out, *cameras in*," she scoffed. "He was hiding cameras in meters to take pictures of credit cards, to steal the identity of innocent men and women. Do you ever actually *read* your files?"

"I was making a rhetorical point."

She burst into laughter. "I'm sure you were."

My cell hummed against my thigh. I couldn't answer or O'Connell might storm away. I prayed that if it were Zhukov my phone would capture his new number.

I said, "Can I ask you a question?"

"Do you need me to school you on whether identity theft is a felony or misdemeanor?"

"Funny."

"Or do you even know a felony from a misdemeanor?"

I said, "I've been trying to sell you on this ridiculous theory that you've got the right name but the wrong guy. So why are you even giving me the time of day?"

She threw her head back as if to laugh, but nothing came out. "You've *really* got your client's ass. Can I get your business card in case I ever do a crime and have a hankering to spend some time in prison?"

"I'm just trying to be honest with you, hoping you might do the same."

She sighed. "Okay, so one of your client's dingbat co-conspirators accidentally took his own picture." Laughter escaped, like Irish chimes, though her incisors were sharp as a piranha's. "We open the meter and there it is, an idiot's selfie. Or is idiot's selfie redundant? The imbecile gives up the name of the kingpin of the meter scheme, a guy he swears he never actually met, because selfie twit is just a basement-level crew member, which is not exactly a surprise. He says the kingpin is this guy Zhukov out of Brighton Beach, not long in our country, and not legally. So we go to our mob informer at the Beach, 'Do you know any Zhukov, maybe connected to Bratva, maybe not?' He gives us your client."

"So basically, you arrested my client on the word of an imbecile and an informant, without a witness or evidence, apart from the smoking gun in his parents having named him Anatoly Zhukov."

"I've done with worse," she huffed. "Was there some exculpatory evidence you wanted to show me or may I resume my life?"

"If you hold off arresting my client," I bargained, "I may have something a lot hotter than a meter pirate. Could be a career-changer, open your own defense shop."

"I'm perfectly content where I am, thank you. Certainly don't want to waste my days defending your lot. And if you don't show me something within the next ten seconds I'll make sure your client never sees daylight again. Nor will you for wasting my time."

Again my cell phone chimed. I glanced at it: St. George. The clean CAT was probably ready to get over to the commissioner.

O'Connell said, "Don't you dare take that call."

"What I have to offer in exchange for a little more time," I told her, shutting down St. George and pocketing the phone, "is a crack at some high-profile names."

This time her laugh made my soul curdle. "Like who? Homer Simpson? A Kardashian sister?"

"Has anyone told you you're not the most likeable person to do business with?"

"It's why I wake up in the morning." She turned to head down the stairs. "Now if you'll excuse me."

The new line I crossed, the one I swore I never would, I crossed for Cipka and Shatterproof, for Rafe and Kendra: "Don't you recognize my name?" I called. "Krakow. As in Arthur Krakow? The Mayor of Brooklyn."

She turned back around with a skeptical hand on a hip.

I said, "I'm his son."

"Krakow," she said, as if all the defendants she'd ever prosecuted had suddenly issued a joint confession.

I said, "When I tell you I can deliver big names..."

"The Mayor had a spawn. Who would have guessed? In the old days they would have chained your sort in the root cellar, a family's secret shame."

She had this trick of becoming less attractive the longer you talked with her. "So do I have my extra time?"

But she'd already turned her back on me and disappeared down the stairs.

·   ·   ·

"Your fighter's got a subdural hematoma."

In view of what St. George and I would be discussing, I'd waited to call him until I was far from the courthouse with its cops and prosecutors, as far as Columbus Park, so public it was private. It wasn't official winter yet but a light snow was falling.

"There's no other way to say it but to say it." St. George's tone seemed almost tender.

"How bad's the bleed?"

"In terms of his fighting Saturday? It depends on how much money you've got tied up in him, or how much you enjoy funerals."

I sat on a frozen bench in the heart of Brooklyn's court district. "How can you even know?" I said. "*How can you know?*"

"Hey, I'm not the janitor; I can read films."

"But you're not a radiologist."

"You're around it long enough you pick it up. Anyway, I'm giving you a heads-up—or a heads off, considering the state of your fighter. You can hear me or you can ignore me, that's your call."

"Does he need surgery?"

"Nah, he's not pumping blood. But a bleed's a bleed. He should have an MRI on top of the CAT."

I watched the snow collect on my suit jacket; underdressed for the cold.

St. George, impatient to finish, rushed me back to business. "I'm sending the clean scan by messenger so you can hand it in with the original signature of the radiologist. You'll also find a report from Dr. Liang confirming the read."

My voice, thin and shaky, came from somewhere far from Columbus Park with its crisscrossing judges and stenos, clerks and perps and families of perps, and of course, lawyers, some in cashmere overcoats and some in rayon, scowling and rushing and clutching battered satchels or Redwells. I realized I'd forgotten about mine.

"And the other scan," I asked. "The one with the bleed?"

"What other scan?" he said, and then he was gone.

THE CASINO, THE CHURCH & THE BLIGHT

Courtesy of Cliff, my computer was finally humming and I was able to access Westlaw. I printed out the case of _Luna Park Casino and Hotel Development Corporation with Empire State Development Corp., v. The Church of Saint Jude the Apostle and Los Mansos Heredaran_, and Googled whatever newspaper articles I could find. I didn't think I'd read the name Anatoly Zhukov anywhere, and I was right.

The case was being handled by way of a condemnation hearing. The fight was about that raw parcel of beachfront Coney Island where Cipka had renegotiated with Zhukov; the church under scaffolding, called Saint Jude the Apostle. The Luna Park Corporation wanted to tear it down to use the land for a casino and hotel. But a firebrand named Gonzalo Guerrero and his outreach group, Los Mansos Heredaran, which Google Translate said meant "the meek shall inherit," were dead set on keeping the property and restoring the church, which had been their headquarters. Their dream was that Saint Jude would expand to include a walk-in health clinic and a neighborhood community center, with classrooms for teaching English and basic legal rights to new immigrants, business skills for the entrepreneurial minded, a senior center for card games and bingo, lectures, book readings, and volunteer choirs. Space, too, for a daycare center for the children of single mothers.

Empire State Development, a government agency, was in the case as partners with the casino, because only the government had the power to condemn. A developer looking to wipe out a neighborhood for his pet project needed the state behind him. The judge, Biaggio Perella, was tasked with determining whether the church and surrounding parcel should be condemned because of the blight caused by Hurricane Sandy. If condemned, Luna Park argued, it would invest a billion dollars to cure the blight and bring to Coney Island all the jobs and tourist money a Las Vegas-style casino hotel can promise, along with, for good measure, plenty of new public housing and even a school to go with it.

But Gonzalo Guerrero and Los Mansos insisted that the only blight was in the hearts and true intentions of Luna Park, the state, and the cabal of rich developers who couldn't care less about the people of Coney Island or the long-suffering victims of Hurricane Sandy, and had no intention of building a school or public housing, or of hiring from the community, unless it was for janitors and chambermaids.

At the first hearing, Judge Perella had said he was leaning in favor of the Heredaran, an inclination that surprised and baffled me. A casino and hotel in the middle of Coney Island would be a golden trough for Brooklyn's powerful and connected. Luna Park's environmental trial experts described how the storm had ravaged Coney Island with biblical fury. Sand had shifted so violently that it changed the shape of the beach; birds and marine mammals had died by the score—more than a year later they were still at risk. Water mains kept bursting, the wiring that delivered electricity to the area had become skittish and unreliable. Sinkholes threatened to swallow huge chunks of street. Guerrero was certain the disputed parcel had suffered the worst of it, but environmental experts need to keep up with the mortgage payments just like the rest of us—they could find blight in the Garden of Eden.

The casino had been dreamed up by Townsend Meeks. Meeks was a local councilman and entrepreneur, and a member of Brooklyn's rumored "Black Hammer," a group of powerful and wealthy African American politicians and businessmen. He popped up in the news now and then for his habit of using campaign funds to support his passion for buying and flipping real estate, particularly brownstones. A passion accompanied by a comprehensive indifference to zoning, construction, employment, and myriad other obstructionist laws and regulations.

The Black Hammer, Vegas money men, maybe the Russian mob, Councilman Meeks and God knew who else—Guerrero insisted to anyone who would listen, which was pretty close to no one, that Meeks was siphoning the Heredarans's post-Sandy FEMA money to seed his initial investment in the casino.

I closed out Westlaw and shut down my computer. If the Mayor had all those names in a secret file, and if Zhukov got a hold of it, he really could extort his rise to the top.

Then Scottie Walsh walked into my office, carrying a manila envelope. "You should keep you door locked," he said. "This devastation is more than enough, wouldn't you agree?" He handed me the envelope: it was from ARC Radiology. "This was under your door."

"It's always nice to see you, Scottie," I told him, casually tossing the envelope so he wouldn't wonder what was inside. "But I'm up to here with a big case."

"Do you remember when it used to be Uncle Scottie? Or Judge, or Your Honor?

"You seem off your game," I said. "You okay?"

"Uncle Scottie," he sighed, surveying my wreckage. "But your father *was* like a brother to me. They serve a purpose, these formalities, these honorifics. Judge, Your Honor, even, at least, Uncle. So the center will hold."

Scottie was my landlord, but he hadn't dropped by since he'd rented me the place at a rate that reflected an uncle's affection. Was it a reach to assume that the shambles we were sitting in had something to do with his sudden appearance? Or how my rent bill had a habit of not always making it to my to-do list?

"Scottie," I said. "Judge Walsh. Can we catch up another time?"

"This won't take long. Five minutes?"

Scottie had always been known around Court Street as "The Judge From Another Planet," for the philosophical furrowing of his brow as he pretended to be wrestling with angels before coming out with the ruling his clerk had written for him the night before. If his wife Eleanor had tapped her trust fund to pay for his seat on the bench, who can blame a guy, we all used to say, for marrying well?

It seemed he'd had that white hair forever, though his striking blue eyes had gone a bit rheumy with age. But he kept up appearances: that unfailingly erect posture, the custom-tailored pinstripe, silver tie precisely knotted, his silk hanky parted into perfect wings, as though a dove had come to rest in his breast pocket.

He said, "I always liked you, Henry. If you lacked the dark wit and Machiavellian intelligence of your father, well, there was goodness in you, a sort of innocence."

"You like me so much you've come to evict me."

He smiled sadly. "Eleanor, you understand, sent me. This is her property and I have to concur. The other tenants, your neighbors—no one wants to live in a high crime zone. And thank heavens no one's called the police. And you haven't exactly made an effort to clean up." He exhaled so forlornly that I was close to feeling sorry for him, though I was the one being evicted.

"And she has been on me to visit you for a while now," he continued. "About the rent."

"Can I get a running start?" I said. "A month? One month and I'm gone. Now's a bad time. Big trial breaking, about to pick a jury."

By this time next month Cipka would be back with Gabriel, throwing snowballs at passing cars. Shatterproof and his kids would be up north. And Olivia would have let me come home.

"If it were up to me," he said. "But Eleanor...she's fallen on hard times. The thing about money is how badly it needs to be spent. And unfortunately her parents could only die once."

"So how long do I have?"

"Seventy-two hours. She was dead set on twenty-four, but I told her, he's like a son to us. So seventy-two or she's having it padlocked and you can sue her."

He rose from his chair, brushing the dust from his suit. "So says the messenger."

I followed him out the door. We were outside now in the cold. He said, "I wish I could have done more. Your father would have expected it." His pale cheeks turned a livid pink and his eyes watered. "The best way not to be haunted in old age by the ghost of who you might have been is to always *be* the man you might have been."

He turned and walked down my stairs. I watched him head for Canal Street, where he hailed a cab with one hand, the other holding down the hem of his jacket to keep his collar from riding up his neck. Then I took off for Church Street Boxing.

When I got there Shatterproof was pummeling the body armor of a skinny young white guy with Rasta hair while Chulo circled around them barking instructions and criticism, his hand casted nearly to the elbow. Rafe and Kendra weren't around. Shatterproof saw me first, calling out through his mouth guard and waving. Rasta kid, apparently aggrieved at this moment's distraction, pushed Shatterproof hard. Shatterproof unleashed a barrage—the kid nearly flew across the ring. Chulo called for a break.

"What you got in that envelope, lawyer?" Shatterproof said, climbing out of the ring and into a sweatshirt. "Incriminating pictures?"

Chulo had a harder time finding his way over the ropes now that he was down to one hand.

Shatterproof said, "You see what happened to old Chulo the Conqueror?"

Chulo threw me a don't-say-anything look as he dug into his training bag and came up with a bottle of prescription pain pills, wrestling the child-proof cap in his teeth.

Shatterproof kept explaining. "Doing some little chili pepper when her papi strolls in and starts beating on *her*, can you believe that? Chulo the Transgressor standing there pulling on his sweats, and papi beats on his own woman?"

Chulo took his pills without water, glancing at me again as he swallowed with a look that said go with the story if you know what's good for you. Shatterproof dragged over a metal chair, too caught up in Chulo's story to notice.

"But before papi's finished pounding on his woman, Chulo goes all *Taken* on papi's ass." Shatterproof shook his head and laughed. "Jacks the man's woman and gives him a beatdown." He smiled appreciatively at his trainer. "Some *cold ass* motherfucker."

Chulo smiled uneasily.

Shatterproof continued. "But not so cold he forgets what he's always screaming at me: Keep your head. Cause he slams his fist into the guy's skull, fractures his hand."

"That's bad luck Chulo," I said.

Woozy with sleep deprivation and pain pills, he sat opposite Shatterproof while I dragged over another metal folding chair and tore open the envelope. Chulo and Shatterproof went as still and big-eyed as my imaginary deer on Shatterproof's West Seneca lawn. "Where's the kids?" I asked.

"Afterschool," he answered. Nodding toward the envelope, he said, "Got what you paid for?"

Chulo looked at me as if he somehow already knew.

"You can't fight," I said.

Shatterproof sprung from his chair and paced in front of it like he was sizing up an invisible opponent. "What do you mean I can't fight? The scan was broken?"

"I mean you can never fight, ever again. Abdul...you have a hematoma. A brain bleed."

Chulo sat back. Shatterproof stopped circling.

"I know what a hematoma is, lawyer."

"You need to think about your kids."

"Don't tell me to think about my kids. Who do you think raised them, they're both straight A's? Healthy as Clydesdales. Raised them alone since they were on all fours and shitting their diapers, and now Kendra won a science prize. *Think about my kid.* You a social worker or a lawyer? All you had to do was get me a clean scan. You can't even accomplish *that*?"

"But that's exactly what I got you." I slid the scan picture and report out of the envelope. "It's right here."

"That's a clean brain?"

"Clean as a newborn's."

He looked me dead in the eyes. "So how can you say I've got a bleed?"

Halfheartedly, Chulo added, "Yeah, you got a clean scan there, how can you say he's got a bleed?"

But I wasn't taking the punches alone on this one. "Chulo's cousin has a gym up in West Seneca and can use a trainer."

Chulo furrowed his brow and rubbed his bad fist, rooting around in his bag.

"What's your cousin's name, Chulo?" I asked.

He brought out the bottle of pills and popped a couple while telling me with his eyes that he was a sucker for thinking I could be trusted. "Manny," he said.

I continued, "You move the kids up north, train fighters, help him manage the gym. The air up there is clean and the schools are good, better than here. It's a whole different world. A fresh start."

"Chulo's cousin?" With a slow burn Abdul turned toward his trainer. "So you're in this too, your cousin Manny? Trying to get me to quit?" Chulo shrugged. "Why are you *shrugging*, chico? Something's on your mind, spill it. Don't *shrug*. Be a man. Jesus! Be that macarra who broke his hand on the guy he was cuckolding."

Chulo sighed. "You got the jumps."

"*Jumps*, that's bullshit. You know I'm susceptible to chills when I'm sweating."

"Everyone's got to hang the gloves up some time."

"I'm only thirty-five. You see brothers fighting—look at Foreman, beating the belt off Moorer at fifty or whatever."

"Or Ali," I added. "He can walk across a room in what, a week and a half?"

"I got years in me," Shatterproof said in a way that made me want to protect my face with my forearms.

Chulo said, "He does got years in him." Then, as if to mollify me, "Anyway, how's he going to start fresh with no stake?"

Shatterproof rose again. "I don't need a stake. I have a job. I'm a fighter." He tossed a small envelope at me. "I got you ringsides. Saturday night. For helping out. But you better give Chulo that scan. I distrust him less than I distrust you."

"I don't suppose," I ventured, knowing this was going to be futile but knowing, too, that I had to try, "I can make you a gift equal to Saturday's purse. I've got the cash. Pay your rent, and it buys us time to figure what to do about the bleed." Quickly, I added, "Like a loan. Or an investment."

Chulo shifted forward in his chair and turned to Shatterproof with his brows raised in hopeful expectation, while Shatterproof looked at me as if I were the one with the hematoma. "You gonna invest in fights you don't want me to have."

I said, "Call it a guarantee you'll have breakfast with the kids Sunday morning."

"I know you're trying to do good, lawyer," Shatterproof said, towering over me. "So I won't pop you for thinking I'd take a handout."

With a long sigh Chulo grabbed ARC's envelope. I was out of ideas, so I turned and walked away, because what else could I do?

It was Thursday afternoon. I stopped short on Chambers with no hearing to rush to, no client to avoid, my Redwell still missing, seventy-two hours from eviction. To save Cipka I was supposed to find a file, ledger, diary, collection of cocktail napkins and matchbook covers, flash drive—Zhukov had no idea what form the Mayor's supposed list of corruptible power brokers was supposed to take. I thought, *If I got my hands on that Ukrainian sociopath ... You would what, Henry? Without Cipka and her breakneck mouth? Cipka and her glass frog? You need someone at your side, to help see this through.*

And one less accident prone than Seal Team Cipka, with Chulo's hand and Rey's bicep. Cliff in mourning for his lost phone.

But I did have a friend, after all. Just as capable as Cipka at smashing heads and spilling blood.

THE NEW FRIEND

I got off at the Brighton Beach station and this time found Helena's building without trouble. Again I faced the bile-colored door with its empty name tag and knocked twice, retreating to the corridor wall to plaster my back against the florid wallpaper. Zhukov's forger opened the door a couple of inches, and at the sight of the jittery lawyer attempting to appear as unthreatening as possible, unlocked the chain and gestured hello by raising a pistol at my head.

It was a small pistol, no bigger than her palm. She kept it trained at the bridge of my nose while she walked backward into her apartment, nodding for me to follow. She was dressed in a two-piece greenish running suit with a white stripe that began at her ankles and ended at her shoulders. Her gun barrel pointed me to the infamous sofa and coffee table (the giant glued-together slabs made it look like an Arctic lake suffering the early effect of global warming.) I upbraided myself for yet another idea not entirely thought through.

"I'm going to put you in my bathtub and fill it with acid," she explained, reaching for the phone. "Even your head will melt."

"Who are you calling?"

"Acid Squad," she said.

"I have a proposition where you might not need to do that."

"No, I need to do it. Where's that crazy ass bitch whore girlfriend of yours? It's a big bathtub."

"Listen, about the crazy ass bitch. And by the way, her name is Cipka and she's my son's nanny. Can you hold off on calling your Acid Squad? Five minutes to hear me out?"

She was already on the phone. "Two, possibly. Two in tub."

She ended her call. "If you bring her to me," she said, "I'll call us clear. And I promise not to touch her until you're on subway, so you won't have to hear her scream."

"Zhukov paid us to rip you off."

She pushed her gun barrel against my nose.

"Cipka, the frog—all Zhukov," I said, talking fast. "Get the ID and not have to pay, that was his plan. He keeps the money, gives us a cut, gets his ID. Zhukov. The whole thing. A setup."

Her eyes widened then went cold.

I continued, "He tried to do the same to me. Paid me in bad money for taking your ID to the D.A. But I caught him at it, I know bad money from good. Your papers are locked away in my bank in a safe deposit box. I also happen to know he's under investigation by the district attorney's office. He kidnapped Cipka to get his papers back."

Her smile was like a boa digesting a bunny rabbit. "Zhukov tried to pass you bad money, *maybe*. But if he kidnapped your Polish bitch it could only be that she tried to rip him off after she ripped me off. Now I almost like her."

"You have two good reasons to make Zhukov give her back to me." Remembering Zhukov's cousin, I added. "In one piece."

"Oh yeah?" she said, her teeth when she smiled matched the color of her running suit. "Like what?"

"The first is payback. He took something from you, you take something from him. The second is that if you don't get me my nanny, I'll turn you over to my good friend the district attorney. But if you deliver Cipka to me unharmed I'll give you your original artwork and it will be like we never met. And you can give Zhukov an acid bath, instead."

She said, "Or I can shoot you, then I don't have to worry about the district attorney."

"If you shoot me," I countered, "The noise will bring the police."

"It's a small gun. Besides, there's always the acid, which is very quiet once I shove your balls in your mouth."

"My law partner is waiting by his phone as we speak, with the key to the safe deposit box where your forgeries are stored, and instructions to take them to the cops if I don't call in fifteen minutes."

For a moment we stared at each other in silence, her gun barrel and I. Finally I asked if we had a deal.

"We'll see. But right now you've got..." she glanced at her watch. "About five minutes until Andrej gets here hoping to give you an acid bath."

•   •   •

A bald slab of a guy in a leather jacket had stationed himself at the subway station. I pivoted and race-walked the commercial strip under the el, trying to blend with the crowd, glancing back for brass knuckles, gun butt, or chloroformed hanky. The tracks finally fell away and I slowed, partly because I was winded, and partly because it seemed that maybe Helena had accepted my offer, after all, since Andrej and his crew never did appear.

It was dark and cold as I made my weary pilgrimage from Ocean Parkway to Coney Island. Olivia rejected three straight calls, but Cliff picked up right away and said he was really sorry, that he couldn't believe how sorry he was, but he'd forgotten to give his mom my message for Olivia how for two days we'd been working around the clock on a case, and he didn't know why, he just did, he forgot, maybe because it had been crazy busy at Verizon that day with everyone accidentally sitting on their phones or giving them the "old toilet bath." He double swore he'd tell her that night.

I passed the aquarium, following Surf Avenue toward Nathan's Famous and Luna Park. Despite the attempt to reinvigorate Coney Island as a genuine "destination," it had the same quality of shabby irrelevance I remembered from when I was a kid, on one of those Haley's Comet-rare Saturdays when without warning the Mayor would decide we needed to get reacquainted, and it was time for a few hours of father and son bonding. Collar unbuttoned, shirtsleeves rolled, tie relaxed, he'd order us two hotdogs each, brimming with mustard and sauerkraut, cardboard boats overflowing with Nathan's extra salty scalloped fries. Sometimes I'd top it off with their exotic but uniquely satisfying chow mein burger, tossing in a handful of crunchy noodles. In summer, if it was too crowded to sit, we'd eat standing side-by-side, bathing in the sounds of the ocean and children laughing, summer classics from radios, mothers yelling at their kids to *stop running around like animals*. Or if we scored a table, he might tell me a war story from his early days in the "trenches." Afterward, we'd walk a half block to where they sold this custardy ice cream. He'd order us each a jumbo-sized cone of pistachio and banana swirl, then he'd stare at the sky over the ocean, eating his ice cream without a word, but with a look of peace I found strange and obscure.

I finally reached the open lot with Zhukov's trailer and St. Jude's church, the proposed site of the Luna Park Casino and Hotel. I nudged the garbage with a foot as I headed for the trailer, finding a broken bottle for protection. No one answered when I knocked, no sound at all from inside. I knocked again and tried the door. It fell open into darkness.

"Anatoly," I called, trying to keep my voice, and especially the hand holding the jagged bottle, from shaking. "Anatoly?" I found a light switch and flinched when the trailer lit up.

In the front of the cab was a cramped office: a small metal desk with a computer that wouldn't turn on, a banged-up file cabinet heaped with Los Mansos Heredaran flyers, buttons, and brochures. An ancient Mr. Coffee that looked like it hadn't been cleaned in a month.

Across the cab, a bare mattress with a pillow and rolled-up blanket were pushed up against a corner. Next to the mattress was a flashlight with a long solid handle that made it look like it was half billy club.

In the middle of the trailer folding chairs were set up in haphazard semi-circle. There was a small window with more brochures and buttons along the sill. The folding chairs faced a whiteboard with names written in Magic Marker. The words FEMA THEFT were written at the top of the board. Under them was what looked like a conspiracy tree of the power players in the casino case.

At the top of the tree was Rick Adelman, a high-flying real estate developer and producer of a string of failed Broadway musicals who'd been in the news recently for dating the winner of one of those TV talent contests, twenty years his junior.

Next to Adelman on the whiteboard, connected by two-way arrows, was Councilman Townsend Meeks. Down arrows connected Meeks to Adalita Sanchez, a state senator, then to a couple of names I didn't recognize, and then the letters ESD, which I figured stood for Empire State Development. Except for Adelman and Meeks, everyone had a question mark next to his name. At the bottom of the tree in big letters someone had written, WHO ELSE?

I pocketed a flyer, borrowed the billy club flashlight, and with the broken bottle, stepped out of the trailer. Cipka just had to be in that church across the vacant lot. I walked over and tried the door. It fell open. My narrow white beam of flashlight shot straight through the nave to a missing chunk of back wall where Hurricane Sandy had blown a hole behind the altar. Scaffolding had been erected against another wall, and a tall A-frame ladder stood open. My light picked up tools and buckets, two hard hats, a cooler surrounded by wood crates, a creature that whizzed by too fast for me to identify (thank God!). But no Cipka. I dropped my sawed-off bottle.

Outside, the only sound was the low exhalation of the ocean. Moonlight siphoned through gunmetal clouds. I pointed the flashlight at my watch: Gabriel and I had missed another bed time. I had no car to get me home. Then I remembered that I had no home to get to.

At the bottom of the flyer was a phone number for Los Mansos Heredaran. After five unanswered rings, someone finally answered. "Yes? Hello?"

Now that I had them I had no idea what to do with them, so I started with, "Los Mansos Heredaran?"

"This is?" He had an unguarded way of asking that guarded question, as if the news, whatever it was, was likely to be good.

"I'm a reporter," I improvised. "A journalist. I heard about your case."

"Against the casino? Can I ask you how? How did you hear about it?" He had a Spanish accent, the kind you didn't hear much, maybe Chile, or Peru, with a cultivated, lilting quality. "We've been trying so hard to get even a little coverage. Only a couple of local newspapers have been willing to tell our story."

Not knowing my name or whether my interest was sincere, he already took my word that I was a journalist. It rankled that he would be so trusting.

I said, "I cover law from a human interest angle. My network of lawyers and judges send word when they've got a story worth reporting."

The night sky arced with stars like shards of ice, then seemed to shudder and let drop a sheet of frozen air.

"The court papers tell a real outrage," I continued. "What they're trying to do to you, to the Heredarans. People love David and Goliath stories. I think I can help."

I was deft and smooth at winning trust; learned it at the Mayor's knee. Knowing not to press too hard, I let him take a moment for reflection, craning my neck until the stars turned to bits of glass and the sky for a moment became a Waldbaum's aisle littered with shattered Del Monte.

He said, "The Church of St. Jude the Apostle, where we had our headquarters before Hurricane Sandy, it's basically an abandoned lot now. Councilman Meeks and the governor and his powerful friends and paid experts claim it's a sinkhole. It's not. The only sinkhole is where our money is going, the money earmarked by FEMA for Sandy Victims. You see, Meeks and his Luna Park Corporation have basically stolen it to use as seed money for their casino project. We're still there, though. On *our* property—but in a trailer. They're not getting rid of us so easy. Do you think you can find it?"

Turning around to look back at the trailer, I said, "I'm pretty sure I won't have much trouble."

"Then I'll see you at—no, wait. Instead, meet me at Mermaid Avenue and West 17th Street, on the side of Mermaid further from the ocean. This is more than some court case. But you can't understand unless you actually see what I mean. We'll meet in the morning, okay? Mermaid and 17th."

I thought about spending the night in the trailer. It did have a nice cot, a Mr. Coffee, and a television. But I wanted to sleep in my own bed, next to my wife. So I took the long train ride home, to tell Olivia everything.

THE TAP DANCE

She wore yoga tights and a pale blue hoody, her hair in a ponytail, her face freshly scrubbed with one of those loofah things that she uses because soap is a "skin killer." In the run up to her forties she was becoming one of those women about whom other women remark, with wonder and envy, that she'd stopped aging at thirty-two. But her eyes seemed tired and careworn, perhaps because she'd opened her door to find me behind it.

"You can't be here," she said.

She was blocking most of the door frame, presumably to leave no angle that I could wedge myself through. I asked if Gabriel was asleep.

"What do you think?"

"Hasn't he asked for me?"

I thought a sob caught in her throat. "It's not enough," she said. "Emma phoned to tell me what Cliff told her, that you and he were working on a case, but it's not enough. Like I'm going to take *Cliff's* word. And even if you didn't, I don't know, bribe him in some way, even if you *were* on a case, it's not enough. Those wrappers were in my car. As if it weren't enough that the two of you...in *my* car, as if you were going out of your way to...to really *hurt*. And now she just happens to be gone."

"How can I explain if you won't let me in to talk?"

"Wrappers. Car. No Cipka. QED, Henry."

"Even a criminal gets a closing statement."

She cocked her head as if thinking it over. "Not here. You're not charm-worming your way into my home. It's a school night, so Reilly's probably upstairs. I'll run and see if she can watch Gabriel for an hour while she does her homework. Meet me at the vegan place."

"But how will I know if Reilly's available?"

"Sit there for an hour or two and if I don't show, that's a pretty good indication."

"It would be so much easier if I just wait inside."

"Don't push it, Henry," she said as she shut the door in my face.

As usual, not much was happening at Om Cooking, so we were able to have a corner to ourselves. She ordered a Buddha's Breath tea. I had a mug of their Morning After Roast, which was basically caffeinated propane.

"My original plan," I said, "was to make you listen and forgive me. Drag you by your hair back to my cave."

"I'd have punched you in the face," she said.

"Which is why we find ourselves at Om Cooking pretending to like Buddha's Breath tea."

She smiled, not wanting to. Then tears began to flow.

"The orange wrappers," I began. Now what?

"You took her to some beach and that's where you did it. In November. Weren't you *cold*?"

Was it adrenaline that was rocking my heart, or the Morning After Roast?

"What makes you think we went to the beach?" I asked.

"There was sand in the floor mats, *idiot*. You could have been more careful. That's what kills me, the casualness. That you don't even care enough to clean up properly."

"The innocent never think about covering their tracks, we have no tracks to cover."

"Sand and wrappers," she said, with surgical precision, her tears having instantly dried.

"Sand and wrappers and something else," I answered, thinking as fast as I could. "And when I tell you, you're going to laugh and beg forgiveness for not trusting me."

"Uh-huh."

"Sand, wrappers, and Cliff Mott."

"*Please.*"

"It's true. When he told Emma we were on a case, we were. Cipka, she's...my client. Obviously I wasn't going to *charge* her. Actually, it's not Cipka, it's this friend of hers, got played by this guy in Coney Island runs a green card scam. You pay up front, he comes back with there's this complication, he needs more money. It's either pay or live a walking nightmare when will ICE show up. So you pay, but he never delivers. Threaten to sue or report him to the cops, he says go ahead, illegal, report me. Cipka's friend goes back to plead with him, she's got this great job lined up and needs that card. He tries to extort sex for it and she doesn't know what to do. So Cliff, Cipka, and I drive down to Sea Gate to confront the guy and convince him to give Cipka's friend her money back. Or if not, I told him, I have a friend at Homeland Security."

Olivia got up and walked away without a word. I thought she wasn't buying my story until she returned with a pecan cranberry vegan scone for us to share. It tasted like it was made of concentrated sawdust.

She took a nibble. "They're closing in twenty minutes," she said apologetically. "But he gave me a deal on the last of the scones."

She forced a knife through the scone while I worked feverishly to come up with an answer for when she asked why I needed Cliff's help with the green card scammer.

"Okay, so you didn't want Bryce's partnership." She called her father by his first name. If I'd ever tried that with the Mayor, Nina would have needed a scrub brush and a box of Brillo to clean my remains. "Male pride, I get it. That's why you're becoming obsolete, men. But you know what I wish? Remember back when I got you that opportunity to come on board P²R³ as house counsel? We'd be happy right now."

"Actually, if I were working for P²R³ , with your career going the way it is, we'd probably be collecting his-and-her unemployment checks."

Her voice broke. "That's not fair."

"But it's fair asking me to be who I'm not. Some *house counsel*."

"You could have been a great lawyer. *Can* be."

"Analyzing contract clauses drier than this scone."

"I just always...I always imagined...the two of us, cabbing to work together, me reading the *Times*, you the *Law Journal*. Then at lunch, or in the middle of a meeting, sharing a secret smile or a dirty look."

"Your dirty looks have been in dwindling supply these days."

"I knew it was a mistake coming here."

"What exactly is wrong with me as I am?"

"*Nothing*. Nothing is wrong with you. I'm sorry." Her eyes said she knew it was pointless to try to force back her tears. "No, I'm not."

Choking down a morsel, I said, "I hope they paid you to take this scone off their hands."

She smiled. I wished I could stop liking it so much when she did that.

"Anyway," I added, changing the subject from my not being the man she'd hoped. "How's my idea going?" She didn't have a clue what I was talking about. "The song. To save Taj's career."

"Morgue-drawered," she said, taking her first sip of tea. "We tried to put a team of ARM analysts in to vet his drafts—*ARM*, Henry," she huffed. "Audience response measurement. To make sure the song will have maximum emotional impact while avoiding any Claymores." Again, she looked at me with pity for my look of confusion. "It's a land mine, Henry. Blows up in your face. But Taj shut us out. He said you'll know what I wrote when you hear it on Spotify. So now we may be going to war with our own client, thanks to you."

"It could still work out. He might come up with a blockbuster."

"Even if it's a hit it won't save my job. I'm on my way out, it's just a matter of when."

"They're not firing you, they'd be crazy. Without you, they're just another flak house."

"Hardly," she blushed.

"Besides, you've got a contract."

"I've got a contract and you know what that's worth."

"They even breathe they're going to let you go, I file suit the next morning."

"You can finish it," she said, pushing her half of scone across the table and rising to stand.

"So I can come home?"

A shadow seemed to cross her face. "What do you think?"

Outside the shop, before she had a chance to sprint away, I said, "This can't go on forever."

"I agree, Henry. The question is, how will it end?"

THE AGITATOR

I woke before dawn on a bed of motion papers and months of unread *Law Journals*, a corner of the "Judges and Courts" section fixed to my chin. I peeled it off and rose shakily to my feet, grabbing a corner of upended desk for support. It was nine. I was out of spare suits; I'd have to sneak one from the apartment.

I had three client voicemails and one desperate text about my having ignored the voicemail. As I shut my office door it hit me that I didn't know whether Scottie Walsh's seventy-two hours to vacate included weekends. Unless Elaine was bluffing, I might be sleeping on the street over a heating grate come Monday.

In Coney Island, on the corner of Mermaid and West 17th, a slight light-skinned Hispanic guy with sandy hair waited with two Styrofoam coffees. He wore a tan jacket over a blue button-down shirt and chinos, jacket open despite the cold. I slowed my approach to size him up, but he saw me coming and turned with an open smile, his expression good-natured and candid.

Extending a coffee, he said, "Gonzalo Guerrero. I hope you don't mind milk and sugar."

He reminded me of one of those perpetual graduate students, with the sort of youthful candor that made it impossible to guess his age. The only mark of dues paid was the weariness in his eyes, but maybe that was the result of sleepless nights worrying over the fate of his Heredarans and their church. I thanked him for the coffee and forced a smile as I sipped: I hated sugar in my coffee and I hated coffee in Styrofoam.

He said, "So you're writing an article on us. At last, someone pays attention."

"Well, researching one. I hope to interest the *New York Times*. How the state claims to serve community interests by exploiting eminent domain. That means its right to condemn."

It was a mouthful, but it seemed to have hit its mark.

His caution gave way to interest. "Believe me, I know all about eminent domain."

"As I said yesterday, I think the public would really get into it. Your Heredarans as David with a rock in his slingshot. But with three giants to slay: Sandy Adelson, Senator Sanchez, and Townsend Meeks."

His face lit up. "You know about Adelson and Sanchez?"

"I told you, I'm a journalist. I do my research."

He started up West 17th Street through a complex of apartment buildings that obliterated any hint of the beach a short stroll away.

"Governor Finney is in on it, too," he said. "I just haven't been able to find even a hint of evidence to prove it. But I will. Justice is never more than a matter of time."

I followed him past the apartment complex into an enclave of small homes made of crumbling brick, and of drywall with cheap siding. Some were separated by fenced lots with brownish sand and patches of half-dead grass, garbage and splintered branches. Some were pressed up against each other so close it seemed that no embarrassing family secret went unshared. Windows were scored with shatter lines. We passed Ottomanelli's Auto Repair. Someone had spray painted SHUT BY SANDY across a padlocked corrugated metal security gate.

A rheumatic tree leaned precariously over a car, its roots like teeth being torn from a mouth. The car had been reduced to three tires and a hubcap. We sidestepped a slab of ruptured sidewalk and walked into the street. A dog snarled, then another; Guerrero stepped back onto the sidewalk and laughed when I declined to join him.

He said, "This is not some corporate wet dream of Coney Island. We're the nightmare you wake up to when the dream is over. Did you know that in Las Vegas hundreds of homeless live in tunnels beneath the billion-dollar hotels? The insiders, the privileged, their grand political philosophy is how can it exist if I don't see it? But what you ignore will rot your soul like a cancer of bad faith. After Sandy, FEMA earmarked millions for us. You can see how the politicians have rushed to actually give us our money."

A car had jackknifed across a lawn and been left there to rust. Two others had come to rest, one's hood on the other's trunk. I said, "They decided why bother to tow, another hurricane's bound to hit sooner or later?"

Guerrero gave a bitter laugh.

Farther down from Mermaid Avenue, awning from a Pizza Garden had come loose to drape across a picnic table. The chairs were upturned and broken.

"We can walk more than a mile in any direction," Guerrero said. "It would all be the same. For weeks there'll be electricity, then it goes out again, and it stays out, and you don't know when it's going to happen or how long it'll last, so how can you prepare? The city still hasn't fixed all the water mains that exploded. They want us to believe that a luxury hotel and casino will revitalize the area, but that's the same promise they made about our FEMA money. Have you ever visited D.C.? Three blocks from the home of the leader of the free world and you think you're in Mumbai."

An old man sat on his porch drinking coffee in pajama bottoms and a sweatshirt. A chunk of his house had been blown away by the storm.

Guerrero called out, "Up early, Ike?"

The old man took a sip of coffee by way of answering.

"He lives in a house with hole in it," I said.

Guerrero didn't answer. For a while he seemed to have withdrawn into himself. "That night," he finally said. "It was a strange darkness, like when there's an eclipse in the middle of the day. The wind was screaming, I mean literally, as if it had a voice, howling from all directions. You couldn't get away from it. Even so, you could hear the cries for help, the sickening blast of cars crashing. Trees being torn from their roots. Sidewalk ripped from the ground, chunks of it tossed through windows and siding. In our ridiculous plasterboard houses we were naked before the power of the storm, and you couldn't tell yourself it will pass. No, it felt personal, like it intended to destroy every last one of us."

The sidewalk narrowed and I followed a step behind. He continued.

"You know what haunts me? I didn't rush out to help. Not at first. I sat in a corner of my house with my head in my arms, weeping with terror. I don't know where you were or what you did that night, but I cried. Like a child before an angry father. 'Why *us*?'"

We stopped where a lawn sign with a splintered wood post lay flat across the sidewalk, filthy with footprints. It read, CONEY ISLAND IS **NOT** BACK. A shard of rusted metal impaled a tree. A foot-high garden fence surrounded the tree, with candles set in the dirt, their crowns a collection of wax stalagmites. Photographs of a girl, seven or so, were arranged around the trunk among the candles, along with toys, stuffed animals, and costume jewelry. A red wagon, mauled at both ends and twisted in the middle, lay on the sidewalk along the fence, as if some giant had picked it up and crushed it in his hands.

Guerrero said, "Her name was Aliyah. She lived a few blocks from her grandfather. His wife had died a year and a half before and was more and more losing touch with reality. That night when the phones went dead, Aliyah's father ran over to bring the old man to their house. But a neighbor said he'd gone out alone into the storm with a flashlight, shouting his wife's name. The family was heart sick, but Aliyah refused to believe her grandfather was gone. The next morning she slipped away to find him. She was electrocuted by a live wire blown loose by the storm. But it didn't kill her; she drowned in the flood water that was running through the streets."

I looked up from Aliyah's memorial at those broken streets shrouded in late October light on which not a soul could be seen. No one walked a dog or rushed to work, no one waited on a curb for the mail or pushed a stroller. "You didn't get any of the money earmarked by FEMA?"

Guerrero exhaled a long sigh and started back toward Mermaid Avenue and the ocean. "Oh, we got. Just enough so that Councilman Meeks could hold his press conference and take credit for wresting the money from the feds for us little people. What Coney Island got, out of ten million promised, was about three. But Meeks waylaid most of that as seed money for the casino. Though we did get some very nice FEMA windbreakers."

I could see Mermaid Avenue up ahead.

He continued. "And the feds? Well, the government is great at throwing money at a problem. Who gets their hands on it, and for what purpose, that's not their concern."

We came out on Mermaid. Across from the Herederans' lot, a Spanish guy in work clothes leaned against a pickup truck smoking a cigarette. As we crossed the avenue he tossed the butt and made a call on his cell. A hundred yards away Zhukov hurried from the church, cell phone to his ear. He stopped when he saw me, reached into a shoulder holster, slipped out a gun, and took dead aim.

Guerrero called out, "It's okay, Anatoly. He's just a lawyer."

"So it would be mercy killing," Zhukov said.

Guerrero glanced back to find me boldly hesitating. "He's not going to shoot you," he said. The tragic fact of the matter is we need security. Powerful people want this Luna Park deal; they're not gambling their investment on the whim of a judge, especially one who's shown himself to be a good man, indicating a preference for people over profit."

Zhukov kept the gun pointed at my head; Guerrero was unfazed. "Anatoly was forced on us as a 'construction supervisor' by the casino people, but they borrowed him from the mob. His real job is to spy on us, and force us out of our home by any means necessary."

Zhukov lowered the gun, warning me with his eyes that he and I had never met.

Guerrero continued his introduction. "But the funny thing is they don't know that Anatoly was actually a labor organizer back home in Ukraine."

"Imagine that," I said, choking back a laugh.

"It's why he came to America," Guerrero explained. "His life was in danger."

"From labor organizing," I said.

"So he's with us," Guerrero said. "A sort of double agent."

I extended a hand to Zhukov, who holstered his gun and lit a cigarette. He said, "You know what Los Mansos Heredaran means?"

"Wolf in sheep's clothing?"

"The meek shall inherit. I believe that they will."

I said, "I can't imagine why you wouldn't."

He spat a flume of acrid smoke. "Today we're on Code Red, because yesterday I learned of betrayal."

I got it: He was terrified of Helena and her Acid Squad, but told Guerrero the Code Red was something to do with the casino project.

He said, "Now violence is coming. That's why I'm strapped."

"*Strapped*," I said. "So they have Netflix in the Ukraine, too."

Guerrero gave a small laugh and walked off toward the church. "I'm a pacifist, but also a realist. And if it were my life alone, that's one thing. But I'm responsible for others, for good people, so I'm forced to resort to men with guns."

Zhukov said, "I'm like fox in their henhouse."

"Yes," I said. "I can see that."

We followed Guerrero under the scaffolding and into the church.

Zhukov flicked cigarette ash at my back. "What's so funny?"

None of the workers turned our way as we walked through the door. Morning sun poured through the hole behind where the altar had been.

Guerrero said, "This was our home until Sandy hit. The home of Los Mansos Heredaran. These men and women work here on a totally voluntary basis, on days when they can't find paying jobs."

"What do you do exactly? Los Mansos?" I asked.

"The thing about the meek inheriting the earth is that we want it now. Eternity doesn't put food on the table, or pay a just wage, or teach what to do in a confrontation with police. We do that. We have, we *had*, a day laborer center, where employers can find good reliable workers. OSHA came to teach construction site safety. We gave English classes, and classes in legal rights."

He arrived at what had been the mid-point of the nave. "Our plan for St. Jude is not so much a restoration as a rebirth. That's why when it's finished we're going to rechristen it La Iglesia de la Resurrección. The Church of the Resurrection. A beacon for the surrounding neighborhoods, our poor souls broken by the storm. To say, you can be born again—in *this* life. But for that we need our FEMA money. Can you imagine a casino as a beacon of hope?"

He stopped again where a couple of laborers were hammering drywall across the hole the storm had blown through the sanctuary.

We stared through it, Guerrero and I, with Zhukov simmering behind us.

After a long silence, Guerrero said, "I could take you back to the trailer to show you our video. I call it *Empty Promises*. The dead, the homeless, business owners dispossessed. It's a year after Sandy, but still at times we go without heat, without electricity. The sewage backup causes terrible sickness, but who can afford adequate medical care? Do you remember all those small businesses closed behind gates? *Empty Promises*. I intend to enter it in film festivals, so that the world can see what's happening here."

I thought about Aliyah and her grandfather, searching for his wife in a gale. About old Ike, sipping coffee in front of half a house. I thought about the laborers rebuilding the church on their own time, believing it would be some kind of beacon. How futile it all was, how we never have a prayer against forces of nature like hurricanes, Councilman Meeks, Sandy Adelman, or the Mayor.

Guerrero turned to lead us out, stopping to speak in Spanish to a woman in a hardhat who was halfway up a ladder. Meanwhile, Zhukov, pressing too close at my back, hissed. "I knew you were putting me on at the urinal that day when you played the virgin lawyer who only wanted to do it the straight way. You think it's funny sending Helena to hurt me, but all you did is cost a forger her thumbs."

"You cut off—no you didn't."

"With a garden shears—when I find her. You're wasting time, mini-Mayor. I want your papa's names. I want those names or the people of Brooklyn will be buying pieces of Helena *and* your nanny shrink-wrapped at Key Food, a dollar eighty a pound."

"So Cipka's in Brooklyn."

A sound came out of him like he'd accidentally swallowed his cigarette. "Don't bet her life on it."

Guerrero turned from the woman on the ladder to lead us out.

"If the state is right," I asked him, "And you're building your church on a sinkhole, aren't you just inviting another catastrophe?"

We'd walked across the plank that lay between the door and the empty lot, and were standing under the scaffold.

"But the state is not right," he said. "I've consulted engineers and environmental experts, honest ones, who assure me that the land is in fine shape, and any scientist who claims that the Luna Park project won't be far more devastating on the environment must be as corrupt as the people paying him. So when you write your story, will you tell these things I've shown you? Will you expose the truth behind the state's claim of eminent domain, and where the real blight is?"

"Well," I hedged. "It's for the *Law Journal*. I don't know that they're interested in anything more than an analysis of the legal issues."

We stepped out from beneath the scaffold.

Guerrero said. "I thought you'd said the *Times*."

Behind me, Zhukov muffled a laugh.

"Of course," I said quickly. "But my contacts at the *Law Journal* are very interested, too, if the *Times* is a no."

"Then we shouldn't be standing here," Guerrero said. "Go tell our story."

Morning had broken out into robust day; it felt like we were wading in sky. The ocean light and salt air held a promise of summer, an assurance of return that I fought, knowing it was November and endless winter lay ahead. It was hard to square that promise of return with the memory of those photos of Aliyah, who would always be seven through infinite summers.

"Yeah," Zhukov echoed. "The hearing is in three days. Why are you wasting time?"

THE RAP PRODUCER'S GIRLFRIEND

Amber Waves waited for me on the steps of my office, blowing smoke rings of cold air. "I miss cigs," she said, standing and brushing off her coat. "But the secondary's bad for Alex's asthma, and besides, it ages you and slows you on the pole."

"You didn't need to freeze." I turned the knob and the door gave way. "See?

She followed me in. "I like to stand on ceremony," she said.

The tilt of her head in her imitation stole reminded me of Cipka, and I felt the bite of a sorrowing guilt.

Amber surveyed the chaos with her hands on her hips. "You didn't tell me you practice law with a sledgehammer."

"High-profile case," I said, scanning the mayhem for the keys to the Jeep that Olivia had neglected to notice I'd failed to return. My plan was to sneak the Jeep past the garage guy while figuring out how to disengage the cell phone alarm, head up to Westchester to visit Nina and ask if the Mayor had kept any personal papers at home, or in a safe deposit box. "Defense lawyers will do anything to learn what you have against their client."

Amber walked across the office and took a chair. "Listen, I know I gave you grief for making me do community service because of Mariano, but I know you had my back and saved me from the nightmare of Alex having to stay with my brother's sick bitch of a wife. Knowing Toya she'd have jacked his Prednisone and tried to swap it on the street for weed. Hell, I'd have to smoke twenty-four-seven too if I had a pushed-in butt-ugly face. So you took care of me, I'm here to care of you."

"*There* they are," I said, reaching for the keys on the floor behind the desk. "You're paid in full. Really. Whatever it was you were going to do for me, I really do appreciate it but…"

She laughed. "Look at you looking like you swallowed an order of bad sushi. I don't mean *that* way. I know you're one of those faithful pup-type husbands."

She didn't wait for me to protest my status as a player of almost epic breadth of anecdote.

"So remember when you told me your wife does Taj's PR? And I went apeshit because he's my favorite artist practically and I choreograph my most popular moves to him? Well my friend down at the club, Paula Vortex—that's her stage name, she's really Cindy Montoya—she's been dating this record producer, a dude called Knox. He comes in one night a couple of weeks ago with his crew buying Freixenet practically by the case and throwing around twenties like confetti. So it gets near to witching hour and things are getting raucous. With all the weed and Freixenet and pussies grinding in his face, Knox starts bragging on how he's actually Taj's record producer but they had a falling out, and now he's going to extract payback."

"What kind of falling out? What did Taj do to him?"

"He didn't say."

"Well, what about his revenge, did he have a plan?"

She shrugged again. "Not like I was in a position to take notes. But see? There's no coincidences in life. That's the butterfly effect. One day a record producer threatens his one-time boy, the next day the poor guy's mired in scandal."

"Can I meet this Knox? I'd like to talk to him."

She hesitated, biting a corner of her lower lip. "Meet him?"

"How else can I help Olivia with her Taj problem?"

"I just thought, the information. In view of how Taj's getting ass raped by the media."

"My wife is going to lose her job and she's blaming me."

"But what do you have to do with it?"

"Not a thing."

"I don't get it, then how can she blame you?"

"You must never have been married. If I could just talk to Knox—but why can't I talk to him? What's the problem?"

"I have to stay clean, you know, for Alex. My sheet. Whatever you've got going."

"I'm just trying to get my wife back. And my kid. I haven't seen him in days."

"Your kid..." She bit her lip again and scrunched her eyes, which I took to be a sign she was working out some deep scruple. I'd never noticed how many charming habits she had, or how good she looked without makeup. Finally, she said, "I'll talk to Paula, okay?"

The keys to the Jeep gave me an idea. "Actually," I said, "it turns out I need one more favor."

· · ·

"Tell you what," Amber said as we stopped at the ramp to Metro Parking, just outside my building. "Next time Alex can stay with Toya, after all. You cost more in favors than I can afford."

She kissed me on the forehead and strolled down the ramp to very intimately question the garage guy on the price of a permanent spot to stash her car, or whether it's better to go month to month, so he wouldn't notice while I removed the little black electronic scanner from the Jeep's dashboard before starting the motor. As I headed for the river it hit me that I probably owed Amber now, which was fine, because she turned out to be a sweet person with a good heart, as long as you didn't drill a peephole in her ceiling.

NINA

I hit the FDR and dialed Chulo.

"The fight still on tomorrow?" I asked.

"Why wouldn't it be?"

"I don't know, a miracle? How's the hand?"

"Popping vikes like jelly beans."

Next I called Olivia, but her cell went to voicemail. I tried her office. Mrs. Mott informed me that Olivia was out at a client's and would probably not be back until evening. Late evening, she added. She also emphasized that the city had any number of troubleshooters I could hire next time my computers went down, because her son had taken early retirement. She suggested ZipRecruiter as a fine source of candidates.

Traffic on the FDR was racing along at its usual six miles an hour. Hoping for a miracle, I dialed Cipka. Her confident, Polish-inflected voice assuring me that if I left a message she'd get back to me soon made me veer across the lane divider, nearly sideswiping a Jag. The Jag's driver popped his head out his window like an enraged Halloween pumpkin, nearly rear-ending a ten-wheeler. I merged onto the Saw Mill River Parkway.

•   •   •

My mother opened her door to find me standing there.

"What are you doing here?" she said.

"What a homecoming, mom. Confetti and tears."

"I thought, seeing you there, that it was Sunday. But of course I knew it couldn't be."

I never dropped in or phoned out of the blue; she was easily flustered by the unexpected.

"I was thinking about you," I told her.

"About me?"

I followed her into the house the Mayor had bought her only after I'd gone off to college, apparently hoping she'd spend most of her time there so he could have the penthouse on Ocean Parkway for himself. Well, not only himself.

She was thinner than ever, a line drawing of a woman. She seemed to have refined her weight obsession to some sort of sacrament, as if her life had become one long Day of Atonement.

"Thinking about you," I said. "And also wanting to get away from the city, to where it's quiet."

"Oh, there are noises all the time. Things running under the bushes. In the trees. Sounds you can't tell what they are. Birds crash against the windows, trees fall against the house. Where's my grandson? Where's Gabriel?"

"It's Friday, mom. He's in school."

"I know the day, I don't have *that* disease. You haven't heard of holidays?"

She made a habit of assuring me that her regular collapse into black holes of bewilderment wasn't *that* disease. In fact, no doctor had been able to name it, she'd confess in her thrilled tremolo, though more than a few had tried. I'd ask how can you be sure a doctor hadn't diagnosed *that* disease--maybe they had and you forgot. She always laughed, and I always pointed out that she was able to appreciate the joke, so how bad could it be? It came and went, she explained.

What the doctors didn't know, she'd always been like this.

"You're not sick, are you?" She turned away and raced to the living room. "You're not here to tell me you're sick?"

The sprawling living room was designed like a ski chalet, with a high wood-beamed ceiling, brick fireplace, and assortment of chairs and love seats. A circular staircase led to the second floor, where you could lean over an oak banister to survey the living area below. There were many windows, but few memories—I was seventeen when we moved here.

I said, "It's just a visit, nothing more. That the Mayor got sick doesn't mean we all will. It was an accident."

"All of life feels like an accident."

One thing was different. Growing up, the only book I'd ever seen around the apartment was a battered copy of John Kennedy's *Profiles in Courage* that for years the Mayor kept alongside the toilet in the master bathroom. Now books were everywhere. The coffee table was colonized by books. Books were sprawled across the sofa and fireplace mantel, and piled on chairs.

"They're thrillers," she explained. "Legal thrillers. I used to get the *Times* delivered but I told them, don't bother, I've had it up to here with your bad news and catastrophes. The weather's turning strange, not like it used to be. Terrorists shooting up schools, people coming over our borders by the millions—where are we going to put them? Crazies shooting up supermarkets. I'm afraid to stack my pantry, but they deliver now, so you only have to worry who they send with your order. I'd carry the bags in myself, but of course they're too heavy, so when he comes I pretend I've been chopping salad and I stand there holding a cleaver."

We sat facing each other on the small bench in the picture window.

"You look good, Henry. Remember how crazy it used to make me, how fat you were, and knowing that everyone thought it was my fault? Your father, of course, no one blamed. But what could I do, I was just your mother. But I like how you've kept the weight off, for the most part."

That was a compliment, Nina style.

She said, "So what does bring you to see me in the middle of a work day?"

"I have a question. After dad died—"

She leaned back away from me.

"Did you save anything from his office? Files or papers? Anything at all? Or maybe at home he kept a safe or secret drawer?"

"You mean the cash?" she said, pushing off the bench to rearrange the books along the fireplace mantel. "I thought Olivia had that wonderful job."

"She does, mom. I do, too. We both have wonderful jobs. But did he leave, I don't know, a diary? Or a sealed envelope?"

She seemed confused, but also guilty. "There's this box of photographs. I've been meaning to put them into an album but you get so busy. I may have a love letter from before we were married."

I was killing Cipka. As a hero I excelled at false starts and dead ends. As an executioner, I was A-list.

"I can do without seeing his love letters," I said. "But *please*—did he leave anything like a diary, or safe?"

"A safe?"

We stared out the picture window at decaying leaves clinging to branches in the hope of a few more days, and dead leaves covering the cold ground like a shroud.

"I knew you would never go with him," she said after a few seconds. "You would never go into the firm. Of course he wouldn't hear it. When you were growing up, he'd say, 'I'm building for the future. Krakow and Krakow—that will be my legacy'."

I apologized for laughing. Gently, I said, "He looked down on men who cared about legacies."

"Not when it came to you."

"And he always said the only reason he wanted me in the firm was to protect me from myself."

She brushed me off with a wave of the hand and a huff of impatience, a lifelong habit. "Do you remember that time when he was so sick he couldn't get off the sofa and he wanted you to do that one hearing, but you wouldn't?"

"I do sort of remember," I lied, hoping to segue with lightning speed to goodbye.

"He had all those court appearances he couldn't do, so he was giving out his files. Shelly Feinstein and Mack and all his friends were going to court to do his cases for him. He was so embarrassed and angry at having to ask."

I began to remember him as he was then, the colossus of Brooklyn reduced to a Gollum beneath his wool blanket.

"He hated needing help even more than he hated asking for it," I said. "Unless it came with an IOU."

"He had that one hearing that none of his friends could do on short notice, but he was too proud to ask the judge for an adjournment. That's why he was so desperate for you to do it."

I saw him again beneath a thin wool blanket, struggling to hand me a file. "Take it," he rasped. "*Take* the fucking thing." But I had learned from the master that life is perpetual war. He tried to push it on me, and I refused him. "Your legacy...all I have to give."

His feet were swollen into clubs; eyes cratered into feverish pools. His shaved head had grown back stubby and raw like the aftermath of a forest fire, with a jagged red crown inscribed by the saw of Dr. Mehmet Polamalu. Finally, he fell back to his sofa pillow, muttering and trying to push the file at me with an extended hand.

I asked Nina, "Why was it so important to him that I appear at that one hearing?"

She stared past me and beyond the dying yard toward that spectral place where the Mayor made sense to her.

I flashed on Cipka hanging from a meat hook. *Don't bother to rush,* she said. *It's only dismemberment and death.*

"I'm sorry," I said, pushing up from the window seat. "Gabriel's getting out of school, I have to pick him up. That file dad wanted me to take—you don't have it, do you?"

"Why would I, it was for you. But...I think I remember...he gave it to Olivia."

"Why would he do that?"

"Of course, hoping she would talk you into it."

"Olivia? The way she felt about him?"

"He was dying, Henry. He was dying."

"And you're sure you didn't save anything: letters, diaries, envelopes, Redwells?"

"Your father was too smart to write down anything he might get caught at. And after anything he might get caught at," she added with a sad smile, "What was left to write?"

She hurried ahead and returned with a book she'd taken from the coffee table.

"Would you like to borrow this? It was written by an actual prosecutor so it's true to life. Maybe it could help you with your career. Amazon ranks it at sixty-nine. That's *very* good. I used to keep pictures of your father on the coffee table. And you, when you were young, and Olivia and Gabriel. But now I don't have enough room for anything but my books. I can't get enough of my legal thrillers. They're like a cuckoo clock. All those gears and springs working together so that in the end, out pops the cuckoo. This one's ranked at nine hundred, so it can't be any good. I don't remember why I bought it. Was it a gift? If it's rated over a hundred it's not worth reading. At first, something terrible happens, too terrible to bear. Murder, incest, rape. Some innocent is facing a lethal injection, only he didn't do it! But then the lawyer comes..."

"What's wrong?"

Her eyes were brimming; she waited for it to pass.

"The lawyer comes to put things right," she said. "Even if he's struggling with inner demons, he's like a hero." She swapped out a book on the fireplace mantel with one on the coffee table. "You're not sick, are you? Did you say if you were sick?"

The doctors told her she had a disorder they could not name. They could not name it, so they couldn't say where it came from. DNA, the drinking water, telephone wires, alien probes. It was just another thing that happens, they said. Just another one of those things that happen.

On the other hand, they had never known the Mayor.

THE GRUDGE

It was Saturday afternoon and I was car-hopping the C train to the Barclays Center where the Nets would be playing the Lakers. According to Amber, I had a small window of time in which to find Knox hawking his CDs before the game began and the crowd thinned out. Alex had a soccer game so Amber couldn't come with me, and in any case her gratitude had run its course, she'd said, but not without another kiss, north of my right ear.

I crossed over to the next car without taking my eyes from my feet as they stepped gingerly across couplers that lurched from side to side. After the next station we'd have three more to go before Atlantic Avenue and Barclays, but I still hadn't found Knox. My chance of redemption with Olivia was disintegrating faster than the rusted train couplers. Suddenly I heard the thunderous sound of a hip-hop anthem. I looked across to the opposite end of the car and saw a boom box held together with black electrical tape. Its hollow, tinny sound made the lyrics as penetrable as the conductor's updates on the public address system. A dude, probably not much younger than me, stood over the boom box with a brace of CDs in one hand and an upturned baseball cap filled with money in the other. A tan corduroy jacket lay rolled up behind the boom box on the subway floor. He wore dark jeans and a T-shirt that read, "4 Knox Productions," with an eight-hundred-number and web address. I put him about fifteen pounds overweight, and uncomfortable about it, like the extra pounds were a recent development. It made his face seem a bit like an overripe melon, which accentuated his popping eyes. He didn't bother to conceal his simmering grudge as he walked through the car pitching his CDs to the uninterested crowd.

"Mr. Knox," I said as he neared me with his upturned hat.

"Working," he snapped, turning away back toward the boom box.

"Paula Vortex told me to look you up."

He stopped to negotiate the sale of a CD, taking a dollar off the already discounted five-dollar price. I repeated that we had a friend in common.

"You don't see me working?"

It seemed less a question than a warning. I dropped a five in his hat.

"It's not *Mister* Knox, Opie. You see the shirt? For-t Knox," he said, hitting the t extra hard. "Where they keep the gold." He shook his cash-filled cap. "Like me. Richie Rich, hat in hand."

He went back to barking his sales pitch as the doors closed on a pregnant woman, opened again so her thigh and shoulder could enter, then slammed shut, content to take some of the pregnant lady to the next stop while leaving the rest behind. She forced open the doors like a female Hercules in red spandex and pushed in, belly first, while the conductor squawked something with the tone of a warning.

Knox sold one more CD, this time at full price. The conductor announced the Barclays station up ahead and Knox sighed, bending to shut off his music.

"Actually I don't know Paula," I told him. "But my friend Amber does. She says you were Taj's producer?"

Knox laid his cap upright on the floor, flipping the CD out of the boom box sleeve and placing it with a sort of tenderness into its jewel case.

"The famous rap guy?" I added.

"I know who he is," Knox snapped.

"Were you his producer?"

He zipped his unsold CDs into a black duffel bag. I put a ten in his hat.

"A lot of things *were*. Okay? Most of life *were*. In about one minute you better hope you were, dentist."

I dropped another ten in his hat. "What makes you think I'm a dentist?"

"You got that look," he said, emptying his hat and pocketing the cash, lifting the boom box and swinging his duffel of CDs around his shoulder. "Or some accountant." Finished with me, he turned to face the door. At the sight of my reflection behind him in the glass, he shook his head. "I never get a break, do I?"

I followed him out. "Not from Taj, according to Paula. You and him have a history?"

"Women can't help but run their mouths. Doesn't mean anything comes out worth hearing. There is no history, dentist. There's only forward."

We climbed the stairs, coming out in front of Barclays.

I said, "You're going to try to sell now, when people are rushing to get to the game?"

"Hell, no. I got an all-you-can-eat ticket. Fourteen bucks. I'll take in the game, feast my ass off, leave middle of the fourth quarter, set up my goods. By then the Nets are usually down by fifty, anyway. Hit the folks with music when they're coming out slowed by Junior's cheesecake and futility."

He stopped at the end of a long security line. "I don't want to keep you from the game," I said.

"Then don't."

I pulled out another ten. "Can I purchase a CD?"

He threw the duffel off his shoulder and within seconds I was the proud owner of *Brass Knoxes: The Greatest Knockouts from 4 Knox Productions*.

"Were you really his first producer?"

Almost before I'd finished the question he'd whipped out another CD, this one featuring a fuzzy, cell phone quality photograph of a younger Taj, not dressed in TajWear silk, Egyptian cotton, or cow hide, but apparently from a bin at the Dollar Store. The name of the CD was *Kevin Russell Raps*. Along the bottom, graffiti-style, it read, "A 4 Knox Knockout."

He said, "What are you, some music blogger on the side when you're not pulling hoppers? Make some documentary about the left-behinds of the music business? I don't give interviews. And if I did you couldn't afford me."

With a grin I pulled out my last five.

"Funny," he said. "Keep it."

The line moved again. We were about ten Nets fans away from the security scanner. I said, "Someone I care about is in trouble over these reports about Taj and child labor."

He kept his back to me. "I got lots of people I care about, and all they have is trouble."

"If someone's setting up Taj," I said, "maybe it's for a good reason. But innocent people are getting dragged into it, too."

"There are no innocents."

We were down to two ahead of us, but the guy at the scanner was logjamming the line, digging into the secret pockets of his army fatigues to unload what appeared to be his life's possessions into the plastic security container.

"Taj'll recover," I told Knox, trying to talk faster than the guy up front could empty his pockets. "It's just a scandal. They all get one, the famous. Like a rite of passage. Take a hit, lay low, launch a comeback. Write a book: *What I Learned*."

The security guard waved Knox toward the scanner.

"I want my wife back! I want her back, Knox."

He spun around with something like interest.

I said, "I don't know if it was you or someone you paid or what, and I don't care."

But he was already unloading his pockets into the plastic bin. My mouth still working faster than my brain, I blurted, "I can help you. Think it through. What's so great about killing his career with some Indian kids a million miles away, if you have to keep serving a life sentence hawking CDs on the subway?"

He looked like he was about to flatten me, security guard or not.

I quickly added, "Or imagine Taj and DeeAna belting out a new song, with production values even God can't match, executive produced by the legendary Knox. Maybe it does so well, Hollywood comes calling to write a song for a new movie."

"So what am I to you, some 'project'? Is this Help a Black Man Month and nobody told me?"

"To be honest, I couldn't care less about you," I blurted.

He stopped unloading and turned to face me, this time with a smile of surprise in his eyes.

I said, "My wife's going to lose her job because of your India bullshit. I can fix it for you with Taj, get you out of the subway."

The alarm sounded as he stepped through the scanner. "Forgot my belt," he told the guard, looking down at his waist and whipping off a large-buckled strap. The guard casually gave him a full body pat down, taking a screwdriver out of Knox's right sock. "Oops," Knox said, shrugging. "Sometimes the radio needs a quick field repair."

The guard threw the screwdriver into a bin along with a blackjack, a set of brass knuckles, two hammers, a scalpel, an assortment of pocket knives, a roll of quarters, and a protractor with its sharp end chicken-winged to a ninety-degree angle.

"I always did find geometry to be lethal," I remarked. No one laughed.

Hitching up his pants and slipping on his belt, Knox looked over to where I held my ground until I got the answer I wanted to hear.

"All right, dentist. Come see me tonight at River View."

"I've got a fight tonight. A client."

"So come after."

"It may run very late. What time do you go to sleep?"

"What time do I *what*? Listen, you either want to help your wife or you don't."

He walked away toward a Bespoke Burgers.

I called out, "What's the address?"

"A-hundred-and-thirty-fifth. River View. Check the web."

"I'm not sure what time I can get there," I shouted to his back. "After the fight I may have to visit a friend in the hospital."

But he'd joined the line at Bespoke Burgers, finished with me for now. The guard said "No loitering, sir" with a look that suggested he wouldn't mind measuring my face with the sharp end of the protractor.

•   •   •

I searched for Gabriel at all our favorite parks until I'd walked as far north as Washington Square. Under the Washington Square Arch a young man in a tux played Beethoven for a small crowd of onlookers who were probably less fans of classical music than they were curious how he'd dragged a grand piano to the middle of Washington Square Park.

Olivia finally took my call. "What do you want?"

As if on cue, the guy segued to "My Heart Will Go On." I forced back a sob to avoid giving her the upper hand. "What do I want?" I echoed.

"I'm driving, Henry."

"It's Saturday and I haven't seen Gabriel in days."

With a catch in her voice she said, "We're going apple picking."

"Without me? How is that even going to work? Usually while he's on my shoulders picking apples, you're on your phone dealing with some new crisis."

"See? What's the point?"

"The point is you're punishing our son for the transgressions of his father."

"So you admit it now? You admit it."

"No. Christ. I meant for my *perceived* transgressions."

"If it isn't true then where is Cipka?"

"You have to believe me, I don't know. I'm working on it. Anyway, don't make this about us. Think about Gabriel."

A guy dressed like Tom Hanks in *Castaway* pushed onto the piano bench next to the guy in the tux. This drew a larger crowd.

"Maybe tomorrow," she said. "We'll see."

The line went dead. I called Guerrero.

"I want to tell your story," I said.

"It's not mine. It's ours, the community's."

"Well I want to tell it, your way. Forget the law angle, focus on the people. It's the *Times* or it's nothing."

"What changed your mind, Mr. Krakow?"

The Mayor had always said find a truth within the bullshit. That's what they'll pick up on, that small nugget of sincerity. Then, whatever you do, don't oversell.

I told him, "It's the girl, Aliyah, who died in the storm. I have a son, his name is Gabriel."

"Yes," he said. "They're all our children. "You're aware who you'll be exposing, and what they have at stake? They'll shut you down. And if they can't do it legitimately, they'll do it with violence."

"The meek shall inherit," I told him. "We may even get a book out of it."

"Are you free tomorrow for an hour or so? I want to show you something."

In a few hours, Shatterproof would be fighting. I was trying to remember if he had a religion, and what its policy was on whether there's an afterlife, and I imagined my conversation with Olivia when I said of Rafe and Kendra, standing shyly behind me, "Oh, *these* kids. They're ours now."

I asked Guerrero, "Will it help me figure out who's behind the development of the Luna Park Casino?"

"Definitely it will be a start," he said. "Here's the address where to meet."

THE FIGHT

Chulo was wrapping Shatterproof's hands in a storage area in the basement of the Church of Saint Ignatius of Loyola in Alphabet City. Shatterproof sat on a fold-out massage table that had a balky front leg, Chulo working the yellow wraps with his one good hand, fingers jutting out of the cast on the other, and doing a surprisingly smooth job of it. We were cordoned off from Shatterproof's opponent, Jhonny "Dogfight" Gomez, by a hospital curtain on wheeled rods. Chulo had to half whisper his strategy reminders in view of Dogfight being no more than a flimsy curtain away. Immediately beyond our "locker room," the church basement had been converted for fight night, with a ring in the center of the floor and rows of folding chairs. Food and bottled beer were for sale on a table against a wall. Fluorescent lights buzzed like mosquito zappers.

"Who's watching the kids?" I asked.

"Babysitter," Shatterproof said, foot tapping the concrete floor, jaw clenched. "And never bring up a man's kids before he fights." Then he gazed off to a future where Jhonny Dogfight Gomez was flat on his back, a heap of blood and melon-size bruises, begging the ref for a few more seconds and he'll surely remember his name.

Which fighter would wind up not knowing his own name was my concern.

"Chulo?" I said.

"Now ain't the time," he snapped.

I emptied my pockets of Zhukov's money and my emergency fund and tried to hand it to Shatterproof. Chulo pushed me against the wall.

"You don't do that to a fighter," he hissed. He inhaled a long breath through his nose, held it a second, exhaled, and took a step back, though a small one.

"No, no," I sputtered, thinking fast. "I'm putting it all on Abdul, every dollar. Tonight's going to pay for my kid's college education."

Chulo said *Lawyers*, as I pushed back the hospital curtain to find my seat, Shatterproof calling after me, "Hey! Thanks for tonight...I owe you."

The curtain dropped back between us. The first two rows of seats were roped off and marked reserved. These were for press, the fighters' family and friends, and "premium" ticket holders. As part owner of Abdul Rahman and the procurer of his clean bill of health, I got to sit ringside. Two beefy heavyweights in the seventh round of a ten-rounder kept circling each other with wary exhaustion. According to my program, one was Ray "First Responder" Drummond and the other was Toney Montana, who, his bio informed me, adopted the last name in tribute to the bloodthirsty fictional drug lord of the film, *Scarface*, Toney's personal hero. Every now and then when the crowd, impatient with all the circling, seemed about to rush the ring to do to the fighters what they were disinclined to do to each other, Drummond and Montana would suddenly toe-to-toe it, clubbing each other with haymakers for a second or two until they dropped back to heave in oxygen as sweat puddled around their feet.

The bell mercifully sounded the end of the final round. Each heavyweight raised his arms in victory, collapsing onto his corner stool while the judges deliberated. First Responder won by a slim margin, improving his record to 114-112. The fighters were hustled off before Montana's fans could wreak havoc, and a ten-minute break was announced so the crowd could rush the concessions while the ring was cleaned. I checked my cell phone in case reception had magically become available in the basement, in hope of hearing from my new partner Helena that Zhukov was dead and Cipka was safe at home.

The MC brought up the next card, first introducing Abdul Rahman, the great "road warrior" (Chulo's euphemism for journeyman), whose footwork was "like watching Michael D'Angelo paint the Sistine Chapel." He declined to bring up Shatterproof's Faberge egg of a chin.

Then he introduced Dogfight, and the ref rang the ring bell, and the two men went at it. It seemed I wasn't going to be able to draw a breath except when the silicone-inflated card girl strutted across the ring. Shatterproof did a fine job of dodging, weaving, and clutching. Apparently he couldn't get Rafe and Kendra out of his thoughts, either.

By round three neither fighter had landed much in the way of a punch: It was more like a benefit for the American Ballet Theatre than a boxing match, and the crowd was becoming hostile. Dogfight tried to force the issue, shoving Shatterproof off him, then bulling back close to his body for an onslaught of uppercuts and kidney slams. Shatterproof's head jerked back a couple of times; I kept gazing at the CPR unit leaning against the base of the ring: Had anyone bothered to test the thing? Also, if EMS had to be called, my phone showed only one star of cell reception—how would that work?

By round eight, Shatterproof had somehow avoided getting hit again. Instead, he flattened Gomez, who almost didn't make it up for the count. But Gomez shook it off and spun Shatterproof's head to a clean ninety degrees, making him walk a dazed circle. I estimated the ratio of Gomez fans to Shatterproof's at roughly five to one, and now Gomez's people were smelling blood. The calls to "finish the bitch" roused Gomez into a flailing attack. Shatterproof backed against the ropes, cradling his head in his forearms. I heard someone shout STOP THE FIGHT over the crowd noise. I realized it was me when Chulo swiveled with a look that could have knocked Gomez out for the count, Chulo never even throwing a punch.

Shatterproof managed to push Gomez off, Gomez tripping over his own feet, which gave Shatterproof a moment to clear the fog. Then he went on the offensive, stalking Gomez and battering him to his knees. After the final round, Shatterproof being neither in a coma nor flat on the canvas twitching with the jumps, I considered that victory enough, but when the ref gave him the fight and he started bounding around the ring, I fell into a sinkhole of despair: Now his faith that he could bob-and-weave brain damage would be through the roof, and he would fight and keep fighting. So perhaps the ref had handed him not just the win but a date with that CPR machine, after all, some night in the near future. One thing was certain, I was through getting him clean scans.

Also certain: There'd always be someone else willing to oblige, as long as Shatterproof could raise the cash.

"What do you think, lawyer? I kicked ass, didn't I?"

He was slumped on the massage table while Chulo removed his hand wraps, Chulo keeping his back to me the entire time.

"Big time," I said.

"Ordinarily, I'd say you fucked up good, spooking a fighter with some bullshit bleed a day before a fight. Fact is, you motivated me to kick ass. *Doctors!* You know they got to tell you something bad so you keep coming back until you got nothing in your wallet but air."

I said, "At least we're past this one, this fight."

"Now it's Jhonny Dogfight needs to retire," Shatterproof said.

Suddenly he cocked his head as if he'd heard a noise. Caught the panic in my eyes and snapped, "Chulo, where's my sweatshirt, man?"

"Right next to you, loco."

He gazed with surprise at the dark blue sweatshirt draped over the table. "Damn Chule, you know I get chilled."

"That you do, champ," Chulo said, quickly packing and zipping up his equipment bag, passing me on his way out with a look that was both an indictment and a surrender to pure defeat. "That you do."

THE JILTED PRODUCER

I passed Knox's River View twice because it was less like a brownstone than a pile of bricks painted with graffiti. On my third pass I finally saw it: "The River View," chiseled bas-relief into stone set just beneath the roof, barely legible under decades of soot and traffic exhaust. The only visible river was a patch of Hudson way down 135th Street under a hazy midnight moon.

There was a locked gate in front of the main entrance with no way in that I could see. The only windows were on the upper two floors and they were planked over. I walked up the dusty stone steps that led to the gate, through a cloud of reefer and a gauntlet of neighbors who appeared less than welcoming. There was a narrow door several feet left of the gate. Above it, someone had spray-painted the giant hand of a white God giving the finger to a black baby Adam, a shout-out to Michael D'Angelo. The door knob gave way and I crossed into a dark vestibule and an underworld lit by bare dying bulbs. The walls were a kind of black tar, the floor was wildly uneven—I thought it would cave any second. Crates were piled on crates, water stained and mouldering. A guy fetaled-up in a corner snored against a rolled-up coat for a pillow. Flyers tacked to the walls and piled on a table announced legal rights clinics, safe sex clinics, worker justice marches, and an Occupy Wall Street parade. The table also held a large plastic fishbowl filled with condoms. I hoped I wasn't about to learn why. Pushing through heavy curtains, I entered a rectangular room with a small stage and a photo art exhibit along the walls. Immediately to my left was a coat rack on wheels and stacked folding chairs. I called out for Knox but no one answered. Someone had painted the glyphs for male and female on a door behind the coat rack. The door was open to a toilet that had seen its share of traffic, a plunger leaning against the bowl.

I called for Knox again, followed rap music up unlit stairs. The higher I climbed, the clearer the rap. It was something about the mark of Cain, Esau and blood, and a snake in sheep's clothing, Joseph and his brothers who stole his colors and shanked him in the back. Someone clearly harbored a grudge.

"Knox?" I called again, my voice crushed to a whisper under the 18-wheeled tires of thumping bass.

I came out on the first landing. It consisted of four apartments separated by pus-colored walls along a creaking warped floor. The music was coming from behind a door with a flyer nailed into it that read, 4 KNOX JAMS. I knocked, "Mr. Knox?" Banged harder, and, finding it unlocked, inched it open.

A gun barrel roughly the size of the Lincoln Tunnel, with Knox at the other end, welcomed me.

"*Dentist*," he sighed, locking the safety.

He was sitting on a piano bench at some sort of console with lots of knobs and levers.

"Never sneak up on a brother like that." He set the gun on the piano bench near his thigh. "Didn't think you'd show. No one can say you ain't motivated, I'll give you that. Pull up a chair."

There were no chairs to pull up, so I dropped onto the sofa. "A lock would be a much better deterrent to unwanted visitors," I suggested.

"Yeah," he laughed. "Might."

He threw me a yellow plastic folder. Inside was a flyer with a grainy headshot of Knox throwing a punch, the knuckles spelling out his name. Bold black stencil across the top read, *Knife In Your Back: aka Brother Love.*

"My CD cover," he said, with pride and resentment. "Another week of mixing and I'm going to drop this bomb like shock and awe. It's Knox's time now. My voice, my rhymes. He started rapping: "It's my time/my rhymes/coming out the shadows shouting I am." He nodded to himself as if to say, *Art and justice, all in one line!* "You spend your life pulling D-league rookies off the streets with their home brew demos. Like ballers who think they got royal balling blood: '*Work* at it? Don't you know who I *am?*' You teach them, you school them. As much mentor as producer. And you produce the *shit* out of them. Then they hit and it's what was your name again? How do we know each other? Holding their nose like they're stepping over some wino blocking the door as they swagger into the VIP room at Club E. Like the virgin birth, born hot product. Fell out of their momma's pussies fully formed for drawing down coin."

I said, "That song you were playing before I came in—it *was* an actual song, right?"

"Look at you! Combination dentist and stand-up comic. That's what they'll engrave on your tombstone. It's called *Joseph and His Brothers* and it's the first single off my album. My Grammy. *Destroy the charts.*"

"And that's what you did for Taj?" I said. "Produced him to a Grammy?"

"Made Taj. *Made* him."

Ever since Amber had told me about Knox's drunken rant at Crème de la Cream, an idea had been brewing for how he might lead me back to Olivia. It still wasn't fully formed, and it was hard to see how Knox could have known that TajWear was using child labor in India, but I felt *this* close to putting it all together.

I pressed harder. "So I guess what Knox makes he can unmake?"

Paydirt. He bolted from the console and was standing over me before I had a chance to flinch. "Messing with the internet's a federal crime. My sheet's white like Tide, dentist. Probably cleaner than yours, putting your dick in their mouths while they're out on laughing gas. Probably got a collection of selfies."

"Actually, I'm a lawyer."

"*Shit.*"

"But the kind of lawyer who helps people." He snorted. "I'm not with the DA or the feds or anything like that."

"Hell, I know *that*," he said, disappearing around a corner.

There was the sound of glass banging and a fridge closing. He returned with a couple of beers. The label on my bottle read, *Evil Twin Lil' B.*

"Craft," I said.

He glared at me. "What'd you think it was going to be, Colt in a forty?" Then he said, "You're what, a traffic lawyer? Kiddie pervs?"

I shrugged it off. "Listen, time is running out on someone I care about. I can help you, but I need to know: That night at Crème de la Cream when you talked about a take down on Taj, were you just bragging?"

"How'd you know about that? One of the girls?"

"What does it matter, I can help you."

"You can help me what?" He still loomed too close for comfort, but at least now he was only pointing the *Evil Twin*.

I said, "My wife happens to be vice president for a company that does PR for Taj's charity."

Again he laughed. "You watch the news? There *must* be a line of work she's better suited to."

"She can get me a few minutes; I can talk to him."

"Make sure to get an autograph. But bring a fifty, 'cause nothing's free with Taj."

"If it was you leaked that story, you need to know you hurt more people than just Taj. You hurt my family."

He fell back on the sofa, holding the bottle between his knees. "I didn't leak nothing."

"But you know who did."

"Didn't say that."

"You want revenge, but success is the best revenge."

"You just make that up, dentist?"

"Lawyer."

"Same difference, except a dentist gives you laughing gas before he drills you."

I stood. "I don't have time for bullshit. Like I said, people are getting hurt." Handing him my business card, I said, "Call me if you want to know how to get *Joseph and His Brothers* worldwide distribution from day one."

As I reached the door, he laughed, "Worldwide distribution. How you going to do that?"

I turned. "Or you can grow old hawking it on the subway."

He studied me over a long hit of *Evil Twin*. Put the bottle on the floor and pushed off the sofa. "Follow."

We climbed the stairs to the final landing and stopped before an apartment door that looked like it could have been a coffin cover stolen from a low-rent funeral. The wood was scored top to bottom with political manifestos: "Justice by other means...Power is what the enemy thinks you have...No bulls no bears just pigs...Revolution begins at home." Dead center at the top of the door, it read, "WE ARE THE INVISIBLE."

Knox banged, shouted, "It's me! Open up!"

The door opened and a skinny kid, maybe twenty-four, was standing there looking like we'd roused him from a bad dream. Rust-colored dreadlocks fell past his shoulders. It was hard to tell if he was black, white, Hispanic, Asian, or a little of each. But for all the crust and daze, there was something soft about him, and I guessed he wasn't long out of Five Towns or the Upper East Side. In the dark hall his board shorts were a burst of some rare tropical flora. His yellow T-shirt looked like he'd been wearing it twenty-four-seven since the start of summer. It was tie-dyed with a picture of a shirt and pants with no one in them. The empty shirt read "We Are the Invisible."

"Knox," the kid mumbled. "What's up?"

They shared a street handshake and a hug. "Trace, my brother," Knox said. "Mind if we come in?"

He didn't wait for an answer. I followed him into a one-bedroom apartment. "Trace, meet a business associate of mine." He squinted at my business card. "Henry Crackhead."

Trace threw himself down on a Salvation Army easy chair facing a high-def TV that spanned most of the room, and resumed playing a video game where two guys were going at each other with scalpel and chainsaw. I scanned his apartment. It was a jumble of pizza, Chinese food and cereal boxes, piles of clothes and newspapers.

Trace chuckled, "Crackhead. That's a funny code name."

"It's Krakow, actually."

He showed no sign of having heard me.

Knox said, "I need you to show him the room that isn't there."

Trace was absorbed in his game, where a lead pipe was giving rise to some considerable blood spray.

Knox stepped in front of the TV. *"Trace!"*

Trace put the game on pause. "You sure?"

"Business," Knox told him.

"For reals?"

"You can trust him. Besides, I've got his card now. I know where to find him."

Trace didn't look happy, but he led us into the bedroom. A computer was stacked on cinder blocks, a laptop on another set of cinder blocks. Everything else was a snake farm of wires.

"Who you working on now, brother?" Knox said.

"That rich dude Philipousis from upstate who's trying to buy his way to being governor. His factory's a truck stop toilet for union busting and labor violations. They've had two deaths in three years and a woman lost her fingers. Can you imagine someone like that as governor? He'd roll back the minimum wage, wipe out safety regs, bring back the white man in hiring preferences."

"What are you going to do to him?" I asked, though I already suspected.

"I don't *do* anything, they do it to themselves. Me, I just shine the light of truth."

I said, "So you're some kind of internet terrorist."

His sleepy eyes flashed with anger. "I take down terrorists."

"So what's the Invisible?"

"Huh?"

I nodded to his T-shirt.

"Oh, that's me. Me and my crew. We work the net, but you never see us coming and you never know we were there. All you know is the pain."

"That's why the name Trace," Knox said.

"Cause I never leave one."

"But you printed up T-shirts," I said. Trace didn't look like he was following. "T-shirts that tell everyone who you are."

He grinned. "I could silk screen a map to this apartment on a T-shirt they couldn't catch me if I didn't want them to."

"So you find dirt on people like Taj, for instance."

"In the cause of justice. Sometimes you need to put a finger on the scales, sometimes a fist."

"That's genius, boy," Knox laughed. "I'm going to steal it for a rap."

Amber Waves's gift had just paid off in spades. "You're the one who took down Taj," I said.

Knox rapped, "Sometimes a finger, sometimes a fist."

"If dirt's there," Trace said, putting up a finger, "I find it. If it's not, but the cause is righteous..." He curled his hand into a fist. I hated his self-satisfied grin.

Knox continued rapping. "Sometimes a finger/sometimes a fist/sometimes an Uzi for the truly blessed."

"But what wrong were you setting straight," I asked. "If the child labor charge was all a hoax? Where's the justice?"

Knox said, "Was it justice for Esau to grift Jacob's legacy? For Joseph's brothers to jack his coat? I was his producer, I *made* him. Then he hits and it's like now he's one of those half-man half-woman jobs. Hermaphrodite. Kevin Russell bangs his own pussy and out comes Taj, draped in gold. Miracle man. Then it's Knox? Knox? Who's that? So then you've got to find a new brother, a true one, like Trace."

Trace and Knox shared a nod of confirmation.

"And if you hurt people who never hurt you?" I asked. "For instance, my wife?"

Trace didn't answer. Knox said collateral damage.

"Collateral damage," Trace echoed uncertainly.

I said, "Another couple of days and those kids in India will be a distant memory. All anyone will care about again is Taj's abs and DeeAna's booty, and you'll be selling your CDs in front of the Barclays Center, hoping to raise enough cash for an all-you-can-eat."

He glared at me, but, like Shatterproof, I kept coming.

"You know I'm right. It's not justice people want, they want heat. They like the fever of righteous indignation, but the cure for injustice takes too long, and it's boring."

Knox looked like he was about to jump me, so I got my idea out as fast as I could. "I can get you off the C train. Get you comped at the VIP room in a blue chip strip club, not like Crème de la Cream, but one where ballers and rappers toss thousand-dollar bills. A house in the Hamptons and a Bentley. But you have to make a sacrifice to get it. You have to give up kicking Taj's ass. Isn't it worth it? One ass in exchange for the world?

· · ·

I came out of the grindhouse atmosphere of River View into a cloud of marijuana. The party on the stairs had picked up heat. Someone pushed a joint at me the size of a kielbasa, but I declined. It was just after one in the morning and the streets seemed to promise something dark and wonderful. But I had a toehold on my way back to Olivia, and I wasn't letting go. My plan was to hike down to Shatterproof's. If his window was dark I'd assume it was because he was asleep and not in intensive care. But if his light was on, I'd stop in to rehash highlights of his fight with Gomez while secretly checking to see if his eyes were trying to roll up in his head.

On the way, I dialed Zhukov to see if Helena had disposed of him yet. She hadn't.

"I want proof of life," I told him.

"I was forced to put trip alarms around trailer," he said. "And you think I can sleep? The minute I nod off, boom! Jump awake because I think I hear Helena's cousins coming for me."

"Let Cipka go free, I'll get your names."

"Now I have to find time in my hectic day to assassinate Helena. But I can't just put bullet in her head or I have to go to war with her cousins. And I can't go to war with her cousins because I have to keep low profile for casino."

"*A* bullet," I reminded him.

"*What?*"

"You said you can't put bullet in Helena's head, but you should have said *a* bullet. You forgot the article. And you've been doing so well up till now."

From his end, I heard a sound like the gargling of a lit Winston. He said, "Why are you wasting your time on Gonzalo Guerrero? The clock is ticking on your ass whore if you don't bring me your father's file."

I said, "Give me proof of life or you can forget that file."

"Or I could torture your son and rape your wife in front of you."

"But that would bring more than a little police attention, wouldn't it? Plus, you gimpy wannabe Russian, fish-eye lowlife wharf rat..." He made a sound like the Winston had lodged in his windpipe. "You don't know pain until you've pissed off a lawyer." I switched gears and segued into my counselor-at-law voice. "In any case, proof of life is customary in these situations."

A taxi barreling down 129th onto Broadway nearly sideswiped me, the driver shouting a suggestion regarding my cell phone and my ass.

Zhukov said, "Do you have FaceTime?"

"Do I have what?"

"FaceTime," he spat. "Why is everything so hard with you? Hang up and add me as contact and then wait."

By now I was standing across from Shatterproof's. His light was on, but I couldn't see anything in the window. Then my cell asked if I would accept FaceTime with Zhukov. Suddenly Cipka filled my phone. It felt like I hadn't seen her in months; I put my fingers on the screen as if I could touch her through the glass. She looked groggy, like she'd been drugged.

"Cipka!" I shouted at my phone. "It's me, Henry. Are you all right?"

She gave me a look that said I must be kidding.

"I'm working on getting you out," I said. "I promise."

"Fuck them, Mr.K. They haven't got two balls between them."

Suddenly there was a blur, along with the sound of crashing and garbled cursing. Then Zhukov was standing behind her with a knife against her cheek. He was bandaged from ear to jaw, the gauze held in place with large strips of tape.

He said, "Stop wasting your time with Guerrero. Don't you think if he knew anything about your father's list I would have tortured it out of him by now? Get me those names or instead of taking her ears and nose, I'll ship her back to Ukraine for sex slave."

I asked him, "What happened to your face?"

He went whiter and his pupils concentrated to pinpricks of black. "She needed to pee."

Cipka flashed a defiant smile.

Zhukov started shouting, "Turn it off, Andrej! I'm sick of this shit. Turn it off, moron!"

The next thing I saw was an extreme close-up of puzzled Andrej trying to figure out how to turn off his phone. I made it easy for him by turning off mine.

As I was crossing the street to Shatterproof's, Chulo came down the steps.

"What are you doing here?" he said in a hoarse whisper. He seemed to have aged a decade since the fight, lugging a gear bag heavy with the hopes and tears of too many road warriors over too many decades.

Above him, the light in Shatterproof's window went dead.

I said, "I had some business uptown, so I figured I'd look in."

He drew his head back and squinted at me. "What kind of business you got uptown this time of night? Nah, don't tell me, I might lose my other hand." He leaned back against the wall near the apartment buzzers. "How's the girl?"

"Still intact. I'm working on getting her out. Chulo...thanks for asking."

"Truth is, I can't get her out of my head. Hanging there like that. What kind of twisted cabrón does that to an innocent girl? Almost young as my niece Rosita coming home from Catholic school?" We let his question hang in the air while I pondered the unlikely notion of Cipka as a Catholic schoolgirl. He said, "I wish you never show'd me her."

I didn't know what to say, so I asked him how Shatterproof was holding up.

"Sometimes after a fight he can't sleep. And sometimes after a fight he really can't sleep. I guess that's maybe a good sign, he ain't passed out in a coma."

"Aren't you the one who gave me the evil eye over worrying?"

"Not worrying's the official position." He bent to drop his bag, but kept his grip on the handle. "I need to get out of this business, but I got to wait till seventy for my Social Security. Too many years the same damn thing. Nothing you can do, it's just life." He held up his casted right hand. "Nothing you can do or you break your hand."

"I'm getting her out," I said. "Your man upstairs, too. I'm not sure how yet, but he never fights again." I backed away toward Broadway to catch a cab for home. "They're going to get free. Cipka and Abdul, Rafe and Kendra. I just need to work out a plan."

"Hey lawyer." He threw the gear bag over his right forearm, lifting his good fist into the air. "If you do? I still got one left."

THREE-CARD MONTE

Guerrero walked me down Washington Avenue in Clinton Hill, a pristine boulevard that was an entirely different Brooklyn from the one on life support we'd toured a couple of days before. Sweeping townhouses looked out over Underwood Park, a mini Arcadia of tree-lined walkways behind iron grille fencing designed to keep out undesirables.

"We're about fifteen miles from Coney Island," he said. "But wherever you are in this city, it's possible to walk one block in any direction and go from hopelessness to BMWs and million-dollar brownstones."

Even in outrage his tone was mild. It seemed he was more naturally inclined to sorrow than to anger—or maybe he believed that the haves would, in time, instinctively self-correct to the side of justice.

I said, "But isn't this what everyone wants? A poor man wins the lottery, does he give most of it away to the people he left behind? No, he buys a townhouse in Clinton Hill and a BMW."

"That's different. I'm not saying he's right, your selfish lottery winner. But I'm talking about those who'd do whatever it takes. Men with no limits. We weren't put on this earth to feed off each other like some Jurassic-age predator."

"But people do make it," I said. "Some people do break through."

He sighed. "You ever see those guys who play that card game in the street? I believe they call it Three-card Monte. They let you win a couple of games, so you'll believe you've got a fair chance at a jackpot.

We know exactly what they're up to, yet we keep playing." He stopped in front of a freshly restored brownstone.

I had no choice but to deal from my own Monte deck. "I believe you and I'm with you. Councilman Meeks and Rick Adelman diverted your Hurricane Sandy money to rig the condemnation hearing and build their casino. But it can't only be them. To get all the licenses cleared, the building permits, to fight off lawsuits and threats of lawsuits, and the environmental stuff, they need help. Insiders, people with influence. If you know who they are, those insiders, people not on your white board, if you give me names..."

He turned to face the brownstone and let out a deep sigh.

Hold on, Cipka, I thought. Guerrero is about to set you free.

He said, "This is Meeks's place, renovated by the architect Fleet McMasters. He did the Google building in San Francisco and the President's getaway in Martha's Vineyard. Meeks had to have *the* house in Clinton Hill; he was counting on a spread in *Architectural Digest*. He's a councilman and his wife stays home with the kids: How can he afford to live among movie stars and hedge fund managers? He rubs his corruption in our faces. He laughs at us. Do you know how many investigations and threats of indictment this man has survived? The Luna Park deal will make him so rich there won't be anything or anyone he can't buy. Do you think he'd let someone like me get in his way?"

"Have you been threatened? Tell me their names and we'll expose them."

"I need to know you're committed to telling our story, no matter what happens. If they get their way the land where our church and headquarters now stand will be nothing more than an island of neon surrounded by acres of the usual futility and despair. I don't care what happens to me, but I need to know you'll follow through, no matter what."

The Mayor would have said don't push, play the long game. Start soft, close hard. But the long game takes time, and I needed those names to give to Zhukov: The clock was running out on Cipka.

"You've got to give me names," I said. "I'll protect you. But I need to know who the players are."

He said, "The subway's a few blocks from here. I'll walk you. Our lawyer, the one who's handling the condemnation hearing, she's very good and she means well. I believe her heart is with the fight. And they say Judge Perella has a reputation for scrupulous honesty, and he's already said he's leaning in our direction, but...there's always that, always a *but* when you're dealing with people like Rick Adelman and Townsend Meeks. Where there's millions to be made and millions more to come." He took my hand, cupped it in his palms. "I'll do what I can to get you a name."

Henry Krakow, master navigator of blind alleys and dead ends. Cipka, why did you have to choose *me* to save you?

"But I need to know," Guerrero continued. "If something happens to me...I need to know you're in this. That I can count on you to be there even if I'm not."

With the penetrating sincerity learned at the knee of a master, a lesson that had consigned me to a life sentence searching for the Xiaos, even though they were almost certainly long dead, to beg forgiveness, to tell them I didn't know, I was only a kid, I looked him in the eye and said, "I'm with you, Gonzalo. Get me that name. I'm definitely with you."

THE FILE

An hour later I was at Cercle Rouge on West Broadway. Gabriel took a flying leap into my arms singing, "Daddy, Daddy," and for a moment I forgot that his nanny was hanging next to a side of beef, and about Shatterproof's jumps, and how Scottie Walsh's wife was a day away from evicting me from my office.

Olivia had chosen Cercle Rouge for our reunion because it was one of her favorites. She liked its French name and polished elegance, and how they breezed her through even without a reservation, because of some reputation-saving work she did for the owner during his high-profile divorce. So there we sat, eating oeufs and saumon, and staring at each other in clenched silence.

Ragidy Supreme was the other reason Olivia had chosen Cercle Rouge. Ragidy was a magician who worked the back room on weekends so parents could enjoy their Bloody Marys in peace, or in our case so Olivia could respond with unmodulated hostility to what I had to tell her. It would take some coaxing to get Gabriel into the back room, since he hated magic and was terrified of Ragidy. But when I reminded her of that, she said, "No, he loves clowns," in a tone that froze my orange juice in its glass.

"The look you've giving me, you could get prison time," I said, when Gabriel was finally in the back room quaking in terror as Ragidy pulled a quarter from his ear. She was wearing her red sweater, the one that accentuated her eyes and summer corn hair; hair bound severely behind her neck so you could see the tension along her forehead, but that kept coming undone, until she gave up fiddling with the snaggletooth clip, tossing it on the table.

"I'm only here," she insisted, "Because Gabriel deserves to see his father. But I'm not certain he wouldn't be better off without you."

I jumped in. "I can fix things with Taj. All you need to do is get me in the same room with him."

"I knew this was a mistake," she said, biting off a sliver of oeufs en meurette and pushing back her chair.

I didn't want to tell her all the details, because I was afraid she'd try to kill my plan in its sleep. But without her there was no plan, so I let it rip. I told her about Amber and Paula Vortex, and how they'd hooked me up with Knox. About his subway CDs and the River View, and Trace, and how if I could just sit down with Taj for thirty minutes I thought I could make the scandal disappear and save her career.

She swallowed a morsel of meurette and gestured to the waiter for a second Bloody Mary. Then she looked me in the eye and said, "I'm coming with you."

"I don't think that's a good idea. From what I read Taj is a pretty volatile guy. It has to be presented in just the right way."

"So present it in 'just the right way', but I'm still coming with you. And don't think you're off the hook, not nearly, about Cipka."

"Yeah," I said, pulling out my cell phone. "About Cipka."

I showed her the video and walked her through everything. Even told her about *Anarchy*. Everything but the stuff on Cipka's bed and under the boardwalk.

She said, "I don't think I can ever forgive you for what you've done to us."

"But I didn't sleep with her, isn't that the main thing?"

She gulped the Bloody Mary and shot daggers at me. Gabriel bolted from the back room, colliding with only one waiter as he ran—a developmental milestone. We watched him plow through a plate of off-the-menu pancakes.

"By the way," I said, "do you have anything from when the Mayor was dying that you may have forgotten to give me?"

"Why would I have something of *his*?" she asked, looking like the butter in her meurette had curdled.

"A file maybe? Near the end when he couldn't get off the sofa, he'd asked me to argue a motion, but I wouldn't do it. Nina said he gave it to you hoping you'd talk me into it."

Gabriel looked up with syrupy lips and said, "Let's go to the 'seum, Henry."

Olivia seemed to hesitate; she drained the rest of her drink.

"I want to see the dinosaurs," Gabriel said.

"I'm working on it," I assured him. "Maybe next week. Let's say definitely next week." I glanced at Olivia in her red sweater; she was studying her empty glass. "Daddy's betting big on daddy."

He was mollified at the prospect of going to the 'seum, even if it meant waiting a week. I said Olivia you look like you remember something. She stared into her drink and spoke slowly, as if the scene materializing at the bottom of her glass would disappear if she pushed too hard.

"He was cursing," she said. "Which was hardly a surprise, given how he usually treated you. He wanted you to do some hearing, but you stood your ground. He was dying and couldn't have weighed more than ninety pounds, but he got so angry it turned him into, well, what he always was. A monster. Your father was an angry man, just full of rage, and the rest of it, the charm, the charisma, it was all an act."

"So, there was a file?"

"Nina came to see me. Maybe she assumed, because he was dying, that I would talk you into giving the monster his last wish. And that you would listen to me, which is amusing. When have you ever done that?"

"And you decided to save me from myself, and from him, by not giving me the file."

"No...no, I did give it to you. I'm sure I must have. Why would I not? It was only one hearing and I'm not the monster. The man *was* dying."

The waiter came and we paid the check.

"You're remembering wrong," I said. "Because there's no way I ever did a hearing for him."

"Be that as it may."

Outside Cercle Rouge, while Gabriel leaped off a bench, Olivia and I shared a moment of acute discomfort, neither of us sure how to say goodbye.

"Just remember I'm coming with you," she finally said, "when you meet Taj."

"It's a mistake," I told her. She turned away. "But yours to make."

She studied the ground for a moment. "Henry, I... Wouldn't it be nice... if we could be like we were?"

"But how nice could it have been, if this is what we've come to?"

"Fine. So I wish we could be like we *thought* we were."

I was about to say how much I did, too, but Gabriel was trying to play hide-and-seek in the potted evergreens. She took his hand and walked away, and I headed back to the office.

Two large men in olive jumpsuits were boxing up my files.

"I still have time," I said. "And besides, it's Sunday."

They turned to me with blank expressions, then went back to flinging my files and loose papers into cardboard boxes. They'd turned my desk right-side up and rolled my chair into place.

"You can't evict people on Sunday," I insisted.

The larger one stooped to grab a fistful of files, like a reaper. "We ain't moving you, we're only getting ready so it goes smooth tomorrow."

"Those files contain client secrets; you're breaking, like, a dozen privacy laws."

The smaller of the two glanced with interest at his fistful of papers, shrugged and tossed them into a carton. The larger one said, "Talk to Mrs. Judge."

"Who?" I said.

"The old lady that's married to that white-haired guy who's a judge."

"Ah," I said. "Eleanor Walsh."

He said, "What kind of man is called Eleanor?"

"Shouldn't you be wearing name tags or something?" I asked. "What's the phone number for your company? I want to talk to your boss."

"We don't have a company. The old lady has our number. Sometimes she calls us for a job off-the-books."

"I could call the police. You can't just stroll into someone's office and take his personal effects. Plus, I could call the IRS if you're off-the-books."

Eleanor's hit squad gazed at me thoughtfully, then went back to boxing my files. I scanned the pandemonium from which I had to find a single file that, if I'd ever had it in the first place, I'd probably tossed long ago. I figured I must have accumulated close to a hundred and fifty files. At roughly a minute a file it would take me about two-and-a-half hours to get through them, with perhaps an extra half-hour for upturning the cartons the hit squad wouldn't stop packing, then filling the cartons back up so the hit squad wouldn't get mad.

About an hour later, I found something. A blue file folder in a sea of blue file folders, except it was the only one with no client name written along the margin. Maybe I did sort of remember wrestling with indecision, "It's only one hearing, his dying wish," until it was too late, and he died, and time went by, and it was buried over by my own files, more and more every day.

I opened it and leafed through his papers. A hearing notice for housing court, notes scrawled inside the cover. A series of letters from one of those hundred-lawyer firms addressed to one of the Mayor's clients, a Martin Braun at 3M Properties. Letters that seemed to escalate from dispassionate expressions of concern over the way 3M and Braun were treating their tenants, to profanity-saturated character assassinations and threats to shut the "profiteering" Mr. Braun out of New York real estate altogether and forever. The last document was a letter addressed to me, typed on his letterhead:

"Henry,

You don't want what I've built for you, and I have to live with that (though not for long—so cancer has *something* going for it). I respect your right to choose your own path, though you're only cutting off your nose to spite your father's face. But I'm grateful you've agreed to take time out of your busy schedule to do this one, big, five-minute hearing. To "sacrifice" your principals for your old man, even if I did have to get cancer and die to get you to do it. While you're arguing the motion, I'll be on my sofa with a smile on my face. Krakow and Krakow, if only for a five-minute hearing.

Since you've been good enough to do me the favor of handling the Braun hearing, I'll do one for you. Martin Braun and his company, 3M Properties, have a field manager, this guy named Freddy Severino. Freddy will be at the hearing, standing in back. When it's finished, he'll come up and introduce himself and tell you something. That thing he tells you is my legacy, all I have to leave you. I couldn't convince you to grab your destiny by the balls and come inside with me, so I hope you'll at least accept the gift that Freddy's holding in trust, that you can't have until after you've argued my motion.

Perhaps I don't win the prize for Father of the Year. But then, who does?

Love,

Artie

That was it. No names, no evidence of a borough-wide conspiracy. Just a guy named Freddy.

"Hey, Attorney Krakow?"

It was the middle of the afternoon, but the guy standing half-inside my door looked like he'd only just been woken by a rude burst of sun through his bedroom window. Both he and his hair were lanky and sallow. He carried a number of serious-looking cameras around a shoulder.

"If you're a process server," I told him, "Attorney Krakow is in Geneva, at an international law conference, accepting a prize for human rights and universal justice. He won't be returning until next spring."

The smaller of Eleanor's men giggled.

"I'm the photographer from upstairs, Max Lichteroff," he said. "Lichteroff Studios?"

"What's happening?" I asked, but figured he was visiting my office for the first time to ask me that very question.

"I've always meant to come in and say hello, but, you know. Anyway, Ron says you're a good guy, despite being a lawyer."

"Ron?"

"The accountant." He seemed tentative and nervous. I assumed he was feeling embarrassed for my sake, given the state of my office.

For the benefit of the movers I said, "How much would you charge to photograph the carnage, for when I sue Mrs. Walsh for wrongful eviction and conversion?"

I wasn't sure whether I had a case for wrongful eviction or conversion, but they sounded like something you wouldn't want a case of. Lichteroff looked bewildered. Eleanor's hit squad never faltered in their steady rhythm of assembling the origami-like cardboard boxes and packing up my life.

Lichteroff said, "Thing is, since we're neighbors I figured I owe you. I'm a studio photographer, and maybe this isn't news, but, I shoot porn, too."

Eleanor's movers stopped to stare at Lichteroff with keen interest.

"Not here in New York," he quickly added. "I'm only *based* here I don't *shoot* here, I fly to L.A. for that. Anyway, I've been going back and forth whether to tell you this, 'cause you probably already know, but, that hot young piece you've been running with? The one with that parchment skin and swagger. Definitely Polish or German, right? Czech?"

I froze with the file in my hand. "My son's nanny."

"Sure thing, sure. So anyway, Friday night I get this message on my Lichteroff Studios International email—that's the name of my porn company, Lichteroff Studios International, as opposed to my straight photography, which is Lichteroff Studios, without the international. Maybe ten seconds of a clip of this girl hanging in a meat locker. She's got, like, nothing on, practically, and her eyes have that look that says I'm here but I'm not here, so you can tell she's on some heavy shit. I knew it was her, your 'nanny'. Even though I only saw her that one time coming out of your office, she's the type brands herself right onto your brain tissue. Some women, when they strip for the camera that first time, they discover the promised land. Looking at her, I thought, this one will blossom like an orchid in my amateur series, *Naked and Lovin' It*. Then it plays through again and I think shit I've seen this girl. The clip comes with a message says the full vid's for sale at auction.

You have until Monday morning to bid, call this guy Bogdan. So I think, *Bogdan*, uh-huh. It's that lawyer from downstairs, running a sideline."

I thought, Bogdan my ass—it's that psycho Zhukov.

I said, "Why would anyone buy a ten-second video of a woman in a meat locker?"

"Well, first of all, the full video's supposedly an hour. And second, a lot more is supposed to be happening than her just hanging there, but you got to buy the hour to see what." He squinted at me. "You sure you're not Bogdan?"

"How can you know there's more?" I heard myself shouting.

He jumped back. "I'm just saying that's the pitch. And the auction is to put it on your website and clean up on downloads."

"Why would you think that I was this Bogdan, selling a woman for downloads?"

He shrugged with the shoulder that wasn't weighed down with cameras. "The solider the citizen, the deeper the kink. So anyway, I say to myself, this lawyer dude's having an auction, I want in."

"You *bid* on her? You bid on Cipka?"

"No! What the hell! Of course I didn't bid on her. Bogdan has this accent and it seemed pretty real, so I'm not, like, a hundred percent sure he's you, and the girl does have that drugged-out look. My girls, they get off on posing naked, that's why the *lovin' it* part. I never venture into the dark side."

The larger of Eleanor's crew sighed with awe, "Oh, man, he's the real shit."

Lichteroff blushed and shuffled in place. "That's why I thought, you know, I should tell you about it."

I was out of my chair, almost nose-to-nose with him. "But you didn't see the full hour? You only saw those ten seconds so you can't say for sure what they did to her. *You can't say for sure.*"

With his right hand, the photographer touched his heart and raised an open palm. "Hand to God. Why do you think I'm here?"

"And the auction is open until tomorrow morning?"

"Yeah, through the weekend until tomorrow at nine."

For a long minute I didn't say anything, working through the possible outcomes of the scenario I had in mind. Finally, I said, "You're going to bid on her."

Eleanor's crew stopped to gaze at me with wonder. Lichteroff looked like he wasn't sure who was crazier, me or Bogdan. I continued, "But you're not just going to bid, you're going to throw up a preemptive number, so that you're not only guaranteed to win, but will make Bogdan stupid with greed."

"Listen, it's not that your girlfriend isn't super hot, but Bogdan will never buy it. There's a million reasons no respectable porn studio like mine is going to bid on a tape from an unknown source."

I showed him my brick of cash. "Bogdan might surprise you. Meanwhile, I need you to do exactly what I say, word for word."

THE NEW OFFICE

I was laid out in a coffin, work boots shuffling around at eye level. I panicked thinking I was one of those poor bastards the medical examiner calls death on only he's not really dead. Then I remembered I'd fallen asleep in the hollow of my desk.

An upside-down face swelling like an eggplant said, "Time to wake up, bud. We gotta take the desk." It was the larger of Eleanor Walsh's two movers.

I crawled out on my hands and knees, unfolding in stages until I was more or less standing straight. "That desk was a gift from my wife; where do you think you're taking it?"

"Storage." He and his partner hoisted it toward the door. Outside my window, a van was double-parked with its back doors open. "The lady judge said you have two weeks to make good on your arrears, then it's going on eBay."

"You realize this eviction is completely illegal, and you will be personally named in my lawsuit."

They eased my desk out the front door. "Do what you got to."

They'd lowered my computer from the chair onto the floor where my desk had been. I sat cross-legged, balanced it on my lap, and began downloading the hard drive to my cell phone. They came back in, pulled the plug from the wall, and carried my computer to the van.

"The lady Judge is not a judge," I called after them. "Just so you know."

Needing to get out of there fast, I decided to run to the Starbucks on Chambers. As I leaped from the last step and hit the street,

O'Connell called and Lichteroff shouted down to me from his window. I asked O'Connell if she minded hanging on for a second, and when she said of course I do, put her on hold anyway so I could hear Lichteroff's news.

"I did like you said," he shouted. "Bid crusher high, then told him look, the money I'm bidding, I need proof what you have is the real shit. I want to see the girl in the flesh."

"And?"

"He's got to think about it."

I shouted my cell number up to his window, reminding him that I had to be away from my office for a while, possibly forever. Then I apologized to O'Connell for making her hold, but she'd hung up. I called back.

"I don't get put on hold," she said. "Lose my number you do that again." Then she told me she was calling to cash in on my promise to have something for her so that she wouldn't have to arrest Zhukov. I told her there'd been a development, and what I had now was probably even bigger than what I had a couple of days ago, could she give Zhukov another seventy-two hours? I'll bring you criminals that when you're done putting them in prison you can run for governor. At some point in the middle of all that, she'd hung up on me. I phoned Zhukov.

"You have what I want?" he asked.

"Closer than ever," I said. "By the way, the D.A. might be sending cops to pick you up. I'm not sure I can hold her off anymore."

Way too evenly, he said, "Straightway, the minute I hear Miranda rights, my cousin ships Cikpa to Ukraine, and your son accidentally drowns in his bath."

Before I could describe what I would do to him if he touched Gabriel or Cipka, Zhukov was gone.

At Starbucks, I ordered a sandwich, a Rice Krispies Treat, and two coffees to give me an excuse to sit for a while and use the place for an ad hoc office.

Guerrero phoned. "I'm just calling to say that you've inspired me to dig harder, to spend every minute of my day finding names for your article. I woke this morning with a strong intuition that things can be set right. Judge Perella said he's inclined to vote for us, but we don't have the luxury of counting on a maybe. And even if we win, it's only the first in an endless series of battles. We need friends like you, and the *Times*, to help us. All we have are volunteer lawyers; the casino's lawyers will overwhelm us with motions and paperwork. But your article—if we expose the whole network, top down, that will be our death blow to them. We'll wipe everything clean."

I pushed my Krispie aside; suddenly I wasn't as hungry as I'd thought.

There was silence from Guerrero's end. I hoped we were finished for now. We weren't.

"We're still mainly strangers," he said. "But together, I have a feeling, we're going to make a change for good."

I said goodbye, but he still wasn't finished.

"Henry?" he said. "The meek really will inherit, won't they?"

Finally, he hung up. The milk had curdled in my coffee; I swallowed it down. Then I Googled 3M Properties and dialed the phone number. When I asked if Freddy Severino was around, the receptionist said he was in the field. "Which field is that?" I asked. She said she wasn't sure, either the India Street development in Greenpoint, or dealing with an accident at the restaurant Bobby De Niro was opening next month in Williamsburg. I told her I was a lawyer and Freddy had something for me, so she gave me his cell number, but he didn't pick up, so I left a message.

Then Chulo called. "What's happening with the girl?"

"I may have something," I told him.

"You either have a thing or you don't," he snapped. "Sorry, but I told you I can't get her off of my mind. We were supposed to rescue her but we failed. It's eating at me, all the time. I told Abdul, I had to."

"You told Abdul?! Why?"

"I don't know, to get it off my chest? Maybe I thought, two heads, we could figure out a way to get her free. Now his head's up his ass about her, too. I want him to see the video. We're at the gym, can you come?"

I was thinking how Shatterproof had said he owed me for the healthy scan. And how, now that I was homeless, there was a way he could pay me back. "I'm choosing a jury," I said, swallowing the last of the Krispie treat. "But I can take a break."

Olivia called as I was hustling through the cold to the gym. "I got us your meeting with Taj," she said. "You know the Gansevoort?"

"No."

She sighed. "It's a hotel in the Meatpacking District. He's giving us ten minutes. One AM in the lobby bar. One, Henry. You better make this work."

"It'll work, but I need a favor. It's an easy one. Can you bring me my coat? I'm freezing my ass off."

Shatterproof was doing a light workout, alternating three-minute rounds of speed and heavy bags with jump roping. The bags had burst wounds held together with soiled strips of electrical tape; it seemed like part of the challenge of working them was enduring the reek of sweat seeped into the leather. Chulo sat backward on a metal chair, arms crossed over his chest, staring out in the distance, fighter and trainer each off in his own world.

Chulo cocked his chin. "Show him it."

I handed Shatterproof my phone. After a while he said damn and Chulo said that's right damn, that's what I told you, and Shatterproof said if you'd brought me along you wouldn't have fucked up the rescue. Chulo said I told you already, it wouldn't of made a difference bringing you along, lawyer here's kid who ran intelligence was not so intelligent, unless what you want to rescue is a smoked ham. They lapsed into morose silence, Shatterproof staring at Cipka, until he whispered, "She's so beautiful." He touched a finger to the screen. "Got a sweetness to her."

"Put her in a habit," I said. "You couldn't tell her from a nun."

They looked at me like they weren't sure I was kidding.

Shatterproof said, "No, there's just something about her."

He handed me the phone and nearly punched the speed bag off its chain.

"Not the bag," Chulo told him. "The rope. You skipped a round."

Shatterproof turned from the bag to start skipping rope. Chulo gazed passed him as he danced, talking more it seemed to himself than to us. "I failed her. I can't believe I failed her." Turning to me he said, "Anyway, what do you got?"

I asked him what he meant.

"On the phone, before coming over. You said you may have something, so what do you got?"

I didn't want to involve Chulo again, and now that Shatterproof was involved, there was no way I was going to put the two of them anywhere near the path of Anatoly Zhukov.

"Nothing," I said. "Cliff again. Another false alarm."

Chulo rested his chin on his arms. "You need to fire his ass."

Shatterproof pummeled the heavy bag until the electrical tape started to blister. "You're not training for another fight?" I called, to deflect attention from the topic of rescuing Cipka.

"There's always another fight," Shatterproof said. "Always. But hey, that scan got me a side hustle. Good money, too. Cash money."

"Oh yeah? How so?"

"For the guy who runs the scan place, Perry something, and some doctor who's Chinese *and* a brother. Serious off-the-books cash just for running packages and sending messages."

Though I already suspected the answer, I asked him what was in the packages, and what kind of messages.

"The kind of messages that can only be delivered by a motherfucker with lethal weapons for hands. And the kind of packages that you don't want to know what's in them. That's why it pays top dollar."

Chulo sighed. Shatterproof snapped at him. "I said I can handle it and I can handle it. Now maybe the kids can go to summer camp this year somewhere it's green, not dodging crack needles and perverts to play in a concrete fountain."

Chulo said, "Yeah, and you can send them postcards from the Riker's Island gift shop."

Shatterproof stopped to stare down Chulo. "What did I say about going down this road, Chule?"

"Yeah, yeah."

"Just remember," Shatterproof continued, stopping to recall whether he was supposed to be rope-skipping or speed-bagging. "You never had kids, you don't know." He took up the rope and started dancing at warp speed.

Chulo turned to me, "He always ignores I have a daughter. Doesn't like how that robs him besting me when we talk about his future. If you do get something on the girl, you're going to let us know, right?"

"Trust me," I lied. "I'm not doing any rescuing with Cliff alone." He gave a small laugh. I called to Shatterproof. "Hey Abdul, remember when you said you owe me?" An uneasy look played over his face, but he never lost a beat on the rope. I explained how I'd been unjustly evicted by Olivia and Eleanor and had no place to sleep. He laughed but came through anyway, told me to look in his bag for the spare key he kept for when one of his kids lost theirs, told me where to find a blanket, that I could sleep on the floor across from his sofa, and reminded me to be careful not to wake his kids if I came in late, because if I woke them on a school night, he'd give me a boxing lesson without the pads.

All I had to do now was wait until one for my meeting with Taj, so I headed up to Shatterproof's to answer a few client voicemails I'd been ducking, shower, and hopefully catch up on some sleep before heading downtown again for the Gansevoort Hotel.

GRUDGE MATCH

Olivia and I met at ten to one in front of the Hotel Gansevoort. She'd remembered to bring my overcoat, a good sign. She wore a black skirt cut to the thigh, with a hot pink jacket over a sheer blouse. She clasped the jacket shut with her fingers when she caught me gaping.

"You don't get to look yet," she said.

"I'll take the yet as a morsel of hope. Meanwhile, I'll just feast on the memory."

She laughed and blushed and changed the subject. "Is Cipka okay?"

"As good as."

Her expression darkened. "She can never come home again, you know that."

I took that as another hint that I might come home again, if tonight went according to plan.

She thrust her hands in her pink pockets and her eyes reflected the lights gleaming from the hotel lobby. "I can't remember the last time we got to be out so late and I could dress a little tarty."

The afterglow of the lavender neon pillars that framed the entrance to the Gansevoort daubed from her face the years of PR crises and crazy clients, of office politics and struggling to be the perfect mother. And of living with me.

"Plus," she continued, "I love the espionage of it."

"I love the espionage of it, too," I said, fighting with everything I had not to chance a hug.

"Don't tease." She pushed my shoulder, but lightly. "Let's go in. We're supposed to meet in the lobby bar by a pool table. Taj is obsessed with pool these days. He's practically world class at it."

"Remember, you're only here to observe. I'm the lawyer, let me do what I do."

But she was already through the door. The lobby bar was the highest of high-end, leather sofas and deep-cushioned chairs, glimmering cherry wood and gallery-quality paintings, with a massive chrome-rimmed pool table at center stage. We staked a place across from the door, near windows with copper blinds. By ten after one, he hadn't shown. "Don't worry," Olivia assured me, plunging her hands into her pockets again. "He's famous for being late."

I reminded her how the problem with Taj's being late was the timing of Knox's entrance. It was vital I get ten minutes alone with Taj to make my pitch about Knox's broken heart and feelings of betrayal, about Trace and We Are the Invisible and internet revenge, and my beautiful plan for reversing both his and his one-time mentor's fortunes. How if he did what I was about to ask, it would pay off big time for both of them.

But Knox walked in at the same moment I was explaining to Olivia how bad it would be if Knox walked in before I got to talk with Taj. He was wearing what I figured was his one good suit, a purple pinstripe that needed letting out an inch or two, over a pale lavender shirt unbuttoned to his chest. The one he'd probably worn at Crème de la Cream the night he'd bragged about taking down his old friend and ex-producer.

"He looks nervous," I said, as we watched him scan the room for us, though we were right there across the floor. Olivia suggested that I'd be nervous too if I was about to confess to probably a dozen federal crimes. "He's not confessing to anything," I said. "He's here to save your career."

Knox finally caught us at the window and strutted over. "Who's she?" he said, staring frankly at Olivia's cleavage. Before I could explain that my wife was not Paula Vortex and he should eye-level the gape, I saw over his shoulder that Taj had stepped in and was heading toward us. He wore a black suit, the silk shimmering like it had been woven from the larvae of glow worms. Under the jacket, his shirt was white as sugar snow skimmed from the Alps. A simple gold chain glimmered from his neck. A turquoise, silver-lined hanky jutted from his breast pocket, folded so sharp you could slice a ribeye with it. Heads turned and there were heated whispers, but this was the Meatpacking District and everyone had to pretend that celebrity sightings were no big deal.

Taj slowed and cocked his head at the sight of the half-familiar back of our purple third wheel. Olivia's panicked expression made Knox spin around just as Taj reached across the pool table to cup the red three ball in his fist. Knox stepped back on his right heel, like he was getting ready to throw a haymaker, while Olivia kept whispering *this isn't happening.* Knox swiveled his head looking for a makeshift weapon to counter the pool ball, and when there was none, balled his hands into fists.

Taj looked angry enough to crush that three ball until dust ran through his fingers.

Knox went into a fighter's crouch. Taj flipped him the ball and grinned. "Straight, or nine?"

Not skipping a beat, Knox told him nine and Taj racked the table. "Dollar a ball?" he said.

Knox said, "What do you mean, dollar a ball? I won't pick up a cue for less than a honey per."

Taj shrugged. "Just thought you'd fallen on hard times, is all."

"*Hard times,*" Knox said. They chose their cues and shot for the break. "I'm not the one needs the favor, Kevin."

"Stevie," Taj countered, "I'm here for a business meeting with one of my PR crew and an attorney, I don't *look* like I need any favors in my hand-sewn Testonis, do I?"

Knox won the break, thundering the cue ball home. "Yeah, I know a few Chinamen knock off Testoni stitch for stitch. Sell them from a carton on Mott and Canal."

"So," I said cheerfully, "Here we all are, ready to talk business."

"Never mix business with pleasure, attorney," Taj said. "Everything in its time."

A waitress came to take our drink orders. When I tried to give her my credit card, she smiled at Taj and said it was on the house. Olivia and I watched the game from a leather sofa. They took what felt like an hour lining up each shot. Taj pocketed ball after ball, but Knox kept up with him. With Knox only a couple of points behind, he peered down his cue in the hope of catching an impossibly shallow angle to nudge the yellow ball down a side pocket. Just as Knox drew back his cue, Taj turned to me and said, "Hey, lawyer man. You married well."

The yellow ball banked against the corner, coming to rest a millimeter from the hole.

Knox froze leaning across the table, head bowed, not uttering a sound.

Taj didn't skip a beat. "The only reason I'm here is a few days ago I'm sitting in a conference room with a bunch of so-called crisis managers, talking about how to deal with this *bullshit*, child labor in India, every one of them looking like a deer staring into headlights on a country road. But not your lady. She's got this killer idea I should write a song, gather together the cream of the music industry to sing it, like Q did with 'We Are the World,' something about saving kids, helping kids, whatnot. Genius." Olivia blushed. "Don't be shy about it," he said. "Fly your colors."

"That's why I married her," I said. "She always saves my bacon."

She crushed my foot under her heel.

Knox, finished grieving over his missed shot, pushed up slowly from the table, giving me a look that said I had better move things along or child labor would be the least of Taj's problems. I took his CD from my jacket pocket and laid it on the railing.

"You hear Knox's new CD?" I asked.

"I don't listen to busker music."

Knox rose to full height. "*Busker* music?"

"It's the shit," I said.

Taj said, "Anyway, I'm so busy getting listed in *Forbes's* top 100, I don't have time to listen to any music but my own." By now he'd knocked down three straight balls, re-racking for another game.

Knox said maybe if you played it straight this time instead of talking over my shot like a bitch. How can a man look in the mirror, everything he has he got by short cuts, back stabs, or straight-out thieving? Taj said trust me, I have no trouble with mirrors, when you look like this it's impossible not to gaze with gratitude and wonder. And besides, I *never* short cut my art. Never. Knox broke down laughing when Taj said art, and Olivia squeezed my hand to signal that I should take control. The feeling of her hand in mine made me think this whole percolating catastrophe was worth it, no matter what happened. I stood and banged a palm against the table railing.

"You're probably wondering why I brought you two together."

Taj said to Olivia, "What does he mean, brought us together?"

Knox told me, "I don't know why I listened to you in the first place. Court Street shyster."

I soldiered on. "Knox may have a way to make your child labor problem disappear."

Taj faced his old friend with his cue at his side and just stared. Breathing low in the throat, like a jungle cat, not taking his eyes from Knox's, he said, "Now how can he have that?"

Knox told him, "You'd be surprised the pull us buskers have."

Olivia said, "Henry, do something."

Easing in between them, I said, "I think what Knox is saying is that he may possibly know, and may possibly have influence over, the guy who can make your scandal go away."

Taj said, "This fool has influence all right, over Jack. Jack shit."

Knox said, "Watch who you're calling fool in your silk suit, fronting like you're some sort of artist, about as genuine as one of them Rolexes the Africans sell out of boxes in the street, or you'll be the first to rap with no teeth in your head." He did an impression of a toothless rapper: "Umph, mmph, mguh, unh unh."

A few heads turned our way.

Taj gave out a rifle shot of a fake laugh. "Wait, wasn't that your best rap from the old days? Before you got elevated to the status of busker?"

Olivia said, "*Henry.*"

I tried to give Knox's CD to Taj, but he wouldn't even look at it, staring death rays at his old running buddy. "*Listen,*" I said, slapping the CD on the pool table. More heads turned. "You're both businessmen so you're both pragmatists. You can kick the shit out of each other, tear up this bar, and all you're going to get for it is a media feeding frenzy. The past won't make you a dime, but it can cost you a fortune."

"Kleinfeld," Taj scoffed. "He *cares*."

Knox tried to muffle a laugh.

I said, "I saw *Carlito's Way* and I don't do coke or steal money or run guns. I help people."

Taj said, "Yeah, you help."

"Himself to other people's money," Knox added.

"I know the scandal is a hoax," I said. "For a fact. Knox knows it, too." Taj's eyes flashed. I quickly added, "There's this group of political revolutionaries that hacks the internet."

Taj turned to Knox. "Used to be you always said music is the only clean thing. Politics, love, sex—nothing but one big con game. Now you got *political*?"

"Listen to my CD," Knox told him. "See who ain't clean, more than ever."

I turned to Taj. "I was handling some legal work for Knox. Back royalties that were due."

Taj laughed. "Back royalties on *what*? Couple of guys reneged on a promise to put a twenty in his hat?"

Knox twitched and took a step forward; I jumped back in. "We were chilling before a court date and I mentioned my wife does PR for you and how she was suffering over the child labor scandal because she's a huge fan and it hurt her that you were hurting. So Knox says that he appreciates how hard I was working to get him his back royalties, he's going to put me in touch with someone who can hook me up with this social justice group who could maybe help fix your child labor problem and save my wife's career."

Taj wasn't entirely buying it. "Why would a social justice group want to hoax Taj?"

I looked toward Knox. He shrugged, so I shrugged. "Do you want to get past it and write a song for that Hollywood movie and get back to raking in millions?" I said. "Forget their motive. Let it go. Knox has a way out for you, I guarantee it. But being a businessman, you know it can't come free."

Taj laid his cue across the table. "Okay, I'm listening."

Knox took his iPhone from a back pocket, gold Beats plugged into the jack.

"That's right," I told Taj. "Just listen."

Five minutes later, Olivia and I left Taz and Knox sitting side-by-side on a leather sofa, with Taj stone-faced in the Beats, and Knox trying and failing not to search his old friend's face for what he was making of Knox's art.

When we hit the cold night air, she was holding my hand.

"So," I said. "Home?"

"Not yet," she said, but smiling, and with her hand still nested in mine.

LICHTEROFF COMES THROUGH

I woke to the chiming sound of Rafe and Kendra's voices getting ready for school, then drifted back into unconsciousness. When I woke again the apartment was quiet. Shatterproof was in the narrow kitchen eating alone in a ring robe that he wore over pajamas, staring through the rusted metal bars at his window.

He nodded toward the fridge. "Help yourself."

I wasn't hungry. "Got coffee?"

"Never touch it. Macha tea. Kicks the shit out of your free radicals. I can brew you a cup."

"My free radicals are a lost cause," I said, pouring myself a glass of OJ and taking a seat.

He gave a grunted laugh and lapsed into silence. After a moment, he said, "It's quiet after they've run out to school. There are mornings you practically jump out of your skin you can't wait for them to leave. But then they do and..." He took another sip of tea. "Can't imagine what I'll do when the younger goes to college."

"I feel the same way about Gabriel and reform school."

This time his laugh wasn't a small one.

"I'll be leaving soon," I said. "Tonight, actually."

"You can stay long as you need."

"Being in your home makes me realize it's time to get to mine."

I could see he understood, but he said, "Long as you know you can stay."

A black gym bag was sitting on the table. "Going to the gym this early?" I said.

"Uh-uh. Business."

"I have a feeling that fighting again would be safer than the business you're about to do."

"A man needs to have a backup plan, and kids need to have a college fund. Just a few deliveries, no stress. Then a short visit with Dr. Liang to get paid. Easy money."

I wanted to remind him how difficult it can be raising college tuition on a prison work stipend, but I let it pass.

He said, "What about that nanny of yours, any developments?"

I said I might have an idea, but having been disappointed before, I was determined to pursue it without hope.

"Pursuit without hope, sounds like my boxing career."

"I wouldn't put it that way, Abdul. I'd say you've been a proud warrior."

He thought about that a moment, put his Macha down and sat straight up with both palms flat against the table. "That sounds about right. Proud warrior."

Then all at once he was shadow boxing inside again. "That girl in the video... not being able to do anything for her, it hurts."

"It does," I said.

"Like a heavyweight's pounding at my kidneys."

"Well, I've never had a heavyweight pound on my kidney, but it sounds right."

"Tell me about her."

I didn't know what he meant: how she got kidnapped? Her hobbies?

"Just everything. Whatever you know. Big things. Everyday things."

I gave him a tour through Cipka World, leaving out her propensity for scams and frogs, and that killer perfume between her legs.

Lichteroff called, shouting into my phone. "I know where they've got her! This guy Bogdan's like, the deal is you bid on ten seconds of video and that's the deal, take it or leave it. But I say listen, I'm willing to break the bank on this one. Fifty K, *bitch*. Fifty. Only I need absolute assurance I'm not getting Harryed."

"Harryed?" I asked.

"Reems," he said, as if I were impossibly slow. "Harry Reems, the porn god. Don't want to get reamed in some sting. I tell him, give me proof of kidnap, or sell her to someone else for pennies on the dollar compared to what I'm prepared to pay."

"Proof of kidnap?" I asked.

Shatterproof shot upright. I mouthed, "He found Cipka."

"She okay?"

"Just where she is," I told him.

"Put him on speaker."

I nodded no. He leaned across the table to try to hear Lichteroff through my phone.

Lichteroff said, "Pretty cool, right? Proof of kidnap? I should patent it."

"Actually, you mean copyright."

"Yeah, well, anyway. So I tell him, 'Here's what's going to happen, I have to actually *see* the bitch' — sorry about the bitch but I had to keep it real. Guess what? He bought it! We set up a meet."

"Where? What's the address?"

"He wouldn't say. But he told me to meet him in Brooklyn, corner of Montrose and Leonard. You show him the money, he brings you to the girl. We're supposed to be there in a couple of hours. So what's the play?"

I said, "No, no, no, a couple of hours? No, I can't make that work. First of all, I'm not sure this Bogdan is who I think he is, so it's not clear what we'll be walking into. Second, I don't have that kind of cash, I need time to raise it. And third, once we're inside and they have our money, how do you propose any of us get out?"

"They're just businessmen," he said. "They can't go around killing people, no one will want to work with them."

I said, "Call him back, tell him you need more time."

"He'll ghost like Swayze. One minute I'm pumped to bid on his movie, next I need a day to think about it?"

"Tell him...the money's flying in from Vegas. We'll do it all in one transaction: proof of kidnap, payment for the movie, Cipka goes home. That way there's less risk."

"There's no risk," Shatterproof said hoarsely. "Cause I'm going to beat this Bogdan senseless."

I said, "On a street corner in Brooklyn where he's sure to come with a small army? And just as sure to leave an animal behind with a knife at her throat for security?"

He sat back, deflated. "They're not going to cut her, they can't sell her."

On my phone, Lichteroff said, "What army? Are you talking to me?"

I told him, "Buy me a day. The money's flying in from Vegas. I need time to figure out this Bogdan, scout the location. Make it work. You have to."

We hung up and Shatterproof said there's no way I don't help with the rescue, Chulo too. His tone said don't bother to argue, so I told him yes, you can help, Chulo too.

What he didn't know was that the next time we met, Cipka would be home, safe and sound.

"I have a delivery to make," he said. He grabbed his bag and headed out the door.

Zhukov called me five times—I let the calls go to voicemail. His messages went from balls-out rage because the hearing was tomorrow and how could he use my names if he didn't have any, to how he was going to return Cipka to me minus her ears and nose, to a geyser of pure fulminating Ukrainian incoherence.

Then Severino's secretary called to say he was due to check out a project for maybe thirty, forty-five minutes around lunchtime at Jay and Johnson.

"What time is lunch?" I asked.

"Could be twelve," she said in her thick Queens accent. "Could be one. It depends."

"On what?" I asked. "I really need to see him." I gave her my word that I wasn't an OSHA or city inspector or process server, and that Severino didn't owe me money.

"On what time he gets there," she explained.

Shatterproof had folded his bed into the convertible sofa. I hung up and rolled my blanket tight and put it against an armrest. In the bathroom, his rusted shower head randomly spat out searingly hot water and ice melt from the Antarctic. Traumatized but clean, I stopped at the open door to Rafe and Kendra's bedroom, a tiny, windowless amnion as bristling with life and chaos as Gabriel's. I thought about the punishment that Shatterproof absorbed, without flinching, and the risks he took, so his kids could heedlessly and intemperately grow there. Somehow, I heard the squeak of my rocking chair, felt the weight of Gabriel on my shoulder, breathing lightly. Saw Olivia coming down the hall, deep into a story about her day.

It really was time to get home. Home to stay.

I began by calling a retired member of Seal Team Cipka, Catskills Division.

"I promised my moms I'd hang up on you," Cliff protested.

"She's a formidable woman, your moms. But you're a grown man. And what will you tell your mother if Cipka is killed, or worse, and you could have prevented it? And besides, this time what I'm asking doesn't involve field work."

He sighed. "What do you need?"

"Find me a butcher, or any place at all that's likely to have a big freezer, in Brooklyn near Montrose and Leonard. Keep within a five, six block radius. Montrose, Leonard. For every possible target I need a map of all the ins and outs: doors, windows, basement entrance from the street, roof. And what's to the left and right a block in each direction: store, office, residential."

"My moms says you're a menace to society." He sighed. "I wish I could afford my own place."

"She must have me confused with someone else. I'm just trying to make things right."

●   ●   ●

I was standing in the sky twenty stories up between Johnson and Jay, shaking the hand of a hard-hatted Severino and asking him why he hadn't returned my calls.

"I meant to," he said. "But isn't there like an expiration date, or a dead man's rule or something?"

He seemed oddly cowed for a guy who was at least six-four and whose hand when you shook hello had the size and power of an auto crusher at a dead car lot.

"Mr. Severino," I said.

"Eddie."

"Eddie, I feel like I've come late to this conversation." He drew back his head in confusion. "What dead man's rule?" I explained.

"You're here to collect on your pop's IOU."

I had no idea what he was talking about, but he was a giant in a hard hat with a car crusher grip, reduced to a bundle of nerves by my "pops," so I looked him in the eye and said, "The Mayor told me you were absolved. Before he died he specifically said, 'Tell Severino he's off the hook.'"

He nearly cried.

I said, "I know it's been years, and it's probably nothing, but the Mayor was representing 3M in a case, and there was a hearing. It was around the time that he was dying. An eviction proceeding against the residents of a small apartment building in Coney Island, near a church in an undeveloped lot. Do you remember?"

He pushed his hard hat down so the rim shaded his eyes. "Might be."

"He was too sick to work, and I was supposed to do that hearing for him. Something came up and I couldn't, but if I had, you were supposed to be waiting in the back with a message for me."

"What kind of message?"

"That's what I'm standing on this concrete slab with nothing between me and the sidewalk to find out."

He looked around at the sky pouring through the steel girders and laughed at my fear. "I don't remember. I wish I did, your pops absolving my IOU and all. But maybe..."

He lowered his head for a few quiet seconds. When he lifted it again, he was grinning.

JOHN F. KENNEDY'S
PROFILES IN COURAGE

"*Profiles In Courage*?" Nina asked for the fifth time. "President Kennedy wrote books?" She picked at a faded tomato sitting on four flaccid leaves of iceberg lettuce. Behind us, a teapot kept up its harsh prompting. She seemed to take the novelty of seeing me in Chappaqua twice in one week as a sign of far greater catastrophes to come. I had already declined to join her in a salad that appeared to be the remnants of a February harvest, but it didn't stop her from asking again.

"It's a late lunch," she explained, as if I'd criticized her for eating.

"Your tea is boiling," I said.

She turned toward the whistle and back again. "Oh, no, it isn't tea," she said, hurrying to the stovetop. The silence that followed the sudden absence of that insistent shrilling was profound, and, in its way, more disturbing than the shrilling itself. It seemed to emphasize how alone we were, together. She scooped Nescafe into a teacup. "I did try green tea, because of the gingko—it's called gingko, isn't it? Well, something like that in green tea that they're always saying is good for your memory." She removed a carton of skim milk from the fridge and mixed several colorless drops into her powdered coffee. "But it didn't agree with me. I think it's the tanins"

"You can brew coffee now," I told her. "They have these special machines, invented by a gentleman named Mr. Coffee. So it doesn't taste like mulch."

"*Mulch*," she said with a small laugh.

"I could buy you one. They're not hard to use. Even I've mastered it."

She laughed again, with the brushing-away-a-fly flutter of hand with which I had a lifelong familiarity. "Why do I need fancy coffee?"

"President Kennedy?" I said, getting back on track.

"That you would remember something like that, of all things. A book your father supposedly kept in the bathroom."

I didn't tell her that when Severino lifted his head and grinned, it was because he'd remembered that the Mayor's message for me for after the hearing was to read his copy of *Profiles In Courage*. "And don't forget, Severino had emphasized. "It's gotta be *his* copy, the one by his shitter."

I said, "I don't know why, I just remembered how he'd always talk about how great it was. He read it over and over."

"Your father loved President Kennedy. He saw himself as the fifth brother," she added with a small laugh, now that he was gone and laughter came without a price.

"I always wondered what he found so great about it, thought I'd give it a read."

"The wicker shelf is gone in the master bathroom, it wouldn't hold. One side fell; it was just hanging there half off the wall. I realized how ugly wicker is. But I don't remember a book …" She gazed out the kitchen window, and after a long moment brought forth a halting inventory. "Dried-out potpourri—it always dries out, don't you find? All that money and in a week the smell dies, which is not so bad, because it's too sweet, I find. Who needs so much sweetness? A box of Kleenex. A set of keys I could never remember what for…washcloths."

"No book? Nothing that can help me?"

She studied me with something approaching maternal concern. "You never wanted anything of his before."

"Nina, *Profiles In Courage*?"

A few days ago, when you asked if I kept any mementos of his, after you left, I remembered. I meant to call you. There is a small collection, silly things, really nothing at all, photos, birthday cards, cufflinks, in a box in my closet. I can't remember a book, though."

I asked her to bring it down. She returned with a large white gift box. "I haven't opened it since I can't remember when."

I lifted the lid and there among loose papers, envelopes and photos, was a copy of *Profiles In Courage*. She said, "How could that be?" The book cover was hard and metallic. Something shuffled inside. "It's a safe," I said.

"In a *book*?" she said, looking like I'd told her it was rigged with explosives.

It wouldn't open. I asked her where she kept the key.

"I'll never remember that," she said with a worried look. "And isn't it just as well? An old book with who knows what inside?" She put a hand on mine; her palm was as soft as a calfskin glove. I couldn't remember the last time we'd touched. Touching was never her style. "You're likely to be disappointed."

"Mom, if you know where that key is…"

She squeezed my hand and walked up the stairs, and when she returned carried a key threaded by a cheap gold chain.

She said, "Artie told me, save this for Henry. When he was, when you could tell that he didn't have much more, that he knew he was…he gave it to me to hold for you. 'Let it be, Artie', I said. 'He wants his own life. Let him go.'"

She handed me the key and turned quickly to the stove to reheat her coffee in a sauce pan.

"Whatever's in there," she said, "it can only bring you pain. What else could it do but bring you pain, it comes from him?"

I hurried the key to the lock and opened the book. Inside, I found about a dozen microcassettes and several sheets of double-folded paper. The cassettes were labeled with names. I didn't recognize most of them, except for a couple of judges and lawyers, a politician or two. Also Meeks and Adelson. There was a cassette labeled "Mitchell"—that would have been Leo Mitchell, the judge who presided over the hearing where, if I'd granted the Mayor his dying wish, I would have represented 3M Company, and where, when the hearing was done, Severino was supposed to tell me that my father insisted I check out his copy of John Kennedy's *Profiles In Courage*.

Turning over another microcassette I read, "Perella." The famously incorruptible Judge Biaggio Perella. I'd confirmed in my research Gonzalo Guerrero's claim that he had warned Luna Park Casino & Hotel that Gonzalo and the Heredarans had made a compelling case, and that he was inclined to vote against the casino. Now it was clear-- that was a brilliant feint to hide his plan for a last-minute change of heart. If Perella made it seem like he was struggling with his decision, no one would question his motive in suddenly changing sides. It seemed the Mayor was right: "Never trust a man who parades his honesty. The perfume of goodness hides the rot in his soul."

I unfolded the papers and found a cheap Xerox of a stock certificate in the name of the Reading Matters Foundation, for a hundred-thousand shares of something called Barnum Properties. I took out my phone but found nothing when I Googled Barnum Properties. But Reading Matters Foundation was run by Lindsey Holt, the governor's wife. Then I ran my fingers along the embossed stamp of another stock certificate; this one was the real thing, and it was in my name. A hundred-thousand shares of 3M, Severino's employer and my would-have-been client, if I'd granted the Mayor's dying wish and done his hearing. The next folded paper turned out to be another letter addressed to me. Nina flew to the sink to scrub her coffee mug.

My Son,

Welcome to part two of Your Father's Dying Wish. I'm dictating this from my new home on the sofa, courtesy of a body that's eating itself alive. Angie's taking it all down and will type it up for you. She's been with me thirty years and is one of the good ones who can actually be trusted. And besides, I cut her in on a piece of my will. Anyway, I've already talked so much I'm running out of strength, so let's skip the bullshit and get to the point. You're my son and I love you. You won't believe this, but everything I've done to build my empire, it's all been for you. That's the natural order of things, so that we don't disappear. Of course you had to tell me to fuck off. Man is born to challenge his father, to find his own way through life. In time, you would have returned to take your place beside me, Krakow and Krakow. But that wasn't our destiny. Life calls on us, at times, to give nature some help, bend other men to our will, even sons, so that life comes out as it should.

So by the time you read this, we'll be partners, and I can die in peace. Because you will have represented 3M Company at an eviction hearing where Judge Mitchell is, let's say, friendly. And the ultimate beneficiary of the judge's friendship is much larger than 3M. It's a money geyser called the Luna Park Casino and Hotel Corporation, which will rise like an oasis of gold over Coney Island. It's going to make a lot of people—not me, as it turns out, but certainly you, my son—very, very rich.

You're probably having an orgasm of righteous indignation. Thinking you'll turn everything over to the feds. But remember, there's a record of your court appearance before our friend, Judge Mitchell. And remember, too, your name appears on a hundred-thousand shares of stock. Oh, and I forgot to mention that without the stock I've left your mother, she'll have just enough money to get by—but not without being forced to give up her house and move into a studio apartment in some crappy building. That's right, I came into the world with nothing and it appears nothing is what I leave. Except that stock. I never was much for saving and investing. There's so much life out there begging to be lived that there were times I actually couldn't breathe for wanting it all. And trust me, the best things in life aren't close to being free. So when your better angels start whispering in your ear, imagine your mother living in one room and clipping food stamps.

So you're in it now and you're in it deep. Don't worry about getting caught; I've covered the angles so you're untouchable. Those cassettes you're holding contain hours of conversations between me and the key players who have been making sure the casino actually gets built on schedule and there are none of the usual obstacles to progress, like zoning and construction bureaucrats, labor bullshit, etc. Those tapes are the crowning piece of my legacy. They give you leverage. And what is leverage but power? And from power flows everything, whatever you dream, the world and all its riches. Those tapes make you who you were born to be. The Mayor's son.

You're going to be angry, you may even hate me. I've reconciled myself to that. We could have avoided this if you'd come in with me when I'd asked.

You're my son, so I'm your destiny. Unfortunately, I ran out of time to let you figure that out for yourself.

I love you more than I can say,

Artie..

I folded the letter inside the stock certificates and locked the safe. Nina was hunched over the sink like a figure from Picasso's blue period.

"Mom," I said, "you're still washing the same mug."

"Am I?" she said brightly. "Did you find what you were looking for?"

"In a way," I answered. Then, "Did you know?"

"Did I know what?" She set the mug in a drying rack and headed through the kitchen toward the front door, though I hadn't said I was leaving. If I gave the cassettes to Zhukov, she could live in her house forever. Olivia and I could buy a summer place in East Hampton. All would be well again, except for Gonzalo, and his Herederans, and the people of Coney Island.

But as the Mayor would say, "What are they to you?"

THE JUDGE

Cliff had texted me a scouting report and Lichteroff had left a voicemail confirming that the deal was on: We'd be getting our proof of kidnap late tomorrow morning. The minute he stepped out of the butcher shop, he'd call me to confirm that he'd eyeballed Cipka. Then I would tell Zhukov that I had his names, but better than that, I had them on cassette—but I had to see Cipka live and in person. Live and in person or I'd burn the cassettes and take my chances with the cops. If he agreed and told me to meet him at the same address as the one Lichteroff had given me, I'd know I wasn't walking into a trap. Not, at least, if I stuck with step two.

Step two was I'd dress up a blue file folder to look like it held the Mayor's legacy. But when I was in the freezer with Cipka, I'd show Zhukov that it held only one tape. One tape as evidence that I had the others, but I had to walk out with Cipka first. Lichteroff would wait in the park nearby, holding the Xeroxed stock certificate and the rest of the tapes. He'd give it all to Zhukov as soon as I walked safely away with Cipka on my arm.

It was late afternoon, too cold for the park. Gabriel was probably home with Liis. As I approached the Taconic, Gonzalo called. What he said made me swerve off the parkway for a safe place to hit the brakes.

"I got you a name," he said. "But you're not going to believe it."

"Gonzalo, what's the matter with your voice?"

"I promised to get you a name, and I got one, and now I don't know what we're going to do."

"Why are you breathing like that? Where are you?"

"Hospital. We had a fire in the church. All our work, Henry. All our work destroyed, but I got your name."

"What do you mean a fire?"

It seemed he was breathing through a sieve. "A drill must have set off a spark. For some reason the door was locked tight. We couldn't get out. We'd done such a good job repairing the wall behind the altar, the only way out was the door. So we used tools and scaffold pipes to batter it open. But I'm okay, really. Smoke, just smoke. On oxygen and sleep a lot. We'll rebuild. Fire can't stop us."

"Was it Zhukov?"

"My name? No, not Anatoly. It's the judge, Perella. He's dirty, can you believe that?"

"No," I lied. "I can't."

Gonzalo said, "How can we ever prove a man so powerful and devious is guilty? What are we doing to do?"

"I'm working on it. But are you going to be all right?"

He could barely get the words out. "Lying here, I've been imagining your article when it's finally out there, like a great wave of truth washing the city clean."

I hung up without saying goodbye. Soon the jittery sun would begin to set, and where would I spend the hours until it was time to save Cipka and my mother by selling out Gonzalo? Gonzalo and his Heredarans and the people of Coney Island.

What are they to you?

I idled on the side of the road until the blur of cars and traffic sounds carried me away, back to the past, though I tried to resist.

Money for your pain. Big house, Cadillac car.

I merged onto the highway, to search for them again, knowing I would fail, but knowing I had no choice, I was compelled to search, to find the Xiaos, to beg their forgiveness. To tell them, I didn't know. I was only a kid.

What are they to you?

THE XIAOS

I loved the Mayor's office. The musk of blue backs and *Law Journals*. Of fine leather shoes and silk suits. Of Coronados and coffee. Of Old Spice and the Wrigley's Big Red gum he'd chew whenever he was breaking himself of the Coronados. The heat off his copy machines and the heat off his secretaries. Carl Sandburg's *Abraham Lincoln: The War Years* eye level to clients on his President's Resolute desk.

I especially loved our early morning Saturdays, the Mayor and the Mayor's son working side-by-side. Mornings as rare as spring in January or his sleeping at home more than a week's worth of nights. His rows of file cabinets, his cubicles and windowed offices, his waiting room with its photographs of hard hats and migrant workers, all seemed charged with the ghosts of actors fresh from their bows. I was eleven, and could hardly wait until The Law Office of Arthur Krakow was re-christened Krakow & Son.

Those hours watching him work were always a condition precedent to the real treat of the day, a movie "in the city," with a stopover at the Broadway Arcade in Times Square, where he let me fill my pockets with tokens until my pants drooped. The Shangri La-like culmination of our Saturdays: The Stage Deli, where we'd devour sandwiches that could prop open a door, and cheesecake wedges as big as your head.

So I almost didn't mind killing time while he worked on files, or that when we finally crossed the bridge to Manhattan, I often had to wait again, this time for a stop at Kino's, so he could "take care of a little business."

Kino's was on Fulton Street. Paulie Mishkin, a defrocked lawyer, was the owner. The Mayor had helped Paulie get a license to sell liquor despite Paulie's having been stripped of the one that let him practice law. The price for this favor involved something I couldn't quite follow concerning a client's wife, ten thousand dollars, and a gun.

But Paulie drew a line through his IOU at letting a kid be seen strolling into Kino's and pulling up a chair. So I would be forced to wait outside while the Mayor disappeared through thickening smoke to where this councilman or that judge's clerk sat facing the wall, prepared for the sort of conversation that could only be had on a Saturday at noon in a topless bar on Fulton.

I would spend that half-hour pretending not to stare through the picture window at barmaids sporting thongs and nipple tassels. How matter-of-fact they were in their nakedness! How blasé their expressions as they poured and strode and served! I longed for the day when the Mayor would let me follow him through the haze to discover, finally, what "taking care of business" was all about.

Then that day came.

"Are you ready to become a junior lawyer?" the Mayor asked, rocking me awake.

He never touched. Not a kiss on the head, no fingers through your hair. It was strange, with his hand on my shoulder, how gentle he could be.

I leaped from bed and he tossed me a crisp new Yankees jacket. He watched appraisingly while I slipped it on as if it were Martian skin: my only sport was singing along with the cast album of *A Chorus Line*.

"The Yankees," he said. "Can't get more American." Then, as if reading my confusion, added, "Trust me."

As usual, we spent the morning in his office. I passed the time by pushing off on a secretary's chair to break the record for wheeled chair distance rolling. Lenny Horowitz's office won me the Olympic Gold Medal. Then I searched the lawyers' desk drawers for stuff that might be incriminating, or at least edible.

Finally, just as I was deciding that he'd changed his mind and I wasn't going to be a junior lawyer after all, he opened a polished wood box and removed a fountain pen embossed with tiny white gold triangles and capped with a shimmering black cover. He caught me gazing as he ran a finger along the studded shaft. "Never go to war," he said, sliding two fresh legal pads, a handful of important-looking papers, and, finally, the pen, into his leather satchel, "without your finest sword."

As his Corvette hummed to life, all I could see was Paulie Mishkin's look of surprise and the welcoming smiles of tasseled barmaids as the Mayor led me to our sit-down with whomever it was we were meeting to do whatever business.

But we didn't cross the bridge to Manhattan. Instead we drove the Belt Parkway straight into Sunset Park and Chinatown, already surging with purpose while the rest of the city was coming reluctantly awake: a jumble of storefront hieroglyphics, backfire and horn blare, the bobbing of intent faces above a sea of olive clothing. The Mayor seemed to know exactly how we fit in. I could only guess.

As we rode the elevator in a seven-story yellow brick apartment house, he inspected himself in the mirrored wall, notching his tie at his throat, adjusting his gold tie pin, spitting his Big Red into a corner.

"Remember," he said. "A lawyer never opens his mouth until he studies the people in the room and calculates the play. You got that?"

"Yes," I said, wishing for a clue what a "play" was.

"This works out, there's a movie about some kind of alien I wouldn't mind seeing."

He didn't seem to know—or did he?—that among my friends the heat coming off *Aliens* was unbearable, because it had creatures who ate your face, and it had Sigourney Weaver. Looking me over diagnostically, he mussed my hair with a smile, the one that instantly seduced would-be clients, judges, opposing counsel, and any number of women throughout the court district, except my mother.

"My son," he said. "My son."

What a strange Saturday this had become. But now I felt ready, "play" and all. He rang the bell to apartment 5R, and the Xiaos appeared. They seemed as old as grandparents, but they had smooth, delicate skin, and fine black hair. Mr. Xiao leaned on canes, holding them at his waist as if they could protect him from whatever catastrophe, official or otherworldly, stood in his doorway in a silk suit with matching tie clasp and cufflinks.

"I'm from insurance," The Mayor nearly shouted, reaching for a business card. "Guardian Accident and Life."

He handed the card to Mr. Xiao, but Mrs. Xiao grabbed it, studying it as if it were a warrant.

The Mayor gave a small bow—I'd never seen *that* before. I also couldn't understand why he spoke like an English primer. "You filed claim. Insurance has money for you. Money for your pain."

Life with the Mayor had already ingrained me with unusual caution. I didn't even lean to see how his card could say he worked for an insurance company. We had money for the Xiaos, that was the important thing. Money for their pain.

Mrs. Xiao glanced my way for the first time; somehow I knew to try a shy smile. Her eyes seemed to soften—we were there to help, after all. Then Krakow & Son followed the Xiaos to the kitchen, which was just large enough for a round Formica table and appliances that looked a hundred years old. A dreary sun diffused through the window blind.

A girl appeared without a word to stand at a chair near the window. She seemed to be around my age—at least I hoped she was. Her complexion was the color of a Caramel Cream, her eyes brimmed with intelligence. An entirely different order of female from a Kino's barmaid, or my classmates with their bewilderingly changeable weather of gossipy whispers, skirmishes, flurries of pop songs and laughter—that always, to me, seemed mocking—and who unsurprisingly wanted little to do with a bookish asthmatic who couldn't catch a fly ball if you placed it in his palm.

I sort of made eye contact with her and straightened my collar as if to signal that a junior lawyer had come to the rescue. She gave no hint of knowing I was in the room. Mrs. Xiao gestured for me to sit. The Mayor's clenched jaw told me it was okay.

Mr. Xiao leaned his canes against the table and lowered himself onto a chair. His daughter waited with eyes averted while Mrs. Xiao settled herself, then waited some more until her mother seemed to allow, with a crisp nod, that she finally had permission to sit.

The Mayor, who was hardly known for restraint, stole a hesitant glance at his hosts before taking off his suit jacket and rolling up his sleeves. Only years later did I see that, the table being round, it offered no dominant position. This left him, as he liked to say, "Behind the eight ball" when it came to establishing a beachhead for his authority. So he loosened his tie and leaned grandly in his chair, arms spread as if to seize the entire room in his embrace. He dropped the fractured English, enthusing about their wonderful apartment and lovely daughter, of whom, he was certain, they must be "more than proud."

The Xiaos nodded and smiled, but the girl never changed expression. Then the Mayor swept his satchel from ankle to table; the authoritative thump of leather on Formica seemed to demand their attention, and they complied. He unsnapped the gold buckle, drew out his legal papers and yellow pads, and made a great show of preparing his special pen for the important work it was about to perform.

The Xiaos gazed as if it all contained some occult secret but hadn't made up their minds whether one best left unrevealed.

The Mayor held the room in a ceremonious silence.

"No man should have to go through this…" he gestured toward the canes. "This tragedy. I can only imagine how worried you are. 'How will I take care of my lovely wife?'"

The Xiaos followed his hand as it squeezed my shoulder and settled on the back of my neck.

"'How can I provide for my lovely daughter,'" he added.

He was right, she was lovely: a beautiful, serene alien, unreachable by me even with Sigourney's spacecraft *Nostromo*. The kind who always sat in the front row in class, pencils sharpened so you could almost smell the shavings, books neatly bound in a plain elastic clasp, never raising her hand but always having the answer (so very different from the alien who stalked the Krakow apartment like the giantess in *Attack of the 50 Foot Woman*, trailing her perfume of Comet and Winstons). Xiao's daughter might never vanquish an acid-spitter with the muscular authority of Sigourney Weaver, but she would surely have it panting at her feet. In her halo of composure, her penetrating intelligence was a force field to which surrender was the only possibility.

Since her parents had never once said her name, I decided to think of her as Cassie.

"But we're not going to let your family go uncompensated," the Mayor continued with his hand at my neck, his eyes flashing righteous determination. "Not Guardian Life. Not me."

"Not *us*," I wished I could add with a manful nod to Cassie.

He asked them many questions about Mr. Xiao's accident. Their English was halting and unsure, but he kept saying, "You're doing great," and, "How long have you been in this country? You speak English better than me!"

Mr. Xiao pushed up on his canes to describe, mainly with excited gestures, how the roof he'd been fixing collapsed beneath him. No crack or groan of warning, no tremor at his feet. How he fell five stories until his hips shattered and a lung was punctured. Mrs. Xiao frequently interrupted to add a detail or correct his memory, and to answer the Mayor's questions about what married life was like now that Mr. Xiao was a changed man. They described how sorry his boss had been for the accident, and how he'd promised to pay the hospital bill and that Mr. Xiao would always have a job when he was well again. And how he'd stopped returning their calls when the bill came due. Their savings were gone, including the money they'd set aside for their daughter's college education. Mrs. Xiao had taken a job as a bookkeeper to make ends meet, but that meant leaving her husband alone to care for himself while their daughter was in school.

The Mayor made a great show of documenting their story in scrupulous detail on the yellow pad, his pen flashing gold as he wrote. The reliving of his accident exhausted Mr. Xiao. The Mayor said, "You have been through hell. Take your time."

Finally, he held out the pen with a gesture that seemed less an offering than a command.

"Big check will come," he said. "Very much money. Big house. Cadillac car."

Mr. Xiao looked to his wife for word whether he should sign.

Maybe it was the magnitude of the moment—the story Mr. Xiao relived dozens of times in thoughts and nightmares fixed on the lined yellow pages. The elaborate pen, promising to write a new but uncertain life. Maybe the urgency of the Mayor's pitch had been too much, had thrown them from the dream of their new house. But Mr. Xiao couldn't sign without his wife's okay.

And she, somehow, couldn't give it to him.

Cassie never took her hands from her lap or raised her head from its slight bow, but she kept staring at the Mayor through unflinching eyes. It felt like it was me she saw, but I wasn't ready to understand why that made me so uneasy.

An intriguing oblong container, blood red and decorated with raised Chinese letters, caught my eye from the top of the refrigerator. It looked like it had been passed down many generations.

Mrs. Xiao rushed to boil a pan of hot water. "The boy is hungry," she said.

"No thank you," I told her, glancing at the Mayor for a sign whether that was the right play.

"It's good," she assured me from a footstool at the refrigerator door. "It's good."

The Mayor laid his pen on the pad and locked his fingers together on the table. "How lucky," he said, from low in his throat. "Henry loves to eat."

Mr. Xiao smiled as if all was right in the world now that Mrs. Xiao had thought to feed me. She tried to hand me the large container.

"Take whole box," she insisted. "Whole box for you."

I gazed into a lake of cookies, each pale yellow with a droplet of chocolate like a Hershey's kiss. If I ate, they would sign. If they signed, what would happen to them? Only the Mayor knew, and I wasn't about to ask.

"You can bring the cookies with us for a treat," he lilted menacingly. "*If* you get to see that movie we were talking about."

I reached to take the container from Mrs. Xiao. It turned out to be made of tin. Her hands were soft as snow. Mr. Xiao nodded eagerly. Cassie never changed expression, so it was impossible to tell if she understood: I had no idea when, or if, there would be another Saturday with the Mayor, or whether *Aliens* would still be around if there were.

The container turned out to be made of tin, but the cookies were good, sweet and light.

Mrs. Xiao brought three cups of tea to the table, only three—her daughter would go without.

The Xiaos watched with satisfaction as I ate.

Finally, Mr. Xiao signed his statement and the letter of guarantee. The Mayor shot up from the table and hustled it all into his briefcase. "I'll be there for your housewarming," he promised, finishing the sentence at their door.

They struggled to keep up, smiling and bowing as if to say that whatever it was he'd said about their house, if he thought it was good, it must be good.

I hugged the cookies to my chest, knowing better than to offer to return them, and glanced back at Cassie, but she just kept staring with her black reflecting eyes.

In the car, the Mayor tore off his tie and gunned the engine. "Your father is a genius! The minute I read the intel on them and saw they had a kid, I knew that was my in. I just saved Guardian a *fortune*. Xiao tells me his story and I write it down, but he doesn't read it. Poor bastard has no idea what I'm writing. They never do. I say sign, they sign. So now Guardian is my friend. And a friend is someone who owes you."

Now I understood why he'd given me the Yankees jacket. Why he'd fixed my collar and mussed my hair.

My first job as junior lawyer was to be a prop.

He ignored the road ahead, elation pivoting to disdain as he studied my expression. "*What are they to you, anyway*?" he spat. "Take care of your own." Rocketing out of Sunset Park, above the roar from his open window, he added, "And next time I take you on business, if someone offers you a cookie—are you listening? Are you listening to me?"

Within days, I'd forgotten the Yankees jacket balled-up at the back of my closet. Most of what I could spare from my allowance went into the cookie container. When it was full, I would get my bike and take it to the Xiaos, hand it right to Cassie. But it turned out to be harder than I thought to fill that tin with coins and dollar bills. Eventually, I spent the money at the Parkway Diner on a succession of banana splits.

But now, in our car heading home from the Xiaos, with the muscles in my father's neck pulsing like live wires, and his question are you listening hanging in the air like a cluster bomb, I nodded yes, I'm listening.

"The next time I take you on business and someone offers you a cookie, you don't hesitate. You don't make me save the play. You damn well better eat the thing, and like it, too."

THE WAY HOME

Olivia stared at her homeless but hopeful husband, hesitating at the other side of their apartment door, clutching his *Profiles In Courage*. Her expression was impossible to read. After a nail-biting few moments she turned and disappeared down the hall. I was home again, but the next sound I heard was the lock in our bedroom door falling into place. I walked from room to room, as if I'd been away for months. Everything was still and hushed on our marital battlefield, the bodies bagged, blood scrubbed from the walls and floor. The wounded slept peacefully under a Spiderman blanket. I lifted him over my shoulder and we rocked together to the sweet squeak of our rocking chair. Gonzalo's hearing was tomorrow at three. I took out my cell phone to call Zhukov. Cliff had sent his scouting report. If everything went according to plan, Zhukov would pay a visit to Judge Perella in chambers before the hearing began, holding the cassette in a closed fist. Lichteroff was standing by, waiting for my go-ahead to make the exchange. Cipka was one speed dial away from freedom.

Gabriel had this way of creasing his eyes and forehead when he slept, as though he were asking a question.

What are they to you?

Gonzalo Guerrero and La Iglesia de la Resurrección, with its blasted walls and sleepy Herederans—didn't he know they would never see that FEMA money, with or without Perella's ruling? Meeks, Adelson, Governor Finney and his wife, the judges and politicians who'd been given a piece of Luna Park Casino and Hotel for their help in rigging it through the system, they had the money and the muscle, but more: They had command of the dark arts of statecraft, the nimble hands of a Monte hustler, the grifter's teeming imagination, the resilience of a subway rat. Gonzalo Guerrero and his Los Mansos Herederan, lovingly and painstakingly breathing life into a church whose inevitable destiny was to be a showplace for hundreds of one-armed bandits. Ike in his house with the roof blasted away. Aliyah and her grandfather. The Xiaos. What did they have? A check from the Metro Insurance Company in the amount of twenty-five thousand dollars to settle a million-dollar case.

I should have known the Mayor would win, that he had to, he'd find a way. So call Zhukov, give him the names and cassettes. Give him Perella. Bring Cipka home. Cash in your stock and start hunting for an Aston Martin and a Hamptons showplace, furnished by Joss & Main.

You're a Player now—you've arrived.

Take care of business, the Mayor used to say. Simple as that. Not an ambiguous situation. The hearing is tomorrow at three. Make the exchange in the morning, walk away with Cipka. Cash in your share of Luna Park stock. Live large.

Gabriel mumbled in his sleep; I pulled Spiderman up over his shoulder.

A Player for a father, can you carry that weight? Should you?

Make the call, rescue the nanny. Take care of business. Imagine what Gonzalo could do with those names, if he were the type to use them.

What Gonzalo could do with those names.

But he would never blackmail a judge to save a thousand Coney Island souls, Gonzalo the Good.

With my legacy as leverage, Zhukov, who had kidnapped my nanny and threatened my child, who had trashed my office and gotten me evicted, who had won Gonzalo's trust in order to destroy him—this sociopathic sender of Kermits and meat locker videos was soon to become untouchable by O'Connell, and Helena.

Give him the tapes and he's a player for life in the Luna Park Casino and Hotel Development Corporation.

But Cipka would come home again. And so would I.

The arm that cradled Gabriel had fallen asleep; he was growing heavier by the day. I moved it to shift the pain; he moaned some fretful dream talk. "Sleep," I whispered, rocking. Sleep as I rock you, rock you to sleep.

Gonzalo the Pure. Zhukov, untouchable for life.

What are they to you?

Unless...

I did make a call, after all. Six of them.

SEAL TEAM CIPKA RIDES AGAIN

When you open your window blinds at four on a November morning the planet seems to have curdled while you were sleeping. Especially if by the end of the day you might be arrested and on your way to disbarment. Or dead. One of Cipka's silvery orange candy wrappers had fallen between the sofa and window. I put the wrapper in my pocket as a charm for safe passage to her new home and new life, the one she'd have if it all worked out. With my legacy under an arm and Olivia's Jeep keys in hand, I left knowing that if anything went wrong, I could never return.

Before falling asleep the night before, the first of my six calls had been to Zhukov. I'd carried Gabriel to bed, tested the door of my bedroom in case Olivia had realized how much she missed me, after all, shuffled back to the rocking chair, and dialed the wharf rat.

He was in a breezy mood. "The hearing is tomorrow at three, midget-Mayor, so you better be calling with good news, or I will make it like you, the Polish twat, and your wife and little boy never existed. Think before you answer, because one hesitation and I hang up and take sledgehammer to this phone. Next time we meet you won't see me coming."

I said, "Here's how this works, and the only way it works. When we meet, I'll give you a small taste of the names, just enough so you know I have them all. Then you'll give me Cipka. When she and I are at a safe distance, my associate will hand you the rest."

There was silence from his end. Then more silence. An ice pick had lodged in my throat. Then, without emotion, he said, "Five in the morning, Sternberg Park in Brooklyn. There's an entrance on Boerum Street with a little brick house with toilets. Go in men's room, door will be unlocked." He laughed. "We end where we started, in shithouse, where all shithouse lawyers conduct business."

"Why a park? Why can't we meet where you're holding her?"

Suddenly, he was fuming again. "Why a park? Because it's open space, moron. I can see cops or Helena's cousins coming from all directions, which I need to do twenty-four-seven because of you. That's why a park."

That had been call one. Call two had been to Lichteroff. Now I pulled up in the Jeep to my office steps, where I found him sitting, head bowed, an open thermos at one thigh and a tan leather photographer's satchel at the other. Rather than honk and risk waking the neighbors, I let the Jeep idle, walked out and stood over him.

"Hey, Lichteroff," I said. "Wake up."

He groaned. "Fifty K cash in the bag but I have to see the girl."

"Lichteroff it's me, Henry," I said, gently shaking his shoulder.

"Not used to waking so early," he mumbled, combing his fingers through his hair. "Now I know why." He sipped from the thermos. "Damn, coffee went cold. We're going to have to make a pit stop."

We refueled at Starbucks then picked up Chulo, who had been call three, then Shatterproof, call four. Cliff was our last pickup. He was shivering on a corner four blocks from his house, to make extra sure he wouldn't get caught by his mother. The five of us made a tight fit in the Jeep. I introduced Lichteroff to the guys, making sure to say he was a part-time pornographer, a short cut to his having to earn their respect. Before I gunned the motor, I twisted around to face my team. "I just want to say you guys don't have to do this. I can still pull over."

Shatterproof said, "Not a man in this car wasn't called to be here. I can't even train right for thinking about her. I just keep seeing her face, how scared she looked."

I asked Chulo how his cousin Rey was holding up.

"He'll mend," Chulo said.

"I'm a little worried about you," I told him. "What we're heading into, and you with one hand."

He reached into a pocket and took out a set of brass knuckles. "Someone's never going to walk straight again, my one hand. Worry about yourself, blando."

Helena had been my last and final call.

I said, "Would I be wrong in suggesting that we never quite got off on the right foot, you and me?"

"You're playing out both sides of your ass," she answered. "First you make a gift to me of Zhukov, then you warn him I'm coming. Now my cousins have to turn over every rock to find him. But he can't run for long. I'll cut his eyes out with Exacto knife. Then I come for yours."

"If I deliver him to you could we consider ourselves even-steven?"

"If you could do that..." she mused. "But why would you?"

"Because I have this thing about Exacto knives."

She thought a minute. "It wouldn't be smart business for me to take eyeballs of lawyer."

"Or his nanny," I reminded her. "You don't seem worse for the frog, and revenge leaves a bitter taste."

She sighed. "Okay, or his nanny."

Having completed the last of my calls, I'd set my phone's alarm for four in the morning, settling down for what would turn out to be a few hours of blissfully dreamless sleep.

Now Seal Team Cipka sped over the Williamsburg Bridge in uneasy silence, guided by Cliff toward our showdown at Montrose and Leonard. "I think my moms would be proud of what I'm doing," Cliff said, finally. "If I don't die."

"I know I ain't doing no dying," Chulo said. "Not today, anyway."

Shatterproof said, "There's worse things than dying—if a woman like that needs you to be a man and you pussy out."

"If you do buy it," I told Cliff, "I promise to let your mom know you went out a hero."

In Brooklyn we slowed at Sternberg Park but didn't stop, so we could scout the round brick building where Zhukov and I would soon finish our business. Then we accelerated to the corner of Boerum Street and Broadway where we took cover behind public housing that blocked any possible sightline from the park, in case Zhukov was watching.

"Cliff, you get out here," I said. "Wait until five, then begin your approach. Remember the script?"

He looked like he was reliving our Sbaglio catastrophe in his head over and over again.

"*Cliff*," I said. "Are we four-by-four?"

Chulo said, "I still don't know why you brung him. Why you can't be the one to stall your guy in the bathroom till me and Abdul call you on your cell when we got the girl safe."

I said, "Look at it from Cipka's point of view. Two strangers come bursting in with brass knuckles after what she's already been through"

Shatterproof said, "I'd never hurt her, wouldn't touch a hair on her head."

"Look," I said. "The plan is solid. I go with you to let her know you guys are friends. Then I hustle across the park to the meet, just a few minutes late. Zhukov may be a psychopath, but he'll wait a few extra minutes to get what he thinks I have."

Chulo said, "It's your call, counselor."

I asked Cliff again if he remembered what he was supposed to say to Zhukov while I was introducing Cipka to Shatterproof and Chulo. He snapped out of his Sbaglio reverie.

"Huh? Oh—yeah. Of course I remember, Mr. K. It's only like five words. I just wish one of you could go with me."

Chulo stepped onto the curb and leaned into the open door. "Out, kid. You got the easiest job of all. I *wish* I had your job." Cliff pushed his way across the seat like it was the last act of a dying man. I gave him one of the Mayor's cassettes, labeled with the name of a bureaucrat in the Department of Buildings. "Show it to him," I said. "Remember, don't *give* to him. He'll have no idea the guy on the tape's a nobody. It'll hose him down a minute and buy me time."

Cliff squinted at the cassette like he was trying to work out how it could possibly help him stall off a maniac. Then he waved to us sadly as we pulled away, Chulo turning and making the sign of the cross to him from the rear window.

Next we dropped Lichteroff at the subway station two blocks from Frank's Meats, where he could pretend to come up out of the subway in case Zhukov had scouts watching. I was sure Zhukov thought I was too straight to cross him, but I wasn't about to bet Cipka's life on it.

"Hey Lichteroff," I said as I pulled away. "Thanks." Even with a fresh thermos of French roast in him, he creased his eyes like he'd just come awake and was trying to remember why he was standing outside the Jeep, alone in the dark, weighed down by a camera bag.

"Nah," he said.

"Well, I owe you."

I was out next, to a corner one block from Frank's Meats. Chulo took my place in the driver's seat. Shatterproof reached into his leather jacket and removed a blue washcloth. He unfolded it on a knee to reveal a huge bloodstained machete. "Borrowed it from the wife of an old friend," he told me and Chulo. "Friend won't miss it he's upstate a while." Reading my expression of pained disbelief, he added, "That angel's coming out in one piece. And so am I. Not doing anything that might make my kids orphans."

I said I hope we have enough time to scout the place and draw a map, so we know what we're walking into. Chulo shrugged, "We're born with no map, we die with none."

I watched in silence as they pulled away and parked a block ahead, a few yards down from Frank's Meats. I checked my watch: We were running a few minutes early.

Lichteroff gave a slight nod and started walking from the subway with the camera bag that was supposedly full of cash, but that he'd actually stuffed with old porn mags. He was also early. Probably nerves. Frank's Meats was a two-story red brick, with bricked-up windows at ground level, and two barred windows above. A metal security gate was drawn down over most of the front, except for a narrow door to the left. To the right, a sidewalk grate allowed for deliveries into the basement. The security gate and red brick served as a canvas where dozens of street artists had sprayed their way to immortality. A sign read, Dangerous Conditions! Do Not Enter!

I let Lichteroff walk ahead and I followed, keeping a few yards behind. When he reached Frank's he tried to raise the gate, but it wouldn't give. He tried the door, but that wouldn't give either. He knocked, then knocked again, and when there was still no answer turned to me and shrugged. I nodded toward the sidewalk delivery grate. He tried that and it gave. Kneeling and holding it open a couple of inches, he gaped down into the abyss, then turned to us as if to say, *You're joking, right?* Finally, he climbed down, the grate shutting closed behind him.

I checked my watch. By now poor Cliff would be locked in the men's room alone with Zhukov.

Next it was Shatterproof's turn to kneel at the delivery grate. Meanwhile, Chulo easily picked the lock on the door. He slipped on his brass knuckles and disappeared into the store. Shatterproof followed Lichteroff under the sidewalk and down to the basement. I stood at the door that Chulo had picked open, shaking from ankles to eyebrows. For courage, I took a final look at Cipka on my phone and told myself, *Go!*

Next thing I knew it was pitch black and I was in a narrow corridor, afraid to whisper Chulo? and praying I wouldn't stumble over his dead body. The corridor ended in a large open shop with empty display cases all around, a long counter with an old-fashioned cash register, a cathode tube TV mounted to the wall, and two wood tables with rickety chairs. Muffled voices argued with mounting violence, one of them Shatterproof's brawling staccato, but I couldn't pinpoint where they were coming from.

Then I saw Chulo behind the counter, a finger at his lips, standing at the top of a narrow flight of stairs. He started quietly down, brass knuckles poised to strike, while I followed close behind, armed only with what I hoped would prove to be a sympathetic way of weeping.

We hit the basement. The lights were at full glare. Shatterproof and Lichteroff were in a standoff with a guy who, despite having a peach fuzz baby face, was built like something out of *Game of Thrones*. He had a knife at Lichteroff's throat, the two of them standing a few feet from a huge freezer. Shatterproof faced them from a safe distance, shoulders relaxed, palms down, fingers draped open like a pianist's. Without looking away from the knife at Lichteroff's neck, Shatterproof nodded toward the freezer and told me, "She's not there," while Chulo with his back plastered to the wall eased behind where Lichteroff and Game of Thrones were locked in their lethal embrace.

"Where's the girl?" Shatterproof barked, to keep the guy from noticing how Chulo was busy outflanking him. "She better be alive and in one piece, and she *better* be unmolested." Thrones pressed the knife harder against Lichteroff's neck, but he seemed unsure of himself. Lichteroff seemed to beg Shatterproof not to reach for his machete. Meanwhile, Shatterproof's eyes flashed to Chulo and back to Thrones. He switched gears. "Think about it, white Shrek," he lulled. "There's three of us and only you."

Thrones seemed even more baffled. Meanwhile, I was panicking over Cipka not being in the freezer, and how Cliff was alone with Zhukov, the clock ticking on Zhukov's patience because of my not showing on time, and Cliff trying to keep him at bay with that one cassette and his stammered promise of more to come.

Lichteroff turned out to be one of those people with surprising reserves of calm. He nodded toward Thrones and said, "I think we found our Bogdan. He was guarding the girl and decided to scam some money for himself on the side by trying to sell video downloads. He used a fake name so your friend Zhukov wouldn't catch wise."

This revelation caused Thrones to heave a knee into one of Lichteroff's, pulling him backward and pressing the knife until it drew a line of blood. Lichteroff's eyes flashed panic, but his voice stayed calm and reasonable. "You don't have to do this. I have Zhukov's money in my bag. All we want is the girl. That's all. Just the girl. We can rough you up a bit to make it look like you got ambushed, and you disappear with all this money while Zhukov goes down on a kidnapping beef."

Thrones thought a moment, then grudgingly loosened his grip and put some space between his knife and Lichteroff's neck. Meanwhile Chulo, easing along the wall, stopped behind Thrones and stood eye-to-eye with Lichteroff. He put up a hand and mouthed, "On five," beginning the countdown one finger at a time.

Lichteroff inched sideways, cooing, "I'm going to open my bag now so you can see your cash." He kneeled as if to unzip the bag, gripped the handle in both fists and hoisted it into an arcing swing that ended in Thrones's face with a clanging sound and a sickening crunch. Thrones collapsed, blood shooting from his nose and mouth, bloody teeth scattered across the floor.

Chulo barked, "*What the...?*"

"Barbells," Lichteroff explained, his bag hitting the ground with more clanging, as if to trumpet the foresight and acting chops it took to bring off a switch of such magnitude. "They were just sitting around the loft. Bought them, like, years ago but exercise never took. You didn't think I was going to bring porn magazines to a shoot-out?"

Chulo shook his head in disbelief and kicked the knife across the floor. Shatterproof straddled Thrones's body, which was sprawled on the floor like a chalk outline of a dead body. "Where's the girl?" Thrones just groaned. "I'm about to work your head like a speed bag, liquify your face bones you don't tell me where she is." Thrones' lips quivered and he pointed a finger toward the ceiling: "Uhsairs."

Shatterproof said, "How many guarding her?" Thrones tried to shake his head, *none*, groaned in pain: "You better hope you ain't lying," Chulo warned. Lifting his camera bag, Lichteroff added, "Yeah, there's plenty more where these came from."

I was beginning to lose it worrying what Zhukov might be doing to Cliff.

Chulo said, "Let's go up slow, just in case," but Shatterproof was already taking the stairs two at a time. We heard a blast—it turned out to be the sound of a nanny-smitten fighter throwing himself against a door and blowing it off its hinges, door and fighter crashing to the floor.

Cipka was on her knees on a bare mattress, wrists and ankles bound in plastic cuffs. Her mouth was taped, and in her eyes I saw a Cipka I'd never imagined existed: terrified and vulnerable and small. She seemed to relax a little when she saw me. Shatterproof told her, "Don't worry, you're safe now." He took out his knife and as he approached she gave a muffled cry, curling up against the wall. Softly, he said, "For the cuffs, for the cuffs." "He's with me," I told her. He stopped moving to give her a chance to look him over: her expression seemed to soften, her shoulders relaxed. They shared something in that silent moment that let her finally hold her wrists out for him, and he leaned gently to her with the knife.

There was so much I wanted to say, but I had to get to Cliff, so all I told her was these guys are my friends and the Jeep's downstairs, they'll get you to a hospital, but I have to go, help someone else, running out of time, we'll talk later. Then I was outside, racing down Boerum parallel to the park, grateful for having rescued Cipka, but hating myself for killing Cliff.

A few yards separated the Boerum Street gate and the round brick building that housed the bathrooms. There was still no sign of daybreak. With my legacy in a file I carried beneath an arm and the forgeries still in my jacket pocket, I pushed open the men's room door expecting to see Cliff and Zhukov. Five heads turned my way. Cliff's was one of them, with a haunted look. He was caught in a crossfire of evil eyes from one irate forger with a bandaged head, two Russian bruisers, one of them wielding an ice pick, and Zhukov, who was also bandaged, from mouth to ear, courtesy of Cipka.

"Cliff," I said. "You look like you're about to die of fear, which given the state of the bathroom floor is perfectly understandable." I turned to Helena. "You were supposed to wait for my signal."

The bathroom was a windowless concrete bunker, so my voice echoed. Behind me to my right were two urinals and two stalls. Zhukov and Cliff stood in front of the stalls, shoulder to shoulder, facing Helena and her bruisers. Behind me to my left was a sink: It once had a mirror above it, but now there were only four screw holes at the four corners of a discolored rectangle of wall. Helena kept her eyes trained on Zhukov, not answering when I repeated my complaint that she was supposed to have waited for my signal.

Cliff said, "I'm kind of scared, Mr. K. May I use the toilet?"

"Get out," I said. "Run!"

Zhukov extended a leg to block Cliff. The bruiser who was holding an icepick turned toward Helena for instructions, but all she did was zero in on Zhukov, whose hand hadn't moved from his jacket's breast pocket.

I said, "They won't hurt you, Cliff. There's nothing they need you for, they're more worried about each other."

He looked at me beseechingly, tears beginning to well. As if I were talking to Gabriel I lulled, "It's okay, it's okay." He stepped tentatively over Zhukov's foot and started for the door. When he'd passed behind me, three feet from freedom, I could see in my peripheral vision that he was hesitating with his head bowed.

"Walk out or I'm going to tell your mother."

"It's not right, leaving you here alone."

"*Cliff!* Get out! *Now!*"

"Okay, Mr. K," he said with a catch in his voice. Then he was gone.

Now that I'd delivered Zhukov to Helena and her bruisers, there was no reason for me to be there either. I kept telling myself to back out, but I'd lost all feeling below the waist.

Zhukov broke the silence. "Where's that little gun you love so much?"

Helena answered, "For cockroach I don't need gun."

Zhukov shrugged, his hand still parked in his breast pocket. "Yet you come with two soldiers. Hey, Straightway, after I carve up these three, I'm going to cut your throat and watch you bleed to death, then walk away with your father's names that you got in that folder, make your crazy bitch nanny my personal sex slave. Your wife, too. Maybe both at same time."

Helena laughed. "You limping fish-eyed wharf rat. You're going to carve *us* up?"

Her bruisers appreciated the irony in her observation.

I said, "Guys, you've got a lot of catching up to do, so I'm *very slowly* going to back out of here."

"You're free to go," Zhukov said. "If you want to be first to die." He took his hand from his pocket and before anyone could react, displayed a brick of crisp bills wrapped in a rubber band.

Helena said, "No amount of money can save you now, Anatoly."

"Oh, well," he said. "It was a thought."

He tossed the cash to the bruiser at Helena's left, the one with the icepick. Icepick bruiser caught the money in his free hand, stepped behind her and stabbed the icepick into the neck of his partner. Blood flumed out around the icepick, spraying against Helena's face. The stabbed bruiser looked like he was trying to figure out what had just happened. When he finally did he raced both hands to his neck.

Icepick bruiser grabbed Zhukov's money, slipped it into his pants pocket and headed for the door.

Helena reached for her gun, but so did Zhukov. The dying bruiser lay on the floor in the fetal position. Zhukov waited patiently until his frantic gurgling became an intermittent rasp that finally ended in silence. "What do you think, Helena? He's dead?"

"Sasha was my cousin," she told him. "First cousin."

Zhukov shrugged. "Was is right." He became downright jovial. "That's past tense, right Straightway? Conjugation of 'to be'. I owe you. You brought me my names *and* Helena." His eyes ranged from me to the garbage bin near the door, and back to his forger.

He said, "What we're going to do is, after bitch is dead, you're going to empty that black garbage bag and help me put her body in it. We'll dump her body in the river."

I really preferred not to put Helena's body in a Hefty bag—and I especially didn't want to empty that garbage bin. Nodding toward the dead bruiser, voice trembling, I said, "But what about him?"

"You're right, there's two. I didn't think of that." His head swiveled from Helena to the dead bruiser and back again. "Wait a minute! Forget river. Police come, think he killed her and she killed him. It's perfect."

"You can't shoot me," Helena told him in a tone that suggested they were spitballing ideas. "The blast will bring every cop in neighborhood. Imagine you trying to limp away on that no-woman-will-ever-fuck-you leg."

Zhukov seemed to be considering whether she was right.

If he agreed it was too public a place for a gunfight, then maybe I should start running?

The problem with running was that Helena had grabbed Zhukov's wrist and was clawing for his gun, blocking my way out. He beat at her trying to pry his hand loose, the two of them inching backward until they bounced off a stall door. Helena took his head in her hands and pushed her thumbs into his eyes, banging his head against a wall. Somehow he managed to slam his gun butt against her ear. Her hands fell and she just stood there blinking, looking whiter than ever, like she might throw up. Zhukov tried to force his gun into her mouth, but before he could pull the trigger, she grabbed his wrist in her hands, contorted her body to avoid the line of fire, and kicked at his bad leg.

With a wild, animal howl she threw herself at him, struggling to force the gun barrel backward to his face.

But Zhukov's free hand had somehow produced a small axe.

He swiped at her cheek, opening a stream of blood. Then he chopped at her fingers until she stumbled backward to stare in horror at the quaking, mangled source of her art and income. "*My hand!*" she keened.

If you're ever in a foxhole and need someone to get your back, I'd go with a Russian forger every time, because they really are indomitable, if she were any example. With another howl she went at him again and again, Zhukov hacking frantically, the two of them spinning and banging around the bathroom until she had no more fight, or blood, left. She fell wordlessly to the ground.

Suddenly I held the gun and was pointing it at Zhukov while he fought to catch his breath.

"I'll shoot," I said. "Believe me."

"Give me the names, I'll tell you where the girl is."

"I'll tell *you* where she is. At a hospital, guarded by my friends." He grinned like he thought I was bluffing. "Where she was," I said, "was Frank's Meats." He went white. "Upstairs. The freezer's in the basement and so was your guard, but we took him out."

His eyes seemed to sink into his head and his voice came from deep in his throat. "Give me the names and my ID and I'll let you live."

"You're not exactly dealing from strength, since I'm the one with the gun."

He came out with a wheezing sound that I decided was a try at a laugh. "You're a pants-pissing lawyer, Straightway. Step on a roach, weep like girl."

"Maybe," I said. "But we never know who we truly are until we're tested. And anyway, all I have to do is aim at a wall, the blast will bring the cops, and, as Helena said, you won't be able to limp away fast enough. You'll do time, lots of time, in a federal prison, not only for killing Helena, but for the fake ID in my pocket. And I'll throw in the dead bruiser over there, too. Tell them you did him along with Helena. So toss me the twenty-thousand and we can both walk out before someone walks in and I can't help you anymore."

"What twenty-thousand?"

I patted the file beneath my arm. "There's no way you were coming to get this thinking I'd give it to you without insisting I see the money. It was the girl and the twenty. That was the deal. The girl and the twenty. So you brought the money to show me, thinking you'd get the names and keep the cash, and what could I do to stop you, nothing but a pants-pissing, straightway lawyer."

I thrust my gun hand out until my arm was fully extended. He flinched and nodded toward one of the stalls. There was a small black bag just behind the door. As I stepped back toward the bag, he took a tentative step toward the axe on the floor. I pointed the gun at the other stall and fired.

It was the first time I'd ever shot a gun. What I learned was never discharge a weapon in an echo chamber—someone had upended the little brick house and was rolling it across the park. I couldn't hear a sound, and I could hear every sound that had ever been since the beginning of time. Zhukov staggered, holding his head, tripped and fell across the dead bruiser, righted himself, awkwardly because of his bad leg. He showed a mouthful of green teeth and lit a Winston. I tightened my arm against the file. The screaming in my head was beginning to subside, but I still had to strain to hear him.

"Okay, you have gun, you have girl. I have no ID and no names to protect me. So I'll take my twenty-thousand and go."

"I'm sorry but I need that money for something."

He smiled sadly, "You can't walk around pointing gun forever, Straightway."

"Tomorrow will have to take care of itself," I said.

He dropped the bag and flipped his Winston at me, turned and walked out. Before the door hammered shut I could see that dawn was about to break. We were down to three in the bathroom, but only one was breathing. I knew I should run, but there was this small problem of my having shot myself in the back of a thigh—the bullet had ricocheted from the stall. It felt like someone had ripped Helena's axe down my body from ass to ankle. I forced myself to push open the door and head for the street. Cliff was running up to me.

"What happened? Are you okay? What's in the bag?"

I tried to tell him it was all nothing, the bag, the leg, just get to the car before the cops came. Cliff, being Cliff, ran back toward the bathroom. People appeared on the streets surrounding the park, and traffic was beginning to get heavy. I couldn't call out that he was going the wrong way and would get us both arrested, so I just kept walking in the direction of the Jeep, as inconspicuously as I could, given that blood was pouring down my leg. By the time I left the park, Cliff ran up beside me.

"Where are you going, Mr. K?"

"Where am I *going*, Cliff? To the *Jeep*."

"The Jeep? What are you saying?"

"Well did you plan to hitchhike out of here?"

We were walking as fast as I could manage. The pain in my leg was searing. I kept a hand pressed against the back of my leg to stanch the blood, knowing it was absurd, but doing it anyway.

He said, "Don't you remember? They have the girl, your friends. In the Jeep to a hospital. The plan was when you showed up in the bathroom, I was supposed to leave and go to work. You were going take the train and meet them there. At the hospital, Mr. K."

I pictured myself sitting on the train, blood seeping across my seat. It would be packed for the morning rush hour, but for my fellow passengers, a lawyer in a pool of blood would be just another commute. We turned a corner and I told Cliff to call an Uber. I'd give the driver a fifty for bleeding into his back seat.

The rest of the team had taken Cipka into Manhattan, to Beekman Downtown. The Uber pulled up and I dragged myself in before he saw my bleeding thigh. Cliff rode along, calling Shatterproof and Chulo for an update, but for some reason they didn't answer their phones, and I'd never gotten Lichteroff's number. For all I knew, Zhukov had a small army waiting outside of Frank's, and they were all dead. The Uber dropped us off outside Beekman Hospital.

I stopped to block Cliff's way into the emergency room. "You're late for work."

"I can't stand around fixing phones all day, not knowing how she is."

I said, "Helena showing up early like that, I'm sorry. I had no idea. But you're safe now, and you're done. Go to work. Go to work, Cliff. I'll call you with an update, I promise. Then I'm going to ask you to forget any of this ever happened."

"It was a blast, Mr. K. And don't worry about my moms, you're cool, no worries."

With Cliff reluctantly off to Verizon, I pushed through the revolving doors into the emergency room. As I limped toward the reception window to ask how I could learn the room number for a friend, Chulo called out "Hey, lawyer!" I turned and saw them in the rows of walking wounded. Cipka and Chulo, sitting near the back of the room, Cipka looking drawn and childlike in Shatterproof's sweatshirt.

"Where *were* you?" she said.

"I had to take an Uber and there was traffic."

She rolled her eyes. "I meant with the rescue. And why are you limping like the Russian douche?"

Chulo said, "Not for nothing, but your girl's a handful. We could barely get her to come here, she kept ordering us to take her home."

It seemed to cost her a lot of effort to talk, but that hardly stopped her. "I would be the one to know, wouldn't I, if there was something wrong with me? So can we maybe cut the chivalry? I'm tired, that's all. I want to go home and sleep it off."

"Where's Abdul," I asked. "And Lichteroff?"

Chulo said, "The photographer left when he realized the girl was okay and the show was going to get boring."

"The girl's name is Cipka," she snapped.

He looked at me beseechingly. "See what I mean?"

A sudden jolt of energy shot through the ER. Cipka raised her head and smiled: A regal welterweight strode across the floor holding a large Styrofoam container, looking like he wanted to hit someone.

"Lawyer," he nodded, taking the seat next to Cipka's. "How you feel, Cip? I was all over this godforsaken hospital trying to find someone with brains and pull to understand you can't be waiting to see a doctor, what you been through. Stopped for this." He handed her the Styrofoam container. "Eggs for protein, a bagel for carbs and to settle your nerves. Food's the last thing you want, I know, but trust me, you'll feel like a new woman, some protein and carbs."

With a weak smile, she took bird-sized bites from the plastic fork. "That's right," Shatterproof told her. "Trust me."

"You don't look so good lawyer," Chulo said.

Shatterproof agreed. "Whiter than usual."

"It's nothing," I said. "A small nick. Though I think I'll hang out here a while. Eventually, a doctor might stroll by."

Cipka asked me how I'd found out where she was and what happened with Zhukov. Then she said forget it, you can tell me later, I just want to go home. She pushed carefully off the chair. Shatterproof locked an arm under hers. "Not without me," he said.

"Okay, 'dul," she told him, with a look that if you didn't know them, you'd think they'd been together a long time. Chulo scoffed, shaking his head in disbelief. They rose up together, the fighter and the nanny, Cipka leaning against Shatterproof, arms linked, Shatterproof gazing at her with worry.

"You ever meet his kids, Rafe and Kendra?" she asked me. "They're so sweet. He showed me pictures."

At once the image I'd been chasing these last days was complete. Hiking the black bag up to my lap, I said, "I don't doubt he's showed you pictures. When he's nose-to-nose with an opponent and the ref's about to say come out fighting, he pulls a wallet out of his trunks." Shatterproof gave a small laugh of assent. I turned to him. "Gabriel loves her, she's like a second mother."

He said, "What are you getting at, lawyer?"

I unzipped the bag and showed everyone the twenty-thousand. There were whistles of amazement all around. Reaching into my jacket pocket, I took out the money Zhukov had given me for Helena, including my fee, and most of my emergency fund, put it all in the bag with the twenty-thousand and zipped it back up.

"Chulo," I said. "Your cousin up in West Seneca still needs someone to help him with his gym?"

Chulo smiled broadly. "He ain't said, but I can personally guarantee you he does."

To Cipka I said, "Considering the circumstances, I can't invite you to resume your employment with the Krakow family." She grinned. "And in any case, Zhukov is still out there running loose."

Her eyes flashed. "Yeah, he hasn't heard the last of me."

"That's exactly what makes my idea so perfect."

"And that's what exactly?" she asked.

"I'd be really surprised if there were no colleges with MBA programs near West Seneca, at least within driving distance. And it sounds like Chulo's cousin and Abdul are going to need someone who understands business, if they're going to take their gym to the next level."

"Well, well," Shatterproof said.

Chulo struggled not to break out laughing. I gave the bag to Shatterproof. "No more CAT scans?" I asked.

He held it in a fist, offered me his other hand. Looked me straight in the eye. "No more CAT scans, brother."

Cipka tore the bag from his fist. "I'll watch over the money, you stick to training fighters."

"Whatever you want, angel," he said. "Whatever you want. Let's get out of here."

They started out of the emergency room. Chulo asked wasn't I coming? "My leg," I said. "Going to stick around awhile."

Cipka turned back to kiss me on my cheek. "It's been real," she said.

"Couldn't have been realer," I answered.

As they pushed out the revolving door, Cliff phoned to tell me he was sending a text with audio and I should listen right away. "I'm sorry I didn't tell you before, Mr. K. What happened was, I was scared thinking about going into that bathroom alone, I didn't know what you were getting me into. So I recorded everything for insurance in case I actually got out of there alive and needed to play it for cops or anything, down the road. My moms is always telling me I need to learn to plan ahead, life's not just about today. But I couldn't stop thinking how you'll probably need it too, and, well, I'm sorry I didn't tell you before, okay? But here it is now."

He hung up and sent a text with an audio file. I only needed to listen for about twenty seconds before hobbling through the revolving door as fast as I could. The three of them were far up the block, heading for the avenue. I called out, "Chulo, I forgot something." He turned and hustled back, nodding his head as if to say, what's this crazy-ass lawyer up to now?

THE LEGACY

My leg turned out to be more than a flesh wound, but nothing that would require major surgery. Without an excess of exaggeration I might get some mileage out of it with Olivia. They dressed the wound and wrapped it, gave me something for the pain, and I pushed through the revolving door into a sparkling November day.

Despite my wounded leg, I felt lighter than I had in a long time, now that I was relieved of Zhukov's money.

Now all I had to deal with was my legacy, which I still carried in the file under my arm. Despite all I'd been through that morning, it was only eleven, more than enough time to get to Brooklyn for the Luna Park hearing and Judge Perella's decision, so I picked up a copy of the *Post* and collapsed in a booth at the Mykonos Diner to fuel up on coffee and a Lumberjack Special. The front page featured an old photograph from their archives: Taj and DeeAna accepting a Grammy Award, Taj holding it up with two arms like a prizefighter displaying his belt. The headline read, "Taj KO's Hacker." The story was on page three:

"A group of self-styled 'internet cleansers' that goes by the name What Is Truth? has taken credit for a 'reputation assassination' against famed rapper Taj, to falsely perpetrate the claim that he profited from child labor in India through his billion-dollar clothing line, TajWear.

The group released a statement by a hacker who calls himself Trace. It reads, 'Social media has turned us all into mindless consumers of info-swill, to stop us from waking up to the systemic injustice that keeps the one percent on top and the rest of us fighting for their leftovers. America, Inc. will turn us into an army of subway rats if we let them, gobbling up their lies and distortions. And when we get too close to the truth, they'll make us declare war on each other. Whatever it takes to keep us from paying attention.

That's why we fronted Taj as an exploiter of child labor. To make you pay attention. But the innocent shouldn't have to pay for the sins of the guilty. We regret using the tricks of our enemy against one of our own. The fact is, Taj is a great artist and a great humanitarian. If the world can be hoaxed to turn against a man like Taj, we need to own up to just how dangerous the web has become. And how much worse it can get.

Sorry Taj—we knew you could handle the heat, but now everyone knows the truth. And now it's all on you, world. WAKE UP AND THINK!"

The article went on to quote Taj as having no desire to pursue prosecution of the shadow group: "Taj doesn't have time to posse up against some small-time hacker. Instead, I'm using the experience for good, putting out a single called "What Is Truth," that's going to break at the top of the charts, win me another Grammy. My good brother Knox is writing and producing it with me, and we're assembling some of the greatest artists around to sing background, just like Q did with 'We Are the World.' After that, my label, TajRap is unleashing Knox's newest CD. And hear me, it's going to tear s#*t up!"

I still liked my idea for a song better. "For the Children" would really have torn s#*t up. But if Taj and Knox got me home again, as far as I was concerned, they were Beethoven, Mozart, and Josh Groban all rolled into one. Maybe I'd drop by River View in a year or two to ask Trace whether he'd actually turned a new leaf, or whether that was all a sham for keeping We Are The Invisible just that. But I probably wouldn't.

Caffeinated and fed and caught up on the day's events, I hustled to Brooklyn to catch Judge Perella in chambers so we could have a little ex parte conversation before the start of his afternoon calendar.

.   .   .

The courtroom was empty, the guards hadn't returned from lunch. I slipped behind Perella's bench, through the door, and escaped into the hall to make an end run for his chambers. He was bent over his desk, peering at a folded section of the *Times*, nose buried in newsprint, a hand draped across a massive hard-bound *Oxford English Dictionary*, so I figured he was riveted on the crossword and that explained why he hadn't acknowledged the stranger hovering in his threshold. I said Judge Perella? He finally looked my way and the pencil he'd been chewing fell into his hand. He pushed his reading glasses up the bridge of his nose. His face looked like it saw the sun only the few minutes every day it took him to walk to the subway. His hair was thinning in some places, and in some places not, in a disordered progression toward old age.

"Good morning, Your Honor."

"The courtroom is where we usually conduct the court's business. Have you lost your way?"

"No sir. I'm right where I need to be. My name is Henry Krakow."

"Krakow? As in...?"

I stepped further into the room—he pushed away from his desk. "Yes," I said. "He was my father." It felt strange hearing myself confess that. "I'm here about a case you're deciding this afternoon."

He studied me carefully. Then he asked, with measured indifference, "Which case?"

"The casino in Coney Island."

He looked down at his *Times*. "What's a seven-letter phrase, in Latin, meaning a communication with a judge made by one party in an action, without inviting the other party into the room, in order to gain an unfair advantage? Ah yes! Ex parte."

"May I close your door? I think you'll want me to."

"Sure. Come on in so I can breach an inviolate standard of judicial conduct."

By now his clerk was hovering at the threshold. He waved her away as I shut the door and moved closer.

"This is an entirely different kind of ex parte. For the benefit of the judge."

He removed his reading glasses and placed them on top of the *Oxford*. "I'm not certain what I'm supposed to make of your sudden appearance in my...I knew Artie had a kid, a lawyer. But he never talked about you. Never said you were part of his business."

I opened the file with its cassettes. "My father left this to me."

He cocked his head and creased his eyes, as if someone had called from another room. Lifted his glasses to his face but didn't put them on. Flipped the dictionary to a random page and ran a finger down the column of words. Lifted his pencil and raced it to the crossword, but placed it carefully across the puzzle, stood and walked unsteadily to the window just behind his desk.

"I'm a good judge," he said, gazing through the iron security bars through a window gauzed over with decades of filth. "Scrupulous. Absolutely scrupulous, but for one mistake. Things go wrong all at once and you...the *pressure*. We're only human. An error in judgment. A moment out of character. One single stain in a stainless life. Wouldn't it be something if it wasn't money that made the world go round, but books, and ideas? When the pressure hits, that terrible money pressure, it *forces* you to act out of character, to stray. Your father, with his Rolodex of names, his reptilian cunning for collecting souls and favors and debts, gets a phone call. My bankruptcy lawyer—at least I suspect, no, I'm sure—how else could the Mayor have known I'd be vulnerable? A public bankrupt, a judge with no judgment in his personal affairs, can you imagine the *shame*? At a charity dinner he takes me into a corner and offers me a way out. Stock in his casino company in exchange for a handful of favorable decisions. You think, I've led a spotless life—maybe it's appropriate to balance the scale. All you lawyers with your Porsches and Hamptons homes. Don't I deserve recompense for decades of sacrifice in service of the law? A modest reward, nothing more than a token, really, for keeping the hyenas and jackals, the wolves, at bay? Protecting our law-abiding citizens from criminals like your father. Like you." He turned to the window and brought a hand against the bars as if to touch his soiled reflection. "One mistake, that's all. Just one, and there's no going home. No going home..." All I could see of him was the ragged hay-like hair in back of his head, his deflated shoulders. Finally he turned around. "So what do you want? In an hour it will be done. Did you really think, just because my heart is with the Heredarans, that I would decide with my heart, rather than my wallet? Did your Luna Park thugs think I was waffling, and send you to threaten me, as if I were a common lowlife?" He studied my expression and a wave of vertigo made him reach for the window sill to steady himself. "Unless...you don't *want* me to decide for the casino? You *want* me to go with the Heredarans? Atone for your father's sins, now that he's no longer around to stop you?" He seemed almost to wish it were so.

"No," I said. "The casino must win."

"Then what?"

In the next few minutes I laid it all out for him. The phone call he would make to Meeks, Meeks's phone call to Sandy Adelson. The shares of stock they would transfer to the Heredarans, equal to the number of shares I held in my name, shares that I would also sign over to the Heredarans. Gonzalo Guerrero's seat on Luna Park's board of directors. If I don't get what I want, I added, these cassettes and stock certificates will become the next internet sensation, and believe me, I have a friend who makes the dark web look like the teacup ride at a kiddie park. Make sure to tell Adelson, tell Meeks, that if they think they can play the long game, I'll always have this," I said, slipping the cassettes and stock back into my file. "My legacy."

As I opened his door he said, "So the new Mayor has finally been crowned. Congratulations. But you don't want to cut yourself in for a piece? They're going to insist on it, for their own insurance."

I turned to face him, holding the file out between us. "You can tell them that some hazards are just not insurable."

"So I was right, it is about atoning for the sins of the father."

"No, it's because I'm hoping you were wrong when you said there's no going home."

He had no idea what I was talking about, which was fine. Before he could ask, I was gone. Turning a corner on the way to the elevators, I tore up the file and threw it into a trash can, along with the tapes. Trashed it all. I had no office, my files were in storage, waiting for Eleanor Walsh to incinerate them. You couldn't walk a block in the city without tripping over a lawyer, so my clients would have no problem finding someone to take their cases where I'd left off. I would ride the elevator down and walk out of the court district for the last time. No legacy, no ghost stalked me now.

The door to the lawyers prep room was propped open by a security guard whose name tag read Jesus. He was sharing a joke with Jimmy Toole, who was famous for scratching out the best closing arguments in the county on the cocktail napkins at Hanrahan's. I'd never met Jimmy Toole, but I'd always liked him, and I thought how sad it would be never again to see him lurch to the jury box after a Hanrahan's lunch.

I turned down the west corridor. The light suddenly was much too bright, as though I'd stepped out of a long spell in a pitch black room. A million hungry, greedy, calculating, inconsolable people stampeded from the elevators, their bickering, scheming, lying and weeping rising to a din. They were insignificant, wayward souls, but what a noise they made. What an extraordinary noise.

Suddenly a seven-foot giant came screaming at me from the elevator. He was dressed in a tailored black suit with a midnight tie studded with white stars. Two chocolate-skinned women all in white stood behind him, their heads bowed and veiled in white. He carried a hand-carved walking stick crowned with a lion swimming in a mane of polished mahogany. The lion had diamonds for eyes.

"Hey!" he fumed. "Are you a lawyer?"

And I just had to laugh.

WARM FOR NOVEMBER

I stood at the gate to Gabriel's favorite playground, not hesitating, just giving myself a minute to watch him play. He was at the top of a slide, debating strategy with a plastic Green Beret. His usual gang of marauders was nowhere to be seen. In the few days I was away, a moment seemed to have passed where he'd somehow grown into the next-level Gabriel, a profound change fully and irrevocably consummated in a hiccup of time. I would have liked to have been there to watch that moment as it happened. The air was June-in-November. Liis held his down jacket on her lap. She looked like Cipka's twin sister, but hotter, if that was possible. She was only temping; for our next nanny I envisioned someone more grandmotherly, perhaps with a slight moustache.

She caught me standing there, so I went over and took Gabriel's coat, sat next to her on the bench. Cipka had called, Liis said, to make sure Gabriel was okay, and to say that she was trying something new with her life, she wouldn't be coming home, but was pretty sure the Krakows would not be asking Liis to stay on. I told her Cipka was right. She shook my hand and we said goodbye, and she said don't hesitate if you ever need a back-up, Gabriel's a sweet kid, and she was gone.

After a while, Gabriel noticed that his nanny had somehow morphed into someone who resembled his father, except bullet-gouged, sleep-deprived, and splattered with the blood of several Eastern Europeans, not to mention his own, still reeking of his first, and last, smoke-filled room. He studied me from his perch at the top of the slide, a disturbingly percipient look on his face, before launching into his customary headlong sprint for my arms. But when he asked if I would play, I told him next time. Maybe next time.

Olivia had left at least a dozen messages. While I watched Gabriel from my bench, I finally called her back.

"Why didn't you return my calls?" she said. "I've been half worried sick you'd been shot or stabbed or something, and dying to know how it all came out."

"I was hoping I could tell you the story in bed tonight."

She didn't respond, but she didn't say no.

"Anyway, there was the smallest of hitches."

"What kind of hitch?"

"The thing with Zhukov in the bathroom, where Helena was supposed to get him out of our lives forever? That kind of went exactly the opposite of what I'd planned."

"So we're never going to be safe? I can't live like that, Henry. I can't."

I looked at my watch. By now Chulo would have kept the promise he'd made me outside the hospital, and paid his visit to O'Connell with Zhukov's forgeries and the tape of the Sternberg Park massacre that Cliff had secretly recorded. I'd thought Cliff had hesitated at the bathroom door because he'd come unglued, but he'd actually placed his cell phone in the sink. Now, if O'Connell beat the Russians to Zhukov, it would be many decades before we'd hear from him again. If the Russians got to him first, it would be an eternity.

I said, "Actually, it worked out surprisingly well. But I don't want to ruin the story by jumping ahead. I'm at Cupertino Playground with Gabriel. Can you maybe get out early? I have just enough money in my pocket for a family dinner."

"Lee pretty much guaranteed me a promotion, so I think I have enough pull right now to manage that."

"Yeah, I saw the article. 'What Is Truth' isn't the worst idea for a comeback song, but I still think 'For the Children' would have bought you and Taj a lot more traction."

She laughed, and that alone was like coming home again.

I said, "So where should we meet? Andiamo?" Andiamo was one of her favorites, a three-star Michelin. Gabriel and I didn't mind the place, but it wasn't on our greatest hits list, despite the Michelins, because their portions were the size of teaspoons. We preferred Ninja, over on Hudson, which was designed to look exactly like a feudal village and the waiters jumped out at you dressed in full ninja gear.

She said, "I was thinking more along the lines of that place on Hudson. Where everyone wears those black costumes, and they scream in your face just as you're putting food in your mouth."

"Done," I said, smiling to see Gabriel playing with his friends again, a game that required running aimlessly before crashing into each other at top speed. "See you there."

Later that night, after our first family dinner in what felt like a year, while Gabriel was giving himself a bath, I agreed with Olivia that it was probably time to get rid of his rocking chair. We'd move it to the spare room rather than send it to storage, just in case we might need it again. But before we did, I kissed Gabriel goodnight, and while Olivia undressed after her long day's work and a dinner with ninjas, I rocked one last time, watching her in the open door. And before telling me how her day had gone, she listened to my blow-by-blow of how I'd rescued Cipka and introduced her to Shatterproof, and Rafe and Kendra, and their deer.

ABOUT THE AUTHOR

Two chapters from *The Money*, published as short stories in *The Hudson Review*, were nominated for a Pushcart Prize and for *Best American Mystery Stories*. The *Pembroke Review* nominated Klein for Best New Poets 2019. Other work has appeared in *Film Comment; Columbia, A Journal of Literature & Art, New York Stories*, and numerous others.

NOTE FROM THE AUTHOR

Word of mouth is crucial for any author to succeed. If you enjoyed *The Money*, please leave a review online—anywhere you are able. Even if it's just a sentence or two. It would make all the difference and would be very much appreciated.

Thanks!
David Shawn Klein

Thank you so much for reading one of
Our Legal Thriller novels.
If you enjoyed the experience, please check out
our recommended title for your next great read!

Fatal Accusation by Marian K. Riedy & Tanja Steigner

"*Fatal Accusation* is a complex multilayered read which takes
you headfirst into the murky world of lawyers and what
justice actually means."

— TBHONEST

Made in the USA
Columbia, SC
20 December 2024

50221688R00152